THE F-WORD
REALITY SHOW

Chris Westlake

Cover design by Elizabeth Ponting, LP Designs & Art
Editorial services provides by Jeff Jones, www.jeffajones.blogspot.co.uk

www.chriswestlakewriter.com

For AJ, my wonderful son who always takes a keen interest in my writing.

Don't worry, Chloe…you'll be next!

THIRTY-SIX YEARS AGO

The sun was only just beginning to welcome a new day when John Davies, a retired businessman and a respected member of the local community, decided to let his beloved Labrador, Rusty, off the lead to stretch his legs. Technically, it was Rusty, and not Mr Davies, who located the dead body floating on the surface of the pond.

Two days earlier, at a few minutes before five in the evening, fourteen-year-old Denise Edwards sat cross-legged on the grass verge about seventy-five yards from the pond, nursing her left ankle with her right hand. An early evening breeze swept through her natural blonde locks, tied in pigtails at the back. Dried horse manure speckled the road that was barely wide enough for the occasional tractor to pass through.

Denise spotted the figure strolling along the middle of the road from maybe three hundred yards away.

They locked eyes from about ten yards. The man's sunken, vacant eyes dropped. Denise knew exactly what he saw. At school, the pubescent, acne-ridden boys leered at her from within the comfort of their huddles. Denise knew that her blossoming body caught the attention of both boys and men. She knew she had to be careful not to give the wrong impression, because – as her mum frequently told her – the male species were the devil, and the devil had no control over his loins.

"You alright, pet?"

White flakes sprinkled the man's slumped shoulders. A damp, brown stain coated the middle of his navy jumper, suggesting he'd haphazardly eaten his Sunday roast dinner. The sleeves of his jumper were rolled unevenly up his arms. His nicotine-stained front teeth appeared blunt and chipped.

"I felt this intense pain in my ankle when I was running. I don't know if it's sprained or if it's twisted." She held the man's gaze with puppy dog eyes. "Can you help me? *Please*?"

The man glanced over his shoulder before his eyes circled Denise without actually looking directly at her. The fair, glistening hairs on his forearm grazed against his forehead. "Don't get me wrong, it's not that I don't want to help, but...but how? What can I do?"

Denise looked up to the skies, observing the clouds that gathered like balls of cotton wool. She held out her hand. "Can you help me up? See if I can walk?"

Sniffing, the man rubbed his pudgy fingers against his jeans. He clasped Denise's hand. Denise was one of the shortest in her year, and her forehead rose to a few inches from the man's grizzled chin. She hopped on her right foot. Sucking in a mouthful of country air, she placed the tip of her left foot on the ground. "Thank you," she said. "To be honest, I didn't know if you'd help."

Grimacing, the man said it was no problem, and he picked up his pace.

"Don't leave me," Denise said to his retreating back.

The man turned slowly, like his mind conflicted with his body. His blue, watery eyes worked hard to focus on Denise's gaze. He uttered no words, but the lines on his forehead posed a host of questions.

"I won't be able to make it on my own. The village is maybe a mile or so away. Can you hold my hand? Keep my balance?"

The man took a second glance over his shoulder. Denise knew what he was thinking. What if someone saw? What would they think? The road was empty though, as it always was at this time on a Sunday. Trimmed hedges outlined the road all the way to the village.

"*Please?*"

The man took Denise's limp right hand.

They walked in silence for maybe fifty, torturous yards. "It's David, isn't it?"

Squinting, David grunted.

"You live in the first cottage out of the village, don't you? I built a den next to your cottage with my friends when I was a little girl. Your mum came out of the garden to see what we were doing. I guess you could say she wasn't best pleased."

"My mum is a difficult woman…"

"It was funny. Don't worry."

A smile appeared from the side of David's angled lips.

"To be honest, I feel a bit of a connection with you, David."

David stopped and turned to face Denise. His forehead furrowed over his eyebrows.

Denise laughed. "Don't worry," she said,

smoothing his arm. "It's nothing bad. The villagers are always talking about your mum, that's all, and because of that, they say things about you too and-"

"What do they say?"

"She always leaves her front door open, doesn't she? We hear her shouting at you. We hear her shouting at herself, to be fair. They say she is mad…"

"She isn't mad. She just isn't well. She has some issues..."

"Exactly. That's why I feel a connection with you. Kids can be cruel, can't they? I should know; technically, I guess I'm still a kid. They're always saying things about me that aren't true, too. It's horrible, isn't it?"

Dropping his eyes to the floor, David nodded.

"My mum is religious, too. Why does your mum say you should go to hell though, David?"

David's eyes flickered in every direction but at Denise. "I made a baby with Jill, didn't I? We didn't mean to. It was the first time we done it. Someone told me you couldn't make a baby the first time. Well, you *can*. The baby will be born in October. *Our* baby will be born in October."

Denise gasped. "A baby? You are going to be a dad? That's amazing. That is a gift from God."

David shook his head. "Mum says I'm living in sin for not marrying Jill, and that's why I'll go to hell."

"You won't. You are a good man. I can tell."

"I *want* to marry Jill. I *want* to be a good dad. But her family won't let me. They say I'm simple. They say I'm no good. And so my mum is right. I *am* living in sin. Maybe I *will* go to hell?"

Denise stopped at the edge of the pond. Behind her, flamboyant lilies floated on top of the clear water.

As a young kid she'd run home from the pond with a jar full of tadpoles. The pond was somewhere villagers retreated to for some space and quiet. It was a place where nothing bad ever happened.

"What's that in your pocket, David?"

Open-mouthed, David glanced at his pocket.

She smiled. "Is it your knife?"

"What?"

"It's fine. I know you have a knife. You use it to skin rabbits, don't you? Your mum cooks a stew in a huge pot. We can smell it from the road. You carry the knife everywhere. You are known for it. Can I see it?"

David dug his hand deep inside his pocket. Denise's eyes widened at the sharpness of the eight-inch blade.

"They say your mum beats you, David. Is that true?"

David shrugged his shoulders. "She is my mum. What can I say? Doesn't every mum do that when their children are bad? Sometimes I deserve to be beaten. She says some of the things I do are evil."

Denise's smile widened. "What do you do?"

David's arms hung loose by his side. "She caught me...she caught me doing something with myself."

Denise arched her eyebrow.

"You know? She caught me...playing with myself."

Denise put her hand to her mouth. "Naughty boy, David. So tell me, what were you thinking about when you did that?"

"What? I weren't thinking about nothing."

"I don't believe you. You must have been thinking about something bad if you mum says you're going to hell."

David's forearms tightened. His eyes reddened. "I weren't. Honest, I weren't."

Denise moved an inch or two forward, close enough for him to inhale the perfume she'd dabbed on her neckline before leaving the house. "Were you thinking about girls like me, David?"

David stumbled backwards. "Girls like you? No. *No.* I thought about Jill. I love Jill. I only think about Jill when I do that."

Taking another step forward, Denise put her middle finger to his lips. "It's okay, David. Plenty of men think about me in that way."

David swung his arm in the air. The weakening sun reflected against the metallic blade. Denise eyed the sharp contours as the knife plunged downwards. "I *don't* think about you in that way! Leave me alone!"

Denise swiped the knife from his hand. David glanced from Denise to the knife and back to Denise again.

Denise smirked. "I *know* you don't like young girls, David," she said. "But I don't think anyone else will believe that now, will they?"

With a single swoop, Denise slashed the knife across the man's neck. Pushing her right foot against his midriff, David toppled into the pond with a hearty splash. Within seconds, the clear water turned crimson, spreading like red wine spilt on a carpet.

Crouching low, Denise washed her hands clean in the pond water. She spun the knife in the air. It landed with a plop, before disappearing beneath the rippling surface.

"It was lovely chatting to you, David," Denise said to the motionless, floating body.

And then, kicking out her two good legs, she began her trek a mile or so back to the village, just in time for her tea.

THE EVE OF DAY ONE

The headline draws me in like smack to a drug addict.

Will Christmas be cancelled?

Maybe it isn't appropriate to take the Lord's name in vain in these circumstances, but – but - Jesus Christ Almighty, anything but this.

The first two cases of the virus were confirmed in the UK on 30 January 2020, and today – Tuesday 22nd October 2024 – the media is talking about cancelling yet another Christmas. There are a few things us Brits just won't tolerate. Firstly, don't fuck with cats. Secondly (and these are in no particular order), do not – under any circumstances - take away our Christmas.

I tell myself to turn away. I tell myself to resist the temptation.

Of course, I don't turn away. I lean forward, making sure I don't miss a thing, sucking in the bad news like sugary soda through a plastic straw.

This really is the bad news to end all bad news. After the hopes of a vaccine gradually descended, so did our liberties, but we put up with that – embraced it even – with a stiff upper lip. Christmas was the light that kept us going through the dark times. And now that light has – potentially – just been blown out, like a candle on a birthday cake.

Turning around, I'm greeted by the gloating, flashing light of my computer screen. If I focus long and hard enough on the emails (my faceless colleagues are constantly badgering me even though we haven't exchanged words using our mouths in days, weeks, *months*) on the screen that ping, ping, ping, then hopefully I'll be able to resist the headlines on constant repeat behind my aching shoulders.

Clutching my mobile, I circle the front room until I do what I always do in these circumstances, when I want to be somewhere else but there is nowhere else I want to go, when I don't want to be awake, but I don't want to be asleep, when I don't want to be dead but I'm not entirely sure I want to be alive either.

I call my younger sister.

She was born just eighteen months after me, which is nothing in the big scheme of things, is it? I've probably spent less time than that trying to get through to my mobile provider. I'll always be her big brother though, and to me that is an important role. My first *ever* memory is of my little sister crawling along our living room's carpeted floor. I was nestled in the middle of the sofa between my dad on my left (dressed as Santa) and my mum on my right (dressed as Santa's little helper). Our fascinated eyes followed my sister as she made her way closer and closer to the Christmas tree. And our fascinated eyes didn't dare look away as my little sister reached out and tugged at one of the prickly branches and (even I could tell this wasn't part of the big plan) the tree toppled to the floor with an almighty thud.

But the felled tree missed my little sister, and so – quite simply – one of my first memories as a kid is of my family laughing hysterically.

"Well *hello*. This is Frances-"

"Frances-"

"I know how much you really want to talk to me-"

"I really do-"

"But I am busy being busy at the moment. Places to go, people to see; I'm sure you know how it is. What can I say? I'm a popular girl. Leave a message and I'll drop all the other important things going on in my life and I'll get straight back to you..."

Rubbing my sleeve across my forehead, I flinch. Am I startled by the sound of my own voice? Just how long has it been? "Frances, I know they keep telling me to stop calling you, that this number really shouldn't be available for me anymore, that it isn't healthy for me to keep calling you, but they're wrong. They're all wrong. Not only am I going to keep calling you, but I am going to keep calling you every single day. I just want to hear your voice. Is that so bad?"

I stumble backwards against the sofa, like I've had too many spins on the merry-go-round. "I just want to say I love you, Frances..."

My middle finger taps the red button. Letting go of the phone, it disappears down the sofa, joining the pennies and the biscuit crumbs. With my back to the television, the red, glaring unread messages multiply on my computer screen. Out of mild curiosity, I click one of the messages.

Andrew. I am sorry to trouble you. It says you are available but I called you and you didn't answer. You still need to be free to take calls when you are working from home. I know you can't be out of the house, otherwise you would be breaking the newly implemented rules. I need an urgent response to a query please.

With the words repeating in my mind that I can't possibly be out of the house, I throw on my jacket, tearing at the metal zip until it grazes my chin. Eyeing the sofa, I tap my toes against the floor a few times before sliding my hand down the crack. What if somebody calls me? What if it is an emergency? Moving to the kitchen, the black cotton fabric on the kitchen table seemingly glares at me. Gulping, I take a few steps forward before turning on my heel and slamming the front door behind me.

The autumn air is mild, and yet featureless layers of thick, drifting grey clouds seemingly graze the floor. Brushing the drizzle from my forehead, I don't bother looking left or right for cars as I cross the road. The Green Cross Code is a thing of the past. With my hands bunched tight inside my pockets, my shoulders sway from side to side. The twitching curtains used to mesmerise me just like the news headlines and the internet feeds. Removing a hand from my pocket, I slide my fingertips down a moist, sloping car bonnet. I used to glance over my shoulder. Today and (probably) tomorrow my eyes fix ahead, indifferent to my surroundings.

Have I stopped caring?

Sometimes as I walk the soulless, deserted streets I imagine that I'm living in an apocalypse. For me, this type of life may as well *be* an apocalypse.

My trainers struggle for grip on the sloping grass embankment. I remove my hands from my pockets to help maintain my balance. Soggy mud cakes the hem of my blue jeans. Despite the occasional shopping trolley and an abandoned plastic bag, to me the canal water is beautiful. The lilies sit peacefully on the surface, regardless of the weather.

The water is surprisingly clear, and if you stop and peer closely, tiny fish gather, kissing the surface. Whatever my frustrations with the current predicament, I reluctantly accept that the wildlife has blossomed. The rain pelts into the water like bullets firing from a gun. The rising bubbles suggest the fish are thriving. My feet retreat from the muddy path and back onto the bumpy concrete.

I focus on the brick tunnel plastered with red and blue graffiti about twenty yards in front of me. Stepping over an abandoned bottle of vodka, I remember that the tunnel offers shelter and a decent hiding place for the drunks and the addicts. The path curls to the right on the other side of the tunnel. I usually poke my head inside first to see if a cyclist is coming from the other direction. Or at least I used to.

From about ten yards, the shadow from within the tunnel begins to expand.

The growing shadow is replaced by shiny, black leather shoes, damp from the rain. My eyes rise. The sturdy, tree-trunk legs give way to a navy sweatshirt, stretched tight by considerable shoulders. The black cotton fabric covering the face cannot conceal the outline of a strong chin.

My fists tighten into balls. I push out my chin. "Do your worst," I shout. "I fucking dare you!"

The shiny, black leather shoes keep moving forwards.

Whoever this is, he'll need to kill me if he wants to take me down. This is it. I've had enough.

"What are you doing?"

I slant my head. What did he say? My coiled shoulders loosen. My arms dangle by my sides.

"You think I'm one of the marshals?"

I don't say anything for a few moments. "Who else would you be?"

Pulling at the straps, he removes his mask. In my mind I'd already created a cartoon character, and yet the jaw line is even stronger – even more ridiculous – than I'd envisaged. The cheeks are void of stubble, and the lips curl at the corners. My eyes glance to the black fabric balled into his pocket. If he isn't one of the marshals, then he must be...

"I am just like you," the man says, holding out his hand.

His grip is firm, but effortlessly so; he doesn't try to prove his masculinity. "You don't feel like you belong anymore? Me neither. There are plenty more like us out there. You just need to look in the right places. I am on your side."

Wrapping his arm around my shoulder, I'm conscious of the lean, rippled muscle. The guy is about the same age as me – forty-four – and he doesn't look down on my 6'2, and yet he is broader; he is stronger. I take a quick glance left and right. It is just me and this man.

The man's arm moves away. Looking down, I focus on the green and white bird shit coating the concrete floor. Some of it is dried; some is soggy and soft. As the initial threat eases, I'm hit by an erratic thought: I don't want to stay in this tunnel for too long in case a bird shits on my head.

"So, tell me; how are you, Andrew?"

I'm unnerved that he stares deep into my eyes, like this isn't just a token, idle question; he genuinely wants to know how I am.

"How do you know-"

"Andrew Macintosh?"

I must raise my eyebrows, for his smile spreads.

"Currently residing at 24 Cornell Road?"

I scan his face for indicators. I don't know if his smile gives any clues.

"Don't worry," he says, holding up his hands. "I have a proposition you might be interested in, Andrew. And it will all start tomorrow..."

DAY ONE

Contestants Eliminated: 0
Contestants Remaining: 50

Morning

Whilst my eyes snap open, the side of my face remains pinned against the pillow. Dried spit coats my chin. Not even shapes and outlines are visible in the darkness of the room. The curtains are pulled tight, just like they were yesterday and the day before. Is it morning, or night time? Stretching my curled legs, I have my first real thought of the morning.

Oh fuck. Another day.

I know exactly how Bill Murray felt in *Groundhog Day.*

Subconsciously I'm aware that I'm not quite awake yet. Sleep clings to me, not quite ready to let me go, like a spawned lover. One day older. One day closer to death. Something is different from yesterday though, isn't it? This isn't the same day on repeat. I just can't quite remember what makes it different, though. It's a Wednesday. Nothing special happens on a Wednesday. Some people call it the hump day, but that's only because there isn't anything interesting to say about the day. But something *is* different. It is like I am leaving the house and I can't quite remember what I've forgotten. Phone? Mask? Key? Wallet? The thought gnaws like an itch that desperately needs scratching.

My back jolts upwards like I've just been stabbed with a needle. I'm startled, like somebody has dropped a medicine ball on a hard, wooden floor. My hands push down against the bed. The alarm clock digits flash green.

5:15.

Exhaling, I raise my head to the ceiling. I have time.

Still naked, I part the bedroom curtains for the first time in days. Returning to the house yesterday, my clothes damp from the drizzle, I spent the afternoon glued to the computer screen, searching everything and anything that could, in some bizarre and random way, be connected to the proposition. Bitter experience has taught me to be suspicious of everything, to always expect the worst; that way anything better is a welcomed bonus. Despite myself, my heart hankered for it to be true. Excitement seeped through my veins; excitement I hadn't felt in a long time. My fingertips tapped the keys. Sucking in the air, I held my breath...

Everything the man said tallied.

"Trust me," he'd wolfishly grinned, like a sales advisor telling me crypto-currency held zero risk, that the value only ever went up and never down. The flurry of zigzagging lines disappeared from around his eyes when he spotted my scepticism. Any trace of humour vanished from his face. The salesman transformed into a preacher promising me that, unless I repented my sins, the only direction I was heading in was down. "Andrew, I know you have little reason to believe anything anyone tells you in the current world. And even though I know a lot about you-"

"You know my name. You know my address. What do you *really* know about me?"

"I know, for example, that in different circumstances you'd long to call Frances this evening, asking for her advice..."

"Don't you dare mention my sister, you hear?"

Whilst he held his hands up – two mighty mitts that could squeeze the life from the average man's windpipe – his creaseless face showed no indication he was surprised by the ferocity of my tone.

"Okay, well I know you don't know *me* from Adam," he said. "That isn't a good basis to trust me, especially with something this monumental. Let me tell you something about myself..."

"I'm not being funny, but you could be making this up, too..."

"I have two children. Zoe is nine and Mia is six. Mia was born prematurely, and she remained on a life-support machine for two weeks. We didn't know if she'd live or if she'd die. I love my girls with all my life. Now I swear on my two little girls' lives that I am telling the truth. Go home and check it out for yourself. I know that's your way. Do your research..."

He knew I would anyway. He was merely giving me the green light to do so. Sat at my computer desk, with the afternoon light fading, I was still riddled with doubts. Why hadn't I heard about the whole thing? I brushed away that notion. When I managed to keep away from the news and the gossip, I deliberately lived in a bubble. For long periods, I may as well live in a cave. It made sense that it meant nothing to me. As Spock would say, it was logical.

Sheltered under the bridge, the wind and the rain gaining momentum, it was like the man had read my mind. He left me with one final question to consider.

"What exactly do you have to lose, Andrew?"

And then he asked me to choose my F-Word.

Instinctively, I recalled raising the F-word to my mum when I was knee high to a grasshopper. The word felt like something dark and mysterious that should never, ever be mentioned.

My darling mum. The other mums always smiled when they passed us on the way home from school. The dads acted strangely around her, though, in a way I couldn't put my finger on. Sure, they smiled, just like the mums did, but their eyes lingered. I got in the habit of glancing over my shoulder after we'd passed. Our eyes connected, for they glanced over their shoulders, too. They looked away, just like I did when Dad caught me in the sweetie drawer.

It must have been autumn when I raised it, just like now, because I recall the soggy leaves staining the pavement a mix of brown and yellow and red, like the awful paintings I brought home that Mum pinned to the fridge.

"What is it, Andy?" Mum asked.

I'd given no indication that anything was wrong. Could she read my mind? I hoped not; it was around this time I started taking an interest in girls.

"Edward got sent to Mrs Lewis's office for saying the F-word, Mum."

Her lips creased into a smile. "*Did* he now?"

We looked both ways before crossing the road. "What else is it?"

"What do you mean?"

"That isn't everything. Tell me what else is on your mind, Andy."

"I just wondered something, that's all. What exactly *is* the F-word, Mum?"

Mum crouched down to my level. My eyes were drawn to the beauty spot on her right cheek, just like Marilyn Monroe's. Frances floated around somewhere at my mother's side. "The F-word is any word beginning with the letter 'F' that you choose it to be. That is the magic of letters. You can create any word you want. The trick is to create a wonderful word."

"So why did Edward get sent to Mrs Lewis's office for saying a word?"

Mum placed the flat of her hands on my shoulders. "Because Edward chose to make his word a bad word, that's why, Andy."

And now, just under forty years later, a nagging thought rebounds in my mind: I hope Mum would think I'd chosen a wonderful F-word.

If *only* I could ask her.

I turned off the computer. Pacing up and down in the hallway, my straightened fingers grazing the wallpapered walls, the question contaminated my mind. I couldn't help but smile when another urge hit me. How did the man know it would be my instinct to call my younger sister? Was I unsettled by his insight, or flattered that somebody actually cared?

The strain seeped away when I heard Frances's voice on the other end of the phone.

"I know this is the type of situation I berate, Frances. I know it is exactly the type of thing I take the piss out of. God, I'm a hypocrite, aren't I? I'm trying to think of all the excuses in the world to ignore it, but there is only one I care about. If I agree to do it then I won't be able to hear your voice for a few days or more..."

Of course, that was yesterday, and a lot can change with a good night's sleep. Showered and dressed, I tiptoe down the wooden stairs. Who am I afraid of waking? I live alone.

Sniffing the milk in the plastic bottle, I devour my cereal, which is like cardboard left out in the rain. Usually I dread returning to my computer screen. Usually it signifies the beginning of another day of monotony.

My conversations with colleagues are well rehearsed.

"How are you, Andrew?"

"Good thanks. How are you?"

"Good thanks. Glad it is nearly the weekend."

"I know what you mean. What are you doing on the weekend then?"

"Nothing. How about you?"

"Nothing."

"Sounds fantastic."

"Doesn't it just?"

The curtains in the front room remain forever open, luring in the darkest sliver of light. Deliberately I allow the room to be visible for all to see (less and less people with each passing day), longing somebody to smash the window and run away with the computer, providing the perfect excuse for doing no work.

It hasn't always been like this. There was a time – in a previous job, in a previous lifetime – when I loved my job, when I liked waking up in the morning.

Whenever possible, I arrived fifteen minutes or so early to class. It wasn't to *do* anything, as such; it was my time; the quiet before the storm, when I prepared my mind for the lecture. I tended to lean back, put my feet up on the desk and gaze at the empty desks, imagining them occupied, picturing the room vibrant with learning.

This particular day I strolled into the room and stretched out my legs, just like any other day. It was about eight years ago I think, when I was maybe thirty-six. I jumped, like I'd spotted a spider crawling across the tiled floor. Only, it wasn't a spider; this creature only had *two* long, gangly legs. The student sat at the back of the class in a navy, shapeless cardigan, his rounded shoulders huddled like he was sipping coffee under the floodlights at a freezing cold Tuesday night football match.

I pulled my legs back underneath my chair and straightened my back. "What are you doing here, John?"

His thin lips gathered into a pained smile and, with a high-pitched voice, he told me he was here for my lecture.

With heat flowing to my cheeks, I shuffled around in my seat. "Sorry. I get that. I mean: what are you doing here so early?"

John fiddled with his pen. "I'm not the most organised, if I'm honest with you. I struggle to plan to get to places. I either turn up embarrassingly early or – worse – I turn up late, and I just cannot deal with all that attention. Truth be told though, I didn't want to miss a minute of your lecture. I find them inspirational, you know? I'm sorry, though. If you have planning to do, then I respect that and I can stand outside and wait for the others to come in."

I felt like a pop star. The classroom was my stage. He'd arrived early to watch me perform. Sliding my chair back and standing up, I was worried my head would hit the ceiling. Of course, I told him not to be ridiculous, told him that he could stay. For the next fifteen minutes we exchanged glances and awkward small talk.

I took more notice of him over the coming weeks and months. I figured that he wasn't naturally anti-social; he just had no social skills. He attempted a smile when the other students arrived, but because it didn't come naturally, his lips merely flickered manically. With his diminutive frame and delicate voice, he remained invisible to the rest of the students. I made more effort in our fifteen-minute periods before class started. One time I asked him whether he longed to mix more with the other students.

"I quite enjoy sitting at the back of the room and listening and observing," he said. "And besides, it helps with my writing."

"You like being a voyeur?" I asked.

John's mouth opened into a perfect circle. "The dictionary defines a voyeur as a person who gains sexual gratification from watching others when they are engaged in sexual activity, sir. Are you suggesting I'm some sort of pervert? I assure you that that isn't the type of image I'm trying to portray."

I held my hands close to my chest. "Oh no. Not at all. I was-"

"Sir, I am *messing* with you."

I realised then that, far from being a potential serial killer, he was actually kind of alright, in an odd sort of way. Strangely, he was just happy being himself. He told me that he did consider dressing differently, maybe wearing clothes that were fashionable within about the last decade or so, but then that wouldn't be authentic. And besides, he didn't want to be just another clone. There weren't many others like him.

One morning he soundlessly shuffled to my desk. I could tell he was there by the shadow cast over my scribbled notes. I waited for him to say something and, when he didn't, I glanced up. John dangled a brown envelope between his fingers. He slid it across my desk.

"I know it is terribly clichéd, but I've started my novel, sir. I appreciate that it is absolutely dreadful, but if you could take the time to read it and give me some feedback, even if you helped make it a tiny bit better, then I'll forever be in your debt."

I gazed at him with his spindly arms and a jumper that looked like it had been left outside in the rain overnight, and I told him that, of course, it would be an honour to read his first draft. For the first (but not last) time, he beamed at me. Secretly, I was honoured that he'd chosen me as the first reader.

All of those hours watching and observing others had paid off. The novel wasn't absolutely dreadful. Sure, the first draft had plot holes, and the sentence structure needed some work, but the characters were engaging, the dialogue was realistic, and the novel was packed with gripping conflict. In summary, it was brilliant. Over the coming weeks I gladly shared what I hoped was constructive feedback, and John keenly made changes. Finally, I closed the final page of the final draft.

"You need to get it published," I said. I wasn't being kind. I meant it.

"I don't think so."

I reassured him that it was good enough.

"It's not that. It's just the novel was only ever intended to be a practice exercise. I want to enjoy the writing process, to practice the craft. And then, when I am ready, I will start publishing my books."

"This book deserves to be read."

John held my gaze. "It has been read," he said. "And it has been read by my target reader."

There was nothing else I could say to that.

It was the last day of term. All of the other students had left, probably filling their mouths with warm, flat beer in the student union. John didn't look like he had anywhere to go any time soon.

"I just want to say thank you, sir."

I held up my hands, my cheeks doubtless flushing. "I just did my job, John."

He shook his head. "No, you did a lot more than your job. I want you to know that I will never forget the help you gave me."

John turned, leaving the room. I stayed with my feet up on the desk for fifteen minutes, the quiet *after* the storm.

I never saw him again.

That wasn't a normal day, and neither is today. Yesterday wasn't a normal day. And tomorrow sure as hell won't be a normal day. Whether that is a good or bad thing remains to be seen. Sinking into the cushioned blue computer chair, my fingers slam down against the keyboard, furiously typing.

I will be out of the office for up to seven days. Go figure. Depending on what happens in those seven days, I may never return. Will you miss me?

My cursor sweeps across the monitor. Messages flash up on my screen. With relish, I delete them. Who knows what they said? Who cares? Not me. Smirking, I realise that my boss, Tony, will only realise I've vanished from the face of the earth when he sends me an email and is greeted with my out of office message.

Suck on my big, fat, hairy cock, Tony.

I scan my phone for new messages (there are none) before pressing the red button to turn it off. I place it on the kitchen table, next to my wallet and my mask. After a quick check of the windows, I take a deep breath and then slam the front door behind me.

******

The orange streetlights glimmer in the darkness. A fox disappears behind a blue bin. Yesterday's swagger is more natural today. My calves are vaguely aware of the gentle, upward slope. Passing street after street, the houses become more and more sparse. I step off the unforgiving concrete and onto soft grass, still moist from yesterday's rain. Looking over my shoulder, I salute the town I leave behind.

The darkness begins to fade just as I reach the field. Perfectly flat, it must be the size of two football pitches. Walking to the middle of the field, I imagine standing in the centre circle at Wembley on cup final day. I glance at my wrist; I am a few minutes early. I inhale a mouthful of fresh, moist air and look up at the sky. Yesterday it was grey, overcast and dreary, and not just in my mind. Today the sky is blue and bright and spotless. I shield my eyes with the back of my hand as the perfectly round orange sun rises from the depths of the fields.

Despite previous attempts to the contrary, right now it feels wonderful to be alive.

What F-word would my dad have chosen? I think it would have been the same as mine. At this time of year as a kid we'd huddle together in the local cafe, sipping hot chocolate, biding our time before heading off to the football. I looked forward all week to those Saturday afternoons. We both enjoyed the simple things in life.

What was that?

With my eyes glued shut, it is like a bee buzzing busily close to me. I picture it edging closer and closer. It feels like I can reach out and flick it away. The ground beneath me begins to shake. The breeze makes me want to pull my arms across my chest. When the noise stops gaining momentum, when it stays level, I know that it has stopped moving towards me, that it has landed.

I've always imagined paddling in warm Mediterranean water on a beachside holiday when a monumental submarine rises from beneath the water, making the bathers gasp and point and scream. I'm reminded of this now as I open my eyes and take in the pristine, polished black helicopter that has nestled on the grass approximately fifty feet away from where I stand.

My calmness vanishes. How crazy was this decision? Suddenly, I am aware how exposed I am, the lone figure in the centre of a large field.

I could be shot dead here and now and nobody would blink an eyelid for days.

My chest tightens. A bulky figure springs from the helicopter. The shock of platinum blonde hair tells me that it isn't the same man from yesterday. That guy was some sort of Adonis, right at the front of the line to play GI Joe or Captain America. From first impressions, I like this guy more because he doesn't make me feel guilty for not hitting the weights every day. The excess cushioning around his midriff suggests that he is no stranger to a doughnut or two. As he picks up the pace from a walk to a jog, I wonder whether it would be a good or a bad thing if he drops dead from a heart attack before reaching me.

His legs are long and his strides are rapid, but still, the seconds pass slowly. I take his outstretched hand.

"Andrew Macintosh?"

"The one and only," I say. Uttering the words, I recall another Andrew Macintosh I met at university.

"Glad you decided to join us. My colleague from yesterday said that you would."

"He told me all about his kids, but he never gave me his name."

"That's right. Anyway, you made the right decision, Andrew."

"We'll see."

"Did you bring anything with you?"

"I was told not to. I only have the watch on my wrist."

The man removes the watch. "Hold out your arms please, Andrew."

His knee digs into the grass as he traces my body from my ankles upwards, paying particular attention to my pockets. "All good. Clean as a whistle."

"Did you want to stick a finger up my arse, just to make sure?"

He stares down at me from just a few inches. There is not even a flicker of a smile. "Not really my thing, sweetheart. You haven't even reached the helicopter and already you're giving attitude. It doesn't bode well, does it?"

"Sorry. It's all bravado. I'm just trying to lighten the mood."

"Did you tell anyone what you were doing?"

"Urm..."

He edges closer. Spittle flecks my cheeks. "I'll repeat my question. Did you tell anyone what you were doing?"

"No," I say. "I was told not to."

He pauses momentarily before nodding. He tells me we have one last thing to do: take a test to make sure I'm not carrying the virus. I tell him the guy took a test at the canal yesterday.

"Good for him. We're taking another one."

With the test completed, the man turns away from me. I spot a bald patch on the back of his head, maybe the size of a tangerine. It grows smaller. Clearly, he has a schedule. Most likely, he has others to pick up. But who? And are they in any way linked to me?

The helicopter's exterior is polished like a limousine escorting the stars. I use my hand to shelter my eyes from the reflection of the sun on the sparkling metal. I stop within touching distance. It feels like my legs are tied down with lead. The man faces me in the doorway, holding out his hand.

"You coming?" he asks. I sense bristling irritation.

Maybe I was right about that schedule.

I don't know where I am going, or who I am going with. I have no idea who or what is waiting for me in that helicopter.

Glancing over my shoulder, I am tempted by the stretch of luscious green grass behind me. The easy option would be to turn and run. This is my last chance.

I'm haunted by yesterday's words, the most brutal of them all.

What exactly do you have to lose, Andrew?

I reach out and take the man's hand.

His smile stretches. "Good man."

There is no turning back now, I think.

******

My cheeks burn when the occupants of the helicopter cheer my arrival. With straight backs, they sit along the outskirts of the helicopter, leaving a space – like a dance floor – in the middle. I untangle my face into what I hope is a happy look, and then, with my head bowed, I find a seat nestled between two others.

"The night is just getting started!" one of them says, raising a glass to me.

At seven in the morning, I guess the guy is deliberately ironic. Pressing my fingertips against my skull, I count the heads. Ten including me. I figure that there are probably another couple of helicopters out there heading in the same direction.

"Fancy a drink, mate? Might help relax the nerves. We've all got them."

The sharp white teeth glisten with moisture. Thick tufts of hair on both sides fail to compensate for the lack of hair on the temple. He is probably ten years younger than me, but he looks older. The man pulls a bottle of champagne from an ice bucket. I hope my pained smile doesn't give away too much, that my raised hands aren't too defensive.

"Bit early for me, thank you."

Another guy leans forward and plants his hand on my knee. "I hope you're not going to be boring, mate?" He winks like a dad conspiring with his son not to tell Mum that he gave him a sweet. "You won't last long if you're boring."

I shrug. Am I going to be boring? Who knows. Am I going to drink? Not today, not tomorrow and not ever. I'm not going to tell him the reason. Reaching out his hand, the guy squeezes hard. His blue eyes hold mine. I don't spot any trace of a smile. "Duncan," he says. "Stick with me and you'll be just fine."

"Andrew," I say, looking away.

My eyes fall on a woman in her late twenties with skin pulled tight over sculpted cheekbones and peroxide blonde hair that falls to slender shoulders. Do we hold eyes for a moment too long? Her face breaks into a smile. I glance at her hands; no, I don't check whether she has a ring on her finger. She doesn't hold a drink either. Does she identify something in me?

With her tanned, flawless complexion and gym-toned body, she's the type of person I normally run a mile from. And yet, here I am, trapped with her in this flying metal bucket. Most guys would follow her around like a poodle; what exactly is my problem?

"This is so awesome, isn't it? It's just a shame I don't have my phone to post a picture to my Instagram."

My teeth jar. "I feel your pain."

Her smile vanishes. Maybe she identifies my sarcastic tone? I long to reel back my comment. I needn't worry. The smile reappears, flickering at the corners. The girl leans forward, holding out her hand like she is the queen. "Hello, stranger on a helicopter. It is fabulous to meet you. I'm Kim."

"And I'm Andrew."

I'm compelled to add to this. That Duncan guy suggested I was boring. Like everyone else in this world, I imagine people talking behind my back, stifling exaggerated yawns. My lips move, but it's like I'm in some dubbed movie; no words escape from my mouth, or if they do, they don't make any sense. Kim – this stranger on a helicopter - sits opposite me with smiling eyes, pouting her plump lips. I'm exposed. "It *is* a shame they took our phones, right?" I say. "Seriously, this would have been a lush photo opportunity."

Even I'm not sure now whether I am taking the piss. I do it so often, and with so many people, that it is almost my natural default. Regardless, Kim's smile widens. "Isn't it just? Honestly, we think alike, Andrew!"

There are no windows. We are sardines in a closed tin. I have no idea what direction we head, or for how long. Are we even in the same country? I recall that the man under the bridge said that if I told anyone where I was going then I *would* be removed.

I try to blank out the call I made to Frances yesterday afternoon.

"What do you do in life?"

The voice comes from beside me. I don't look up. I don't know who the voice comes from, but I do know it is soft, that it is encouraging. What *do* I do in life? I know it isn't what I want to do. The pandemic put an end to that. The pandemic ended so many things.

And now, I tell the man next to me that I work in finance, that it pays the bills, that it could be a whole lot worse. All of this is true. But it isn't who I *am.* I know I'm blessed, because the pandemic took many lives, and I'm still here, and yet – and I hate myself for thinking this - often it feels like I'm dead inside.

A hand massages my shoulder. "I like your holistic view of things," the man says. "You are looking at the big picture, my friend, at the world outside of your own. But I get the feeling that this role that pays your bills isn't what defines you as a person, is it? I'll make a note to explore that further..."

I jerk my head to the side, now interested who says these things, who it is that seems to know me better than I know myself, but I'm distracted because somebody spills champagne on the floor, and it starts spreading.

******

When the helicopter lands, we sit with our hands planted on our thighs, exchanging glances. The door flicks open and the guy from the field peers inside with a big toothy grin. He tells us to leave the helicopter, to please take our time. I wait for the crowd to disperse. I am the last one to leave.

Stepping off the helicopter, there isn't a moment to absorb the outside world before I'm ushered into a tunnel made of white cotton sheets that is maybe ten feet wide and twenty feet high. Blue, velvet rope is clipped to metal rails on both sides; my feet sink into luxurious red carpet. Despite the fidgeting and the whispers, we form an orderly line. There are about thirty people in front of me. The clapping and the cheering – from somewhere behind the curtain – intensifies as the numbers whittle down; it reminds me of walking past a football stadium on match day. I look over my shoulder; there are ten people behind me. Another helicopter must have landed. Most of them are younger than me, but a few are significantly older.

The numbers in front of me reduce to zero. A hulking giant with a shaven head and a pointed goatee leans over the railing, greeting me with a nod. He casts a shadow over the entrance, leaving me with no idea what lies behind him.

"Your turn," the man says, unclipping the rope and moving aside. He winks. "Good luck. Try not to get eliminated too early. There's a good boy."

This is my moment. Sucking in my cheeks, I step past the bouncer and enter the competition.

I'm blinded by the flashlights that appear from the left, from the right, from seemingly everywhere. I shield my eyes behind my raised forearm.

"Smile, Andrew."

"Give us a pose."

"Show the viewers who you really are, Andrew."

After years in the darkness, existing as the invisible man, the spotlight is on me; I'm a caged bird that is released and expected to survive in the wild. The audience is cast into the shadows; I have no idea if there are tens, hundreds or thousands of them. They exist only as faceless, expressionless people.

The photographers, crouched low with their faces hidden behind the cameras, flee like rats down a dark alleyway. A beaming, dark-skinned black lady holding a microphone calls me over with an elaborate wave of her hand. Freckles dust her cheeks; I can't tell if they are natural or painted. I don't dare glance down – not with the cameras on me - but I'm left in no doubt that womanly curves fill her black dress. My lips brush against her right ear as she pulls me close.

"Every man, woman and their dog; let's give a thunderous welcome to Andrew Macintosh!" She turns to the crowd with upturned hands. "So, how are you feeling Andrew? I appreciate that this is a huge moment for you. Don't worry, those nerves are natural!"

I glance at the bulbous, spotted head of the microphone. How close is my mouth supposed to be? I part my lips to imitate a smile. "I was feeling fine until you reminded me this is a huge occasion."

The laughter emitting from the darkness feels almost canned. "You have chosen Freedom for your F-Word. Between you and me, and the rest of the viewing world, of course, there aren't that many of you. For the benefit audience at home, let me remind you that if Andrew wins the competition then we'll transport him to one of the few countries in the world that hasn't been hit by the pandemic, where there are zero restrictions in place. We'll sort out all his documents and administer him with one month's rent. Tell me, Andrew, what would that mean for you?"

I move a few inches closer to the microphone. "For me it is the difference between life and death. I am dead without my freedom."

Dark eyelashes flutter. "You do make it sound

fantastic, Andrew, but I can't help but feel you've missed an opportunity here, sweetheart. If you'd chosen Fame then we'd have set you up with your own YouTube channel with over two million subscribers, and we'd promote you so your subscribers rocketed. Isn't that everybody's dream? And if you'd chosen Fortune then we'd furnish you with £250,000. I get giddy just saying the words. Don't you think you've given up a lot choosing Freedom, darling?"

I hold her gaze. "Those things don't mean anything to me."

The woman pats my shoulder like I'm the three-legged dog at the kennels everybody says is adorable, but nobody takes home. "You are one in a million, you really are. I have a feeling that our viewers are really going to warm to your quirky ways. And of all our contestants, you really do tick the troubled background box. There's so much pain and heartbreak, isn't there darling?" She turns her back, to face the crowd. "We all love a sob story, don't we? And it wins the votes. Why don't you take this opportunity to tell us all about it?"

She passes me the microphone; I hold it like a soggy ice cream cone. Blinking salty sweat from my eyes, I dig the balls of my feet into the carpeted floor. "I'd prefer to keep my family out of this. It isn't about them. And I certainly don't want to use them to win any votes."

"You could really make social media go mad with a few words here, Andrew."

"I'm not interested in social media."

She takes back the microphone. Her smile broadens, plumping her cheeks. "You really are a sweetheart, Andrew. I must say, you are one of my personal favourites. Give me a call after the show and we'll see if we can hook up."

The kiss on my cheek distracts me from the laughter. Cheers erupt around me. I twist my head to the side.

A glass door slides open, inviting me inside.

With a wave of the hand, I take a few reluctant strides. Stepping through the doors, I leave the outside world behind me.

I venture into my new world.

*****

My jaw drops. With my feet glued to the floor, my head rotates 360 degrees. What is this? Put bluntly, my new world is some kind of giant greenhouse.

The tiled floor spans about three hundred feet in length and a hundred feet in width. Aside from the curved ceiling, the hall is cuboid in shape, and apart from a single reflective wall, it is made entirely of transparent glass. The reflective wall has three doors; it's impossible to know what lies behind them.

With the exception of an open area spanning about twenty feet, box bedrooms outline the circumference of the hall. The bedrooms are maybe six feet wide; just enough room for a door and a single bed. The bedroom walls, and the doors, are also made of glass. The beds face the hall, so occupants can sit up and observe everything going on. I can see into the room and out of the other side. We're surrounded by overgrown grass (faded yellow from the summer), brambles and spiralling trees.

There are three cubicles where the bedrooms

end and the glass wall begins; I assume they're the toilets. I arch my head back. The curving ceiling reminds me of an igloo, only instead of snow everything is made of glass. The sky is still blemish-free. The orange sun is now a luminous yellow. I can see everything outside.

And the outside world can see everything that happens inside this place, too.

If only it began and ended there. Big Brother really is infallible. I spot about fifteen cameras; those are the ones they haven't hidden.

I anxiously try to appear relaxed. A few other singletons occupy each corner of the hall, marking their territory like a cat pissing on the lawn. We try not to glance at the small groups huddled together, bonding like they've known each other for years. I can't find Kim from the helicopter. I must be desperate to even look for her. There are between forty and sixty of us; presumably, there were another four or five helicopters.

I know why I am here; but why are *they* here?

Despite my nerves, I stifle a laugh. Who are these men walking around in white shirts, flannel shorts and socks pulled to their knees? Their almost featureless faces are clean-shaven. Short, sensible haircuts part in a straight line down one side. I estimate that they're an inch or two shorter than me, and they have lean but unspectacular builds. I count heads: there are twelve of them. Squinting, I check a badge pinned to a lapel.

Guard.

My throat is like sandpaper. I crave a glass of water from one of the round tables spread evenly across the hall. The glasses of water are outnumbered by the bottles of wine and champagne. I fail to catch a guard's eye. His glazed expression suggests he isn't concerned what I do. This is a good sign.

As I'm pouring water into the glass, a shadow grows close to me, just like it did down the canal. Was that really only yesterday? Looking up, I'm met by a light-skinned black man clad in faded jeans and a leather jacket. Although he is of my height and build, I suspect the ladies – and men – would say he carried it better. Apart from the odd speck of white, his stubble matches the black leather jacket. I could easily imagine him stood outside a rock or jazz club with a half-lit cigarette hanging from his lips. The subtle lines under his hooded eyes suggest he is maybe in his early forties, but something tells me he could still turn heads. Something tells me, on the other hand, that he wouldn't be bothered if he did or if he didn't. His calmness – or maybe it is his indifference – is in stark contrast to the excitement bubbling throughout the rest of the hall.

"I'm Dylan," he says, holding out his hand. "Do me a big favour, mate? Come chew the fat with me for a while. We don't want any of these other contestants thinking we haven't got any friends now, do we?"

Smiling, I take his hand. "Sounds like a plan."

"We could be two lone wolves hanging out together," Dylan says.

I delay my nod, trying to think of a clever retort. Somehow, the silence doesn't feel awkward.

Dylan winks. "Are you going to tell me your name, or am I going to have to guess it?"

"Oh. Sorry. I'm Andrew."

"Good to meet you, Andrew." Dylan moves an inch or two closer. His eyes are Americano with just a dash of milk. "You might need to give me some tips, squire. How you keeping cool in here? I'm a bag of nerves, mate."

I look him up and down. Nervous? The guy looks like he's on a yoga retreat.

Dylan smiles. He must read my mind. "Looks can be deceiving, my friend. I was born and bred in Britain, but my heritage is Jamaican. Damn, my granddad was on the SS Ormonde that sailed from Jamaica to Liverpool way back in 1947, even before the Windrush. And this relaxed look right here is just the way some of us Jamaicans roll. That's probably why cricket is such a religion in the West Indies."

Smiling, I tell him that I'm glad he said that and not me; it sounds like a sweeping stereotype.

"I get what you're saying. But it's what I believe, and I'm too old and tired to sugar coat my beliefs. People tell me that my movements appear fluid, like I have all the time in the world, when often I really don't. And that's not me saying that, that's other people. But you know what?"

My blank expression tells him that I really don't.

"When I head back to Jamaica every year with my family, the locals know that we are British, they know that we are visiting." Dylan releases a throaty laugh. "I may look chilled to you, but to those guys I look like I'm rushing around, like I'm in a hurry to get somewhere I really don't need to go. But my point is – and I'll get there eventually – is that you shouldn't believe everything you see. I may look like I'm ready for a lie down, but really I'm shitting it."

I break into a smile. "I'm shitting it, too."

The side of his mouth breaks into a smile. "Well then. We can help each other, can't we? Truth be told, Andrew, I've been missing my family."

"Wife? Kids?"

"Tick, and tick again," Dylan says. "Two little girls. Eight and ten. I'm in here for them."

Dylan glances at the clock. "The two little terrors will be in school right now, or at least the online version. They're completely different, you know? Sometimes I wonder if they have different dads or something."

A sliver of a smile must cross my face, because Dylan breaks into a laugh again. "I swear that they don't, you cheeky sod. But the oldest girl? Well, she has her life all planned out. She is heading to university. Becoming a vet. Finding a husband who treats her like a person and not an object. The happy couple are having two kids; a boy and a girl, and in that order. And then, when the kids are in comprehensive school, they'll get a dog and live happily ever after."

"Sounds like the idyllic life."

Dylan nods. "Doesn't it just? When she has a bad day – bless her cotton socks - she actually imagines her future, just to pull her through. Being a child is just too – erm – childish for her. She can't wait to become an adult and join what she thinks is the real world. And who am I to dash any of her delusions? But the youngest girl? She lives one day at a time, and she lives that day like it is her first day on the planet. She is so energetic. It is so damn cute, I tell you."

It is fantastic to hear him talk about his family. I'm grateful for it. I just hope he doesn't ask about my life. And – more than anything - I'm hoping he doesn't ask me why I'm here. Please don't ask me. I don't want him to think I'm a lunatic *just* yet. "Where did you tell work you were going?"

I blurt out the question and then instantly regret it.

What if he doesn't work? What if he *can't* work?

"I just took leave, mate. I'm an accountant. You weren't expecting that, were you? Anyway, the work comes in waves. March is the busiest time of the year, as you'd imagine. It tends to be slack around this time of year, so work weren't too bothered, if I'm honest."

I didn't expect him to take leave without his family, but then he did say that he was here *for* his family. I can just tell that he is a fabulous dad. I can't deny my envy. I have no idea what sort of a dad I'd be. What sort of an inspiration would I be?

Dylan spins around, taking in the whole hall. "I'm just trying to piece my thoughts together," he says. "So tell me. What do you think of this place, mate?"

"So far so good," I say.

Dylan thumbs his stubble. "I can't quite put my finger on what's bugging me."

"You're picking up some sort of vibe?"

Dylan's grin is subtle. "You read me like a book, Andrew. You read me like a book."

"What do you think it is?"

"Have you ever received a random email saying you've inherited a fortune?"

I nod.

"And what did you think when you did?"

I pause for a moment. "I thought that it was too good to be true."

Dylan scans the room again. "That's exactly what I'm thinking about this place," he says.

******

The next thirty minutes or so pass without drama. At first, I'm primarily an observer. Duncan, the guy who asked if I was going to be boring, talks relentlessly. The bloke has banter in spades, but it all seems to be at somebody else's expense. I imagine that whatever he does in life, he is probably incredibly successful.

Who else catches my eye? There is a knucklehead in his thirties who looks like he doesn't have two brain cells to rub together. And a tall, broad blonde girl looks like she has taken a break from the gym to join us. Of course, she gets plenty of attention. I'm drawn more to a woman with red hair that falls effortlessly to her waist. I'd guess she's in her early thirties, but then I'm the guy who thought John Cleese was still only seventy. Piercing blue eyes dominate a face sprinkled with freckles. She must catch me looking, for a brief, mysterious smile passes her lips.

The sound of ringing bells jerks the whole room to attention. I count ten rings, just like at the boxing when they announce the main event of the evening. We look to the ceiling when a male voice echoes around the room.

"Ladies and gentlemen, boys and girls, this is the moment you've all been waiting for. We are delighted to introduce your host for the show..."

Silence replaces the chatter and laughter. Straightening my back and loosening my shoulders, I lock eyes with Dylan. He arches a single eyebrow. Seconds pass. I continue glancing around. The faces stare ahead at the three reflective doors, waiting for one of them to open. Kim glances over her shoulder; her face alights when she sees me. She gives me a wave; an infant spotting her dad in the audience at her nativity play. Despite myself, I return her smile.

A gasp fills the hall as the middle door opens.

I let everyone else move forward a step or two. I can't see over their bobbing heads. Heels click on the tiled floor, growing louder and louder. Who on earth *is* this? I shuffle to the side, finding some space. My jaw drops.

I am not sure what I was expecting, but it wasn't *this.*

The woman stood at the front of the hall is probably only five foot tall, even in her four inch heels, and she likely lingers around the size six hangers at *John Lewis.* The red, painted smile appears disproportionately large to the rest of her, like a six-inch dick on a dwarf. Is she mid-forties? Maybe she is fifty? It is difficult to tell, for her forehead probably lost the ability to move back in the nineties. At a push, she is the mate's mum you secretly had a crush on but didn't tell anyone, and for a very good reason, too.

Seconds passed in silence, without the woman saying or doing anything. Her smile stretches her cheeks to snapping point.

"Hi-de-hi, campers."

I stifle a laugh. Now I know how Dorothy felt when she discovered the Wizard of Oz was really just a middle-aged balding fat man hid behind a curtain.

"My name is Rebecca. I am your host for these fun and games. Isn't it *wonderful* to be alive?"

Each and every one of us say that it is.

"Congratulations. You are the brave ones. By agreeing to participate in the show, you've decided to grab life by the balls and give it a good old squeeze. Can you please give yourselves a round of applause, just for being you? "

I look up at a camera. Is it pointed directly at me?

I clap enthusiastically, just so I don't stand out. The other contestants appear to be performing monkeys. Who exactly are they looking to impress? Is it each other, Rebecca, or the cameras? I glance at Dylan. Now, he *does* stand out. With his crotch pushed forward, he thumbs the pockets of his denim jeans. Marlon Brando would take notes from this guy. But what will the viewers think of his behaviour?

"Rules remind me of an *Ikea* instruction manual, so we'll get through them quickly. This is a reality show. You are one of fifty contestants. If you care to look around you then you'll see the cameras dotted everywhere. You are now being filmed. *You* are important. Our show will be screened every night to millions of viewers. The location of the show is, and will remain to be, a secret. Neither the contestants nor the viewers have a clue where we are."

"Do *you* know where we are?"

Heads turn. No surprise; it's Duncan.

Rebecca smiles coyly. "Sometimes I don't know what day of the week it is, let alone where I am, darling."

She quietens the rippling laughter with her upturned hand. "Details of the show, and the contestants, were not announced in advance. Nobody will realise you are participating until they see you up on the screen. You were told not to tell anybody you were coming on the show. If we find out that you did tell somebody then you *will* be eliminated. Did any of you tell anyone you were coming on the show?"

Heads drop to the floor. I shuffle from side to side.

"Silence is most definitely the right answer,

campers. Can any of you remember what the name of the show is?"

Hands rise, like we are back in school. Choose me. Choose me. Rebecca points at Kim.

"The F-Word Reality Show."

"Very good, Kim. And who knows what the 'F' stands for?"

"A naughty word you weren't allowed to utter in school," somebody pipes up. Laughter fills the room. I imagine my mum laughing at this, too.

Rebecca shakes her smiling face. "You would think that, wouldn't you? But, no. It stands for Fame, Fortune and Freedom. You all chose your F-word before you entered the show. That will be your prize if you win."

The chorus of approval leads Rebecca to rub her hands together. "Listen very carefully, for I will say this only once. You will be allocated a daily shower time. The cameras are turned off in this area. Tomorrow morning will be the first slot. At the end of the shower you'll be provided your outfit for the show. Any questions?"

Rebecca takes our silence as a no.

"We'll make an important announcement twice a day, reliably informing you that the cameras will be turned off for an hour. Therefore, twice a day and for an hour only you will be free from the cameras. Understood? Right, let's get things moving."

My eyes wander to the other, nodding, contestants. Most are faceless individuals, replicas of each other. My eyes stop wandering when they reach the young lady with the flame hair. Something stirs inside my trousers. Instinctively, I turn to see if Dylan has spotted her too. Maybe he prefers the tall blonde woman? Dylan stares absent-mindedly into space. He appears oblivious to the female presence. He *must* be a dedicated family man.

Rebecca points at me. "Andrew. You are a team captain for this. Come stand here, please."

She already knows my name?

This time it isn't paranoia. All eyes really are on me. Standing a foot or two from Rebecca, her perfume draws me in. She gives the impression she showers three times a day. Rebecca calls another contestant by their name; she tells him to stand the other side of her.

"Choose teams. Andrew, you pick first."

Thank God I'm the picker. I remember getting picked last for the school football team, not because nobody liked me, but because I'm a terrible footballer. At least this way I'm saved the humiliation.

"Dylan," I say.

More heads join both teams. I'm drawn to the knuckle-head I spotted earlier. He reminds me of a schoolyard bully. The short sleeves expose tree-trunk arms. He thrusts his head forward like a pigeon. This guy would be an asset if there are any physical challenges. I point my finger at him. "You."

I choose the rest of my team based on their apparent sanity; the pool of choices reduces to just two. The final two scan the room, making sure they don't catch my eye. My throat gulps. I spot the reddening, watery eyes.

"Kim."

I lower my head as she joins us. I'm pinged by guilt that I didn't pick her earlier. I'm pinged by guilt that I didn't pick her because I suspect she is both insane *and* irritating.

"Thank you," she whispers. "For making sure I wasn't last."

A frog jumps in my throat. "No problem."

"That's one thing sorted then," Rebecca says. "Tonight is yours to enjoy. We are going to allow you to let your hair down, so you can settle into the show."

I follow Rebecca's retreating back until she reaches the middle door at the rear of the hall. The door opens, and then it shuts behind her.

******

Evening

Sinking into the sofa opposite Dylan, my trousers gather, and my shirt stretches at the arms. I think better of checking for dark circles under my armpits. Dylan still hasn't taken his leather jacket off, but there seems to be no risk of him overheating.

I crank my neck. The tiled floor has been transformed into a dance floor. A couple (who presumably met this morning) gyrate to the music; their hands nestle on the other's hips. Another contestant bows his head, precariously dangling a half-full glass of lager in his hand.

"A penny for your thoughts?"

Dylan stops staring into space. "Apologies, mate. I know I'm not always the best company. I was just imagining what my kids will be up to. I've been thinking about that a lot recently. Oh, and I've been daydreaming about my wife, too."

"How did you two sweethearts meet?"

Dylan flexes his fingers. I get the impression that his wife may be one of his favourite topics of conversation. "We met at the tennis courts. Which is quite ironic really, because it was practically the whitest place in town. Imagine the tennis club in *Trading Places* and you won't be far off the mark."

Stifling a laugh. I ask him if it was love at first sight.

His mind drifts to some previous, wondrous time. "For me it was lust at first sight. I was there with my mate and she was there with hers. I kept accidentally on purpose hitting the ball onto her court, just to have an excuse to talk. But she was the one who came out with some awful, cheesy line."

I lean forward. "Go on. What did she say?"

"She picked up a stray ball and said something about having a handful of one of my balls. She'd probably get arrested in this day and age, but I thought it was hilarious. We met in the bar afterwards, and we just connected, you know? I don't know if I believe in fate, but I swear that we were put on this earth to be together." Dylan pauses. "What about you? You got a wife? Kids?"

I shake my head. "And I don't even know anymore whether it's through choice or not."

Dylan nods. His eyes suggest I've shared some profound wisdom. "We're all different. It's whatever works for you, isn't it?"

I try to make my shrug suitably enthusiastic.

"Got any wider family?" Dylan asks.

"Yes."

Please don't probe me anymore. Please don't...

Dylan leans forward. "What did you think of the rules?"

Relieved that he's changed the subject, I tell him they seemed pretty straightforward.

He smiles. "I think we both know something was missing."

Come to think of it, I *did* think something was missing. "Well, I've been trying to figure out how the contestants will be eliminated. And Rebecca never mentioned that, did she?"

"See. You are clued up. We think alike, me and you." Dylan displays a row of perfectly straight, white teeth. "On the other hand, whilst I'm *clearly* loving your company, I'm not sure you should be hanging around with just me, mate."

I straighten my back. Have I already crossed a boundary?

Dylan smirks. "It's nothing like that. I'm not here to impress anybody but my wife and kids, though. And think about it...how do these shows normally work? Either the contestants or the viewers vote for who they want to stay in the show. Either way, it is a popularity contest, isn't it? You need to get yourself out there and make yourself memorable, Andrew."

My heart sinks. He is right. I suspect this guy is *always* right. I *do* need to make an impression. I need people to like me. I need to win this show. I wasn't lying when I told the interviewer I was nothing without my freedom.

I think back to the canal. That guy knew me so well. He knew I had everything to gain, and nothing to lose. "It was a bit odd how they contacted us, don't you think? Did they contact you..."

A potent waft of perfume interrupts my chain of thoughts. My eyes naturally focus on an unusually long pair of slender legs. I blink away the guilt. Nimble fingers squeeze my shoulder.

"How are *you* doing, Andy?"

"Andrew."

"How are you doing, *Andrew*?"

Kim's lips are about five inches away from mine. I smell no alcohol on her breath, and yet she gives the impression she is high as a kite. Dylan's words – urging me to make more of an effort – recycle in my frazzled mind. "I'm grand, thanks, Kim. How's your first night on the show?"

"Seriously, this is the best night of my life."

I laugh. Kim's face remains placid. She isn't joking.

"Does my face look dreadfully red, Andrew?"

"*What?*"

"Does my face look red and disgusting? I feel it's burning up. I don't want to look silly for the cameras. I know I'm already a monster. I don't possibly want to look any more frightful."

I tone down my audible sigh. "No, your face isn't red, Kim. And we both know you're far from ugly."

Holding my eye, she flutters her lashes. "Do you think I'm pretty?"

I go to tell her that it really doesn't matter whether I think she is pretty or not, but I decide that this will merely prolong the discussion. "I think you're very pretty, Kim. And I guess it *is* exciting times. It is not every day you get to go on a show like this, is it?"

Kim squeezes my hand. "It's blown my mind, babe. We're on TV, Andrew! It's always been my dream to be on TV or YouTube; to be someone. How awesome is this?"

She looks for a response from Dylan. He raises an encouraging eyebrow, which is more than I expected. She turns her attention back to me. "You picking me on your team made you my favourite friend in here, you know that? You could say that you are my best friend forever."

She leans towards me with her mouth open. It reminds me of a shark with bared teeth. I arch my neck back. I consider pushing her away, but I don't want to make it too blatant. It's an overreaction; I'm certain she only wanted a friendly kiss, just a peck. Kim pulls away. Her smile shimmers. She glances at the camera, maybe hoping that the moment wasn't – or maybe *was* – captured.

Kim fires her words out, changing the focus. "You want to know something? You picking me reminded me of my cousin looking out for me at school. I'm being serious."

"How so?"

Kim lowers her eyes. "My cousin was my hero; you know what I mean? She was three years older than me, and one of the most popular girls in the school. She was proper stunning..."

"Do you have her number?"

Kim's look suggests she would *not* give me her cousin's number, and even if she did, there was zero chance she'd accept my call. I wish I hadn't asked the question, especially just after she tried to kiss me; I was just trying to lighten the mood.

"Anyway, before I was rudely interrupted, I was about to say that I wasn't a popular kid at school. If you think I'm an ugly dog now – and goodness knows you probably do - then you should have seen me as a kid. I hit every branch of the ugly tree. If there is a god then he was taking the piss when he made me, I tell you."

"No, I'm sure-"

"I had braces. I had spots. I had everything that is a nightmare for a twelve-year-old-girl. In primary school I blended in. Nobody gave two hoots there, but everything changed when I moved to the big school. It was dog eat dog. We had phones by then; it was all about looking good in photos. Well – newsflash - I *didn't* look good. My old friends didn't want to be tarnished by association. Every day one of the bigger girls stole my glasses and passed them around to other girls. They dropped them a few times. They were cracked and broken."

"Sounds like a nightmare," I say.

Kim takes a fleeting glance at the camera. Water fills her eyes. "Shit happens. Anyway, one day one of the girls stole my glasses, and I was in floods of tears. I was thinking of fighting back when suddenly all the girls froze. My cousin strode in and put her arm around me. She said I was her cousin and she was with me. She told the girls that if any of them had an issue with me then they could speak to her."

"What happened then?" I asked.

"None of them said a word. They all stopped bullying me, too. By about Year 9 I was one of the popular girls in the school."

Looking at Kim now, with her perfect figure and beautiful skin, it is difficult to imagine her as the unpopular girl in the school. Who the fuck *is* she? Maybe she tries too hard to never be that bullied girl again?

"I'm glad it ended well," I say. "But what does it all have to do with me?"

She smiles. "Standing there in the line, with just two of us left, I was terrified I'd be that twelve-year-old-girl again. It was like you put your arm around me and said you were on my side. How cool is that?"

The hairs on my arms straighten. I am not very good at taking criticism, but I am even worse at accepting compliments.

Dylan smirks. "He was just trying to gain popularity, so he doesn't get voted out first."

Kim brushes away his comment with an elaborate flick of her hand. I try to change the subject. "It must have been amazing to have an older cousin like that."

Kim looks away. "Right."

Nobody speaks for a few moments. Something isn't quite right. Fidgeting in the chair, I desperately seek something to say. I'd be useless at speed dating. Narrowing her eyes into slits, Kim nestles her forehead on my shoulder. How does she feel so comfortable with someone she has only just met, particularly when that someone is me? I don't understand people sometimes.

"Can I tell you something?" Kim asks.

"Thought you just did," Dylan says.

"I'm worried about the morning." Pouting her lips, Kim's hands slide to her slim hips. "Well, it is all very well for you guys, isn't it? You don't have to worry about these things. But they have taken away my moisturiser, my makeup, my eye shadow, my *everything*! And Rebecca said that after the shower they're going to put us in an outfit. They could stick us in anything, couldn't they? What are people going to think of me? I'm going to look a mess, boys!"

I smile weakly. I want to ask her why it matters what people think. Luckily, Dylan speaks up. "I'm sure that even without makeup and all those needless accessories, Kim, you'll look absolutely stunning in the morning. You'd look good in a bin bag."

Rising to her feet, Kim noisily squeezes Dylan. She scurries off like a mouse that has spotted some dregs of cheese.

I check my wrist – although I don't really know what I'm looking for – and then I stretch out my arms. "I'm going to hit the sack," I say. "Listen, thanks for tonight. It's been great."

Dylan smirks. "That's the type of thing you should be saying to the ladies, Andrew, you big flirt."

I know I'm one of the first to call it a night, but I just want to hide for a while. I tell myself that tomorrow I'll make more effort, that tomorrow I'll tear this place apart.

There will always be tomorrow.

The bedroom is just a shell, devoid of all personality. I collapse onto the bed; it is neither soft nor hard. I pull the crisp, white sheet to my nose; it smells freshly laundered. Devoid of personality or not, the organisers have clearly made the effort to treat us right, to make us feel comfortable.

With my door shut, I can hear nothing in the hall. The bedroom is completely soundproof. I could scream at the top of my voice and nobody would hear me. I glance at the closed door. Gripping the sheets, I resist the urge to open it.

I need to keep my mind occupied, with something, with *anything*. I recall Kim's insecurities about tomorrow. Her insecurities are all too familiar. I've lived it before.

The first time I realised Frances was unhealthily obsessed with her looks, I was on my bed reading when she barged into my room. She twirled. "Do I look fat in this dress?"

I looked her up and down. I wanted her to know I'd taken my time. Not too much time, of course; she was my *sister*.

"Course you don't."

Frances crinkled her nose. "Why did you hesitate?"

"Why did I *what*?"

"You hesitated."

"Listen. Do you *want* me to tell you that you look fat in that dress? Well, okay then; you look fat in that dress."

I jumped when my sister slammed my bedroom door behind her.

Every day I live with guilt about that comment.

With my cheek plastered against the pillow, I glance through the window. The couple are still dancing. The hands have slid just a little lower now. Sitting up, I eye the empty bed in the adjacent room. When the bedroom is occupied, they'll be able to see everything I do, too.

I'm reminded of the stark, dark reality.

There is really *nowhere* to hide in this place.

DAY TWO

Contestants eliminated: 0
Contestants remaining: 50

Morning

Last night felt like the honeymoon, with cocktails by the poolside and lazy afternoon sex. The reality of married life has hit this morning; we are now living in a world of grocery trips, laundry runs and Friday night sex at 9pm.

Most of the contestants partied like there was no tomorrow. Well, there *is* a tomorrow, and this is it. Bleary-eyed contestants spoon sausages, beans and eggs into their gaping mouths. Nobody makes eye contact.

"You alright, Kim?" I ask.

Kim's trembling lips are still painted red. Black mascara smudges her cheeks. Nodding, she offers me a pained smile. "Ye-yes. Thank you, babe. Just got some anxiety, to be honest with you. It's literally nothing major.

None of this seems to be for the cameras today; she appears genuinely delicate, a child caught in the rain without a coat.

Dylan squeezes her hand. "We all get days like that, Kim. And look on the bright side; just think how terrible the drinkers feel today."

Kim wipes her left eye. "That's the great thing about the pandemic. You can hide away from the world and nobody flutters an eyelid. After all, everybody is in the same boat. Know what I mean?"

My hands grip the edges of the table. The *great* thing about the pandemic?

I recall the glimmer of hope when winter turned to spring and spring turned to summer, and the pandemic began to retreat. And then the summer nights darkened, and autumn edged closer, and I knew that, with a vaccine still a distant possibility, the restrictions would return, replacing all hope.

My university was right to adapt when the pandemic first struck. Either we adapted and did something, or we did nothing and we withered and folded. Work was my lifeline, the nutrition that kept me functioning. I longed to share my knowledge with students, to help them to flourish. Adapting meant moving lectures online and, whilst I was a virtual technophobe, I embraced it because I knew it was our best available option.

At first I insisted all students appeared on camera. I scanned my screen; a few weren't. Keeping my tone light, I asked why, and enquired whether they had any barriers I should be aware of.

"Only that I'm in my pyjamas."

Within a few online lectures, I made cameras optional. One by one the cameras went off, until my mug dominated the screen.

Sure – hands up - I disliked lecturing online; I swear I tried, though. When I lectured online I had no idea whether the students were listening. For all I knew they could be tapping away on their phones or watching Loose Women. My questions were met with silence. I vividly recall slamming my fist on the table when I opened the chat bar to find a handful of students discussing their weekend plans.

And then one morning I glanced at the front page headlines and a light shone from within the darkness of the cave.

The pandemic was easing. Death rates were subsiding. With restrictions in place, we could return to workplaces such as offices and lecture rooms. The zookeeper had unlocked the cage and left the keys dangling, giving us the opportunity to escape and roam the wondrous outside world.

I didn't need a second invite to the party. Ecstatically, I issued the details of the date, time and room for the first lecture. I included in the small print that attendance in person was optional.

As predictable as night following day, I arrived fifteen minutes early. Stretching my legs out onto the table in front of me, I allowed myself a smile. John would have been here by now, eagerly discussing his latest draft. John had left – what was it – about three years before. Glancing at the clock, I untangled my legs and hid them under my chair. Using my fingertips to massage my temple, I released a deep sigh of relief as the door eased open.

"Oh sorry, sweetheart," the cleaner said. "I could have sworn this room would be empty."

Flipping open my laptop, I scanned the students that were online. It was a full house.

Even with the cage unlocked and the door left precariously open, nobody wanted to be set loose.

I typed a message in the chat.

Unfortunately, due to unforeseen circumstances, today's lecture is cancelled. I wish you all the best with your future endeavours.

Wiping a hot tear from my eye, I slammed the laptop shut and closed the door behind me, both to the room and to my days as a lecturer.

But the dreadful irony is that I'm one of the lucky ones; I know that. I had the option to walk away. I had the skills and the experience to take a new direction. Other people had their businesses closed, their livelihoods lost. And yet − still − they aren't the unlucky ones. Not really. The *real* unlucky ones are those who lost their lives, or who lost their loved ones.

I long to raise this with Kim − I fucking *really* long to raise this with Kim − but Dylan catches my eye. He knows the truth − just as I do − that Kim doesn't mean it. It will do no good whatsoever if I raise the matter, if I cause an argument. She needs all the friends she can get right now; she doesn't need her allies turning against her.

"Any more beans, sweetheart?"

Looking up at the waitress, I shake my head, making sure I maintain a polite smile. What is it with these waitresses? They look like they've been transported straight from an American diner. There are five of them, all clad in mid-thigh black dresses, their hair tied back in ponytails, holding a notepad and pencil, taking our orders.

The waitress turns to Dylan. "What about you, handsome? Would you like some beans? Or maybe you're just like me? I don't know about you, but I do love some lovely, juicy sausage."

Grinning, the waitress leans forward, teasing Dylan with fleshy, soft cleavage. I try to catch his eye, to share the moment. He stares straight ahead. I recognise that look. Don't stare at the cleavage. Don't stare at the cleavage.

"I'm good. Thank you."

"Well, you know where I am if you need anything. And I *do* mean anything."

Horizontal lies appear on Dylan's forehead, forming an upside down triangle. The waitress leaves our table.

"Are you alright, mate?" I ask.

"Guess so." With narrowed eyes, he raises his head. "You ever had issues with temptation, Andrew? Have you been tempted to do things that you really shouldn't?"

I stifle a laugh. "All the time."

His face shows no trace of humour. "Me too. And it didn't end well. It didn't end well at all. I don't want my two little girls seeing their dad flirt with a woman other than their mum. That's the exact opposite of what I want from this show."

Wow; this guy really is principled. I'm not sure what he is talking about though; she flirted with him. I decide to shrug, to mask my confused thoughts.

Heads turn as a door at the back of the hall flings open. I rub my hands together, expecting Rebecca to appear. I look again. It isn't *that* door. It is the door to the right. The male voice on the Tannoy is public-schooled, devoid of any accent.

"Good morning, ladies and gentlemen, and welcome to the second day of The F-Word Reality Show."

A handful of us murmur a hello; some are more enthusiastic than others.

"We hope you had a pleasant night's sleep. You'll be called in groups of ten to shower. Your outfits will be ready for you once you've showered. Any contestant who does not shower, or who does not put on the outfit, will be eliminated from the show. We politely remind you that there are no cameras in the shower rooms."

Wiping the underside of her eye, Kim scurries to her bedroom. I don't want to invade her privacy, to gaze inside the room. I imagine her on her bed though, her knees pulled tight to her trembling chest.

The first names are called, and ten contestants disappear behind the door. Fifteen minutes or so later, the door opens. The ten contestants leave and another ten take their place.

I gulp at the sight of the first ten contestants exiting the room. They are dressed all in black, with black shoes, black flannel trousers and black, long-sleeved pullover tops. The men and the women are dressed exactly the same. They have removed any trace of sexuality, all remnants of individuality.

One thought dominates my mind: what on earth will Kim make of this?

Kim is called in the fourth group. I stand in line next to Dylan as we wait for the door to fling open. I try to catch Kim's eye as she exits the room, but her head is bowed. That isn't a good sign. Is she upset? Is she crying? I don't have time to find out. We're ushered inside.

I'm relieved to find myself in a single cubicle, the type you'd find at the swimming pool. I pull across the lock. A folded white towel sits on a narrow bench. It is dry and freshly laundered, just like in a decent hotel. Undressed, I wrap the towel around my naked body. Blowing out a relieved sigh, I note that the towel covers my most intimate parts. This is so much better than I feared, I muse, as I unlock the cubicle door.

I'm at the back of the line, behind Duncan and Dylan. There are five women at the front of the queue and then five men at the back. Chivalry isn't lost in this place. Four guards patrol the area. One of the guards gesticulates to the five female contestants. Turning, he points to the five shower cubicles.

Nobody speaks for a moment. Each of us glances at the showers. We turn to the guard for answers.

"Where's the shower doors?" the first lady asks. "It's completely open. The men can see inside."

The guard takes a step forward. He stops about a foot away from the woman. Bending his knees, he lowers himself a few inches to her eye level. His lips curl. He shrugs his shoulders.

The woman turns around. I bow my head. "They'll be able to see us naked. This is outrageous. You have to do something."

A second woman gesticulates with her hands. "For God's sake, *speak* to us."

The other four guards join their colleague. In unison, they slide their horizontal index finger across their lips.

Of *course*. The guards haven't uttered a single word since I've been in here.

The guards don't speak.

The protests die down until I hear water spraying against naked bodies. I don't *see* anything. I stare at the dimpled floor. I recall the plasters on the brown tiled floors at the swimming baths. There was always some bigger kid slapping his towel against a boy's back. The water in the communal showers covered my ankles when the drains were clogged with human hairs.

"Turn around, ladies. Show us your tits! Don't be shy!"

I look to the guards. With their hands on their hips, their bellies tremble with laughter. Duncan rips his towel from his waist and twists his midriff like he's on the dance floor. The guards pull their heads back, breaking into hysterics. The women pull their arms across their exposed, naked flesh.

"Do something, for fuck's sake!"

The guards don't hear me; either that, or they ignore me.

I need to act. This isn't right. This is *wrong.*

"Show some respect, you dirty little bastard!"

I wish the words came from my mouth. I was too slow, contemplating what to say, what to do, without actually doing or saying anything.

Dylan thrusts his hands against Duncan's chest. Duncan flies backwards with unsteady legs, like he's ice skating in shoes. Smirking, Duncan looks to the ceiling.

"Remember that there are no cameras in here," he says.

Duncan lunges at Dylan with flailing arms. They both fling punches, but the guards decide to act now, throwing themselves between the two men. The pushes subside into verbal threats; it quickly dies down completely.

Moments later, the hot spray is turned off. Gingerly, the five women step out of the showers. Relieved, they engulf their showered bodies within the thick, fluffy towels, before dressing with their backs to us. With bowed heads, they stand in a soundless straight line.

The same guard points to the men. Turning, he gesticulates to the five, vacant shower cubicles.

******

Showered, the outfit awaits me in a neat pile. Even the socks and pants are black and devoid of any individuality. Dressed, I wait for the door to open. The top clings to my shoulders. There is just the right level of flexibility around my waist. Did a tailor snuck into my bedroom in the night and take my measurements?

I look up. Of course, there *are* no cameras in the shower room. They made that perfectly clear, didn't they? They spelt it out to us.

Make no mistake; I despise the cameras. And I don't just mean in this place. Even in the outside world they are everywhere. Watching us. Controlling us. Curtailing our freedom.

And yet – and *yet* – Duncan took advantage when there weren't any, didn't he? He said as much to Dylan before retaliating. Would he have made those obscene comments to the women if the viewing public were watching at home?

I rush outside as soon as the door opens. I need to find her. I need to find Kim.

I peek through the gaps in a group of five or six, huddled together like a rugby scrum. Nothing. Where *is* she? Is she sobbing in one of the corners? I place my hand on the closest shoulder.

I picked the wrong shoulder.

It is the knucklehead guy I chose to be on our team. I've picked up over the past day that his name is TJ. Does he think he's a rapper? Turning to face me, he reminds me of *that* guy in the pub who accuses you of staring at him when – *clearly* – you're actually staring at his girlfriend in her low-cut top. TJ puckers his lips into a kiss. "Why are you putting your hand on me, handsome? It is private property."

This guy isn't going to win any popularity contests; ironic really, as that's exactly what he may have to do.

"I just wanted your attention. Sorry. Listen. Have you seen Kim?"

"Kim? Don't even know who Kim is, mate. She hot?"

"Kim. Late twenties. Ah, just forget it..."

I didn't have time to get embroiled in an argument with this gorilla. My breath quickens as I pace around the perimeter of the hall.

"Andrew..."

I look down at a girl I sort of recognise, like maybe she served me on the till at the local supermarket. I look again.

"Kim. *There* you are. I was getting worried about you."

She breaks into a smile. "*Were* you now? Well, aren't you a sweetheart."

She seems smaller than I remember. Void of makeup, her lips are slimmer, and a red blush coats her cheeks. She is a natural beauty.

Kim holds out her upturned hands. "Well, this is me. No hiding now."

"You look-"

"Naked."

"I wish. I was going to say that you looked beautiful."

Her smile widens.

"But – *well* – how do you feel?" I ask.

"Weird."

"Weird?"

She stands on tiptoes now. "Yeah. I feel totally weird, you know. But then – I don't know - I kind of feel relieved."

I arch an eyebrow. "*Yeah*?"

"Yeah. I have nothing to hide now, do I? Literally, this is as bad as it's going to get. People can take me as I am or they can leave me alone. And you know what? I'm not too bothered either way."

My skin tingles. This is amazing. And yet something punches my chest hard.

If only Frances managed to feel the same way.

An announcement distracts us. We both look up, like the announcement is coming from the ceiling.

"The cameras will now be turned off for an hour. You are allowed privacy. There will be another announcement to notify you of the end of the hour."

My head jerks. Black shutters cover the bedroom windows. I eye the digital timer on the wall, with the digits flashing in neon green. The seconds count down. 60:00. 59:59. 59:58.

My body suddenly feels drained of energy, even though all I have done today is get up, eat and shower. Never before have I longed so bad for the feel of soft sheets clinging to my skin.

"Well, I don't know about you, but I am going to take this opportunity for a nap."

"You read my mind, Andrew."

I flinch when Kim lunges towards me. Her outstretched arms pull me in for a hug.

How long has it been since somebody properly

hugged me? Was it Frances? Or Mum?

"See you in an hour," Kim whispers.

Lying on the bed, my outstretched hands supporting the back of my head and my ears covered by the fluffy pillows, my eyes drift to the closed bedroom door. With my eyes half-closed, I glance at the door like I'm a sleeping duck.

I need to ignore the intrusive thoughts. I need to allow space for them to peacefully co-exist somewhere in my mind, like the rats that go unnoticed behind the bins and the debris. It's futile to try to push them away, to resist them; they'll merely come back bigger and stronger and edging for a fight.

I think back to when we were kids, playing on a patch of grass. I can't remember the exact age, but Frances was finally tall enough to ride the biggest rollercoaster when we'd last visited the theme park. I'd idled for too long, daydreaming about a film I'd watched where the prisoners formed a chain and climbed over the brick wall and escaped. When I returned to reality, my little sister – the girl I was supposed to be looking after – had vanished.

My shouts went unanswered. My breath quickened. As always at that age when faced with a potential crisis, I longed to disappear out of sight within a deep hole. Instead, I ran around in a circle, my ankles grazing against the overgrown grass. I stopped moving. I dug my knee into the muddy ground. I squinted. She couldn't be in there. There was no way she could be in there.

Was she in there?

The dark, circular entrance to the tunnel was about five feet tall and wide, reminding me of the

Blackwall Tunnel from about half a mile away.

I peeked my head inside. "Frances!" My echoing voice just kept rotating and rotating. Nothing else came back.

I unravelled my body and disappeared within the hole, my knees digging into the hard metal. My hands grazed against leaves and other objects, hard and soft, familiar and unfamiliar. I couldn't see any light. I couldn't see *anything*. I kept moving forward, a baby trying to get from one side of the room to the other. I imagined the tunnel shrinking around me, taking away my breath and crushing my body. The pungent water drenched my tracksuit bottoms. My flat hands slipped. I called my sister's name.

All I could hear was my thudding heart.

Thirty-five or so years later, my adult self springs from the soft, luxurious bed. The bedroom walls seem closer than they were before, like I can stand in the middle of the room with outstretched arms and touch each and every side with my fingertips. I don't want to be alone anymore. Taking three strides forward, I pull on the door handle. I just want to leave the door a few inches open, to let some air in, to release some tension.

The door doesn't open.

I turn and turn the door handle, each time harder, with more ferocity, but each time with the same outcome. Pressing my perspiring forehead against the window, I try to at least see moving shapes outside, some sign of life. I see nothing. My banging fists are delicate and brittle against the glass.

"Let me out!"

My shouts merely echo around the room, just like they did in the tunnel.

I glance around the spinning room.

Is it shrinking?

Shaking, I sit straight-backed on my bed. I press my feet flat against the floor.

I glance up. What is that?

It's the alarm. It rings around the four corners of the room. I stay motionless for a second, maybe two.

Pushing myself from the bed, I snap down the door handle.

The door slides open.

I run out into the hall, a tiger released from his cage. Dylan is the first person I spot. Rubbing sleep from his eyes, he smiles wryly.

"The doors wouldn't open! We were locked in!" I say.

Angling his face to one side, he shrugs his shoulders. "You sure? Mine did. I left the room after about thirty minutes or so. I couldn't sleep. I had a quick walk around."

I open my mouth to tell him that of course I'm fucking sure, but I snap it shut again. *Am* I sure? I am not sure *what* just happened.

"You okay, mate?" Dylan's hand is gentle on my shoulder.

I nod. "Yes. Think I had a nightmare. Maybe this place is getting to me."

"Don't worry about it. We're all trapped inside this place really, aren't we? They've thrown away the key, haven't they? We may as well be in prison. This place can make you go mad. It can make you imagine a whole lot of things that aren't real."

Nodding, I tell him that my nerves must have got the better of me. I agree with him that I must have had an odd moment, a glitch.

Truthfully, I've no idea what is going on in this place, or what is going on inside my scrambled mind. I *am* sure of one thing, though.

I am *not* shutting my bedroom door again.

*****

Afternoon

With time on my hands and not much to do, my old, destructive habits begin to creep back in. My therapist warned me that my obsessive behaviour was toxic, that it would lead me to end up prison or a coffin.

I decide to move away from the group. I sit on the floor with my hands pressed on the cold floor, my shoulders leaning against the glass wall.

Why am I so obsessed with Kim? Why am I feeling so protective?

Of course. She reminds me of my little sister. Just the thought of her makes me happy.

Sure, people in their forties make out that they grew up playing conkers and hopscotch in their shorts and knee-length grey socks, but that's just bullshit. We had videos and computer games even in the eighties and nineties; they just weren't so advanced. Admittedly, we did seem to be outside more than youngsters today, though. Often Frances would dig around in the garage or shed for a gadget or a tool and we'd head out in the garden or similar and make our own entertainment.

On this particular day we'd picked up a six-iron, an eight-iron and a handful of grass-stained golf balls and ventured to the park. A group of lads a few years older than me leisurely kicked a ball around in one corner of the park, and so we took the other corner.

Frances swiped at the ball like she was holding a hockey stick; she kept missing by a country mile. It didn't help that she had hysterics. Tears trickled down her cheeks. I remember telling her to keep her eye on the ball. She held her finger up, signalling that she was going to be serious this time. And she was. The connection was perfect. I gasped as the ball flew through the air in a perfect straight line. I followed the ball's trajectory as it rose and dipped and then began its descent, like a flight from Heathrow to Paris. I followed the ball's flight as it hit one of the boys playing football on the back of his head.

The boy rubbed his head, confused and bruised but not seriously hurt. It took a moment before the group realised what had happened. They looked up and pointed in our direction.

And then they sprinted towards us.

I threw my jumper on the floor. I didn't want to fight, but I would if I had to. They gathered like wolves around a stray sheep. One of the boys came close enough for me to inhale his salt and vinegar breath, for me to take in the grey flecks in his brown eyes. With both hands, he pushed my chest. I staggered backwards.

"What are you having a go at him for?" My sister strutted towards the boy with her chest pushed forward and her hands cupping her hips. "I hit the ball, not him! It's me you should be having a go at."

My emotions battled against each other. On the one hand, I'd never felt such intense love for my little sister. On the other hand, I was angry at her; all I cared about was protecting her. If anyone was going to get hurt, it was going to be *me*, and not her.

The boy glanced at his mates. He wasn't the leader of the pack. He couldn't afford to lose face. He pulled back his arm, ready to hit my little sister. He didn't manage to. I lunged forward and tackled him to the floor. I caught him a few times with my head and fists before we were dragged apart.

We both looked up from the grass as the leader of the group stepped over us. I knew him from school. He was a tough nut, and not to be messed with. His dark eyes fixed on mine for a moment. I clenched my body, waiting for the pain. He leaned back, twisted at the hips, and then struck the other boy on the chin.

He grabbed the boy by his lapel. "You never hit a girl. If I see you hitting a girl again then I will kill you. Do you hear?"

We took the opportunity to disappear. I didn't think it was possible, but from that day forwards, the bond I had with my sister was stronger than it had ever been. I knew she would always be there for me, and she knew I would always be there for her.

And that merely made it all the more traumatic, for both of us, when we broke that bond.

It's been two days since I heard Frances's voice. This is the longest I've ever known. She'd have them wrapped around her little finger if she was participating in this show. I need to do better than this, I tell myself. If I don't win this thing for me, then I need to win it for Frances. It was her who told me people are nothing without their freedom.

Staring up at the camera, I force my lips into a smile.

"It has been worth the wait to see you smile."

Startled, I take the offered hand. The palms are smooth and moisturised. The man lowers his lean, wiry frame. He stretches out his legs; I notice they don't stretch as far as mine do. His sloping scalp is completely shaven. "Nothing quite like sitting on the floor," he says. "I've been meaning to speak to you since the helicopter ride – since our journey began – but I haven't managed to find the apt moment."

Of course. The face isn't familiar, but the voice is. The man cups his chin in his upturned hands. His piercing blue eyes are the palest blue I've ever seen. He observes me as though I am a work of art at the Tate gallery. Nobody ever shows me this much interest.

"It is the simple things that make life worthwhile. You could have all the material possessions in the world, but then an act of kindness from a stranger can make your day. From what I have witnessed, you don't smile often. I am not judging, just observing. And so it is wonderful to be in your company when you do smile."

My smile is embarrassed now. I look away.

He must recognise my uncertainty; he holds his hands up. "I apologise. It wasn't my intention to embarrass you. I observe people. Some people paint or embroider; I observe people."

"Hopefully, you don't hang around too many playgrounds then."

His smile appears pained. I decide to quickly change the subject.

"What exactly do you see when you look at me?"

He flaunts a row of straight, polished teeth. His blue eyes sparkle. "Most people aren't usually brave enough to ask that question."

"Should I not?"

"I respect that you have. What do I see? Well, remember that this is only my personal perspective, but in my opinion you have great depth. You are a significant thinker. Maybe the thinking doesn't always work in your favour-"

"You're right there-"

"But you should embrace it, because it is what makes you who you are. And sometimes you pretend that you don't care, but I don't see that as a negative. It is better to pretend you don't care, than to pretend that you do."

I rub my palms along my thighs. "What about you then? Tell me something about you..."

He smiles. "I'm just an average man. You'll find out more about me in due course. But *you;* I'm interested in you. You're hiding great pain, aren't you? Some terrible things have happened in your life, haven't they? I know that, but I don't know what pain it is."

I'm exposed, just like those poor women were in the showers. I shrug my shoulders. "I've had my fair share of pain, but who hasn't? I'm not claiming a monopoly on pain."

"Other people's suffering doesn't reduce your own pain."

"I never said it did. I'm just saying I don't have it any worse than anybody else. I just recognise that I'm privileged in many ways. Look at me. I am a white male, I had two parents, we had food on the table, I went to a good school..."

He shakes his head, but remains silent.

"People go around thinking they are the only ones that experience pain, but that's bullshit. I'm no different from anybody else," I say.

"You hide the pain because you don't want to be a victim, because you don't want to trouble other people with your issues, particularly as they probably have their own bullshit to deal with. Am I right?"

I smirk. "I guess you are right."

"And I don't blame you, Andrew. But I do think there is one area where you've got it all wrong. You view the pain as a bad thing-"

"Because it is. I'm not delusional-"

"Don't be ashamed of the bad things that have happened to you. They are part of what makes you who you are. A wise man once said that what doesn't kill you, makes you stronger. I believe in this. Do you believe in this too, Andrew?"

I absorb the concept. I think it through. "I guess it makes sense. Kind of."

"Too right it does. And if you view the bad things as an opportunity to grow, do you realise just how strong that will make you? The knowledge that you have dealt with worse before and you will deal with worse again is very powerful."

The man holds out his hand for the second time. "I'm Jake, by the way. It has been a pleasure to meet you."

Shaking his hand, I watch as he disappears as quickly as he appeared.

*****

I join Dylan and Kim. The roles have reversed from yesterday; this time Kim sits next to Dylan, and opposite from me. Stretching out her long legs, she rests a slanting shoe against the low table that separates us. There is a colour to her cheeks that wasn't there yesterday; it may just be the lack of foundation, but I doubt it.

"Normally in these shows we get a letter from home or a phone call," Kim says. "I guess that won't happen in this place, because nobody knows where we are!"

Dylan suggests that maybe a mad ex will turn up.

We both flinch, before laughing.

Momentarily, Kim places the flat of her hand down against Dylan's knee. He twists his fingers together. Maybe it is a figment of my imagination, but his leg looks like it shakes for just a fleeting moment. Is he thinking about what his children will think again?

"Maybe I have got this way wrong," Kim says, "but it feels like I can tell you two guys absolutely anything. It feels like I have known you forever."

"Please don't tell us everything. We don't want to know everything."

She jerks her head to Dylan. The curling of Dylan's lips suggests he is joking. Kim purses her lips and slaps his leg.

"What do you want to tell us then?" I ask.

"No, it's alright." Kim crosses her arms across her chest.

"Tell us."

Looking around, she leans forward and whispers, "Okay. If you insist. Actually, this is proper difficult for me to tell you, you know?"

"Don't tell us then," Dylan smirks.

Kim straightens her back. Plumping up her cheeks, she blows out air. "Okay. Here goes. I want to tell you that I've never actually been with a man."

I let the comment sink in. "You like women?"

"You think it's funny?" Kim asks, arching back into the sofa.

"You are not joking?"

"Why would I be joking?"

My first thought – and I try to push it out of my mind - is that blondes are supposed to have more fun. I picture a smiling Marilyn Monroe in her skimpy white dress. But then that isn't a good example, because apparently she was morbidly depressed, living behind a mask that only occasionally slipped. But seriously, though, I assumed she was joking because the concept seems ridiculous. Kim is gorgeous. She is bubbly. She is flirtatious. Why wouldn't she have been with men before?

"Surely you have had plenty of interest?"

Dylan jerks his head towards me. "You are assuming that there is no choice involved."

My skin prickles. I feel like I'm pushed into a corner. "You're a virgin? I mean, that's great. Well done. If that is your lifestyle choice then I applaud you..."

A few seconds pass without any of us saying anything. "This may be a personal question, and tell me to fuck off if it is, but can I ask why you're still a virgin, Kim?"

"It's because she has never had sex with anybody, Andrew," Dylan says.

Kim lowers her head, seemingly ignoring Dylan. "It just never happened," she says. "I had a difficult time when I was younger..."

I block out the thought that maybe I should signpost her to Jake, who seems to be an expert on dealing with bad times. I don't know whether I'd be throwing her into the lion's den, though.

"I mean, life is a struggle now. I wouldn't have called the helpline if it wasn't. But when I was in my teens and early twenties it was a dreadful struggle. And when I did feel just a little better I couldn't find a man I actually *wanted* to sleep with. And then it stopped being a choice. It became an issue. It terrified me."

I look away. My nightmare job would be a therapist. "I understand."

Kim leans forward again. She glances up at one of the cameras. Yesterday she glanced at the camera like it was a mirror, lured by her own reflection. Today she glances at the camera as though it offers unwanted eyes. "Things have changed though."

I raise my eyebrows. "How?"

"I feel more alive than I ever have. This place has awakened me."

I smile. Dylan smiles, too.

Buoyed by our seemingly positive body language, Kim turns her head to a group of contestants on the other side of the hall. "Have you met Christian?"

She's been with him most of the day. The guy has hung on her every word. He looks about Kim's age, maybe a year or two younger. The shapeless outfit drowns his body, but it doesn't take too much to picture snake hips and long, lean legs and arms. His flawless skin suggests a serious moisturising routine. He has an easy smile and a relaxed manner. I can see why the ladies – and Kim in particular – would be drawn to his charms. I resist the urge to fucking hate him.

"No. But he seems nice."

Kim rubs her hands together. "Oh, he is totally amazing! And I don't mean in some meaningless, pointless way, you know? He likes me for who I am. The real me. Do you know how exhausting it is to put on an act all the time?"

I nod. Dylan's face crumples.

"Whilst this place has been totally awesome, I can't wait to get out of here. So I can be with him, you know? I want Christian to be my first and last man."

My heart sinks. Of course, it sounds fantastic, like some black and white film. But this isn't the movies. I've learnt that, just like pigeons, life shits on you. Christian could have his choice of girls when he comes out of this place, particularly if the viewing public adore him. How likely is it that he will want to stay with Kim, however gorgeous and fabulous she is?

"We could be in here a long time," Dylan says.

Dylan reads my mind. We both think Kim is delusional, that she is living in a floating bubble in the sky, looking down at the real world below. Doubtless, they will break up before they get out of this place, but she deserves some happiness, even if it is fleeting. She'll always regret it if she doesn't do something about this wonderful feeling.

I think back to the shower, when I did nothing. We need to do something to help her, whether it is the right thing to do or not. *I* need to do something.

"There is another alternative," I say.

She looks up, hanging on my words.

"Well, you know that we have two sessions each day when the cameras are turned off?"

Kim nods.

"And that during those slots the windows are blacked out, so nobody can see inside the bedroom. I know from personal experience that nobody can hear anything..."

Kim looks at me blankly for a moment. And then she starts smiling...

******

The afternoon hours drift away, like we are on holiday and we are waiting for the dinner serving. And yet adrenaline floods my body. I can't remember the last time I felt like this.

The other contestants appear to have become acclimatised to this easy life. It is no stretch of the imagination to picture them in their pyjamas watching daytime TV, dipping their hands into bags of popcorn. We haven't been given anything to do, and we've become lazy.

The second privacy period of the day is announced.

I imagine an egg timer. The seconds are passing, and every second counts. Kim needs to make a decision; it is now or never. She scans me, with her hands on hips like a disapproving headmaster. Only, her lips slant at the corners. I raise my eyebrows, then glance in the direction of Christian, sat alone in the corner of the hall, seemingly deep in thought.

I am watching a silent movie in slow motion; nobody else in the whole room is watching. Catching Christian's eye, Kim lures him with the wave of her hand. Christian glances around at first, making sure he saves his blushes. I can't resist a smile. Kim appears confident, like an expert temptress. There is a bounce in Christian's stride. His movements become more self-conscious the closer he gets. I move away.

From a good twelve feet, I dare to glance over my shoulder. I smile as Kim takes Christian's hand and then guides him in the direction of the bedroom. Just before they disappear behind the blacked-out windows, Kim surveys me. She holds my eyes for what feels like seconds, and then smiles.

I feel more conscious than ever, even though the cameras are now turned off. I can't help but glance up at one of the cameras, as though seeking reassurance. My eyes turn to Dylan. He merely nods his approval.

My thoughts drift. It is amazing to help somebody else. It has been some time. This isn't deliberate; I've just been wrapped up in my own thoughts and, besides, I've been running out of people to help. A different thought floods my mind, competing for my attention. I'm jealous. Not of Kim, of course, but of what she is experiencing. Whilst it is great to help others, I need to help myself, too. It has been so long since I experienced physical connection.

My eyes wander. Kim pushes Christian down on the bed and then straddles him. She puts a single finger to his lips before kissing his neck.

I smirk. Good girl. She is comfortable. She is confident. She is taking control.

Hold on; what the fuck is happening?

I spring to my feet. I stab my middle finger in the air. I look around with open hands.

"The shutters!"

Dylan looks up at me, raising one eyebrow.

"The shutters have gone back up! Everybody can

see what Kim is doing..."

******

This is like a sick pornographic film, a leaked sex video.

I twist my neck in multiple directions. All the other rooms in this fucking place are blacked out. Only Kim's isn't. I take a fleeting, guilty look through the window; I just need to work out what is going on. Kim's eyes fix on Christian's. She presses the flat of her hand against his cheek. Her tongue circles his lips. Clearly, she remains oblivious to the situation.

Snapping away my thoughts, I decide to act. Now. Pulling back my shoulders, I get right in the face of a security guard. I point at Kim's room. "Look! Are you blind? The shutters are broken. Everyone can see inside the bedroom!"

The hands remain balled behind his back. His unblinking eyes stay fixed straight ahead. If he isn't blind, then he must be deaf.

I raise my voice. "I said that the shutters are fucked! Everybody can see in. There must be a technical fault. You need to sort it out!"

Not a single muscle in his face twitches.

I turn to face the other security guards. Motionless, they are toys that need winding up.

Someone needs to help me.

Dylan brushes past my shoulder. He isn't talking. He is acting, just like he did in the shower room. The white of his knuckle cracks against the window. I join him, if only to do something. My fist cracks against the glass. I am prepared to smash the glass, to leave my knuckles shattered and broken and bleeding, if it means that I can gain Kim's attention, to stop her, to get her out of that awful room.

Kim's lips continue their trail down Christian's body, along his flat midriff, speckled with dark hairs. Kim straightens her back, starts pulling the black top over her shoulders.

"Kim! Kim! Stop...!"

I sense a dark shadow building behind me. I know what it is, but I don't want to face it. I want to push the red bill under the doormat.

I turn around. I have thrown a can of petrol on a burning fire. A crowd of about twenty other contestants have gathered, a mix of both men and women, vultures pecking at road kill.

I lower my voice. I try to stop it from crackling. "Nothing to see here," I say. "Can you please go back to whatever it was you were doing?"

Putting them in the spotlight forces a few to idle away. They don't need me to spell it out that staying to watch is perverted. The majority, though, either don't have a conscience, or they ignore their nagging thoughts. They edge closer in unison, undeterred by my polite request. Their eyes expand; their lips widen. I clench my fists. This is fight or flight. I want to run, to hide in the corner, press my knees hard against my chest, rock back and forth; pretend none of this is happening.

On other occasions I might have taken that option. I just can't do that this time. I need to stand up and fight, if not for Kim then for my younger sister.

I flinch as a wide body jumps out in front of me.

"This man told you that there was nothing to see here. Now go back to whatever you were doing before!"

Through the black top, I can almost sense the muscles in his back straining. The hair on the back of TJ's head glistens with sweat.

One of the men bares his teeth. He keeps edging forward. "Fuck off."

TJ pulls back his arm, like he is loading a gun. His fist connects with the jaw with a thud. The man collapses to the floor, a felled tree. I cannot help but look down. His eyes are snapped shut.

Now I have my answer. This guy isn't all talk.

Expanding his chest, TJ holds his fists up in the air. "I asked you nicely, didn't I? You didn't listen. Now I'll ask you a different question, before things get all emotional around here. Any other of you motherfuckers want to make a move?"

All of the other motherfuckers are suddenly synchronised swimmers. In unison, they bow their heads and look away. My jaw drops as two of the security guards are jerked into action. Working as a team, one of the men lifts the felled man's left foot while the other security guard lifts the right foot. They drag him along the floor like a broomstick, across to the other side of the room. He is clutter. They are cleaning up. De-cluttering.

I stab my finger at them, trying to gain some points. "So you *can* fucking move then!"

I glance to TJ, but he isn't there. My eyes widen as I turn back to the bedroom. Both Dylan and TJ have stretched their arms and legs into the shape of a star, blocking the view. Awkwardly, I search for some space at the window. The three of us stand with our backs pressed against the glass window. All I can hear is my breathing, crackling like a prank caller. I have no idea how many seconds or minutes we stand like this. I look up at the clock.

40:01. 40:00. 39:59...

I question whether I imagined it. I am terrified to tempt fate. The compulsion is too much. I dare to glance over my shoulder.

The shutter has gone down, blacking out the room.

Releasing a big sigh, I press my hands against my knees. I bend forward, gasping for breath, like I've just run a marathon. The room spins. I am not diabetic, but it feels like I need an injection of sugar.

It is as though a minute's silence has ended. The room suddenly cackles with the familiar sound of chatter and conspiring. I'll need to address my conscience later.

I hold out my hand. "Thank you, TJ. I owe you."

He looks at my hand like it is an uncooked sausage. His hand remains on his hip. "Means nothing. They were picking on her. I hate bullies. If I see you bullying, then I'll take you down, too. Didn't do it for you," he says.

I am sure I spot a glimmer of a smile on his face before he walks away.

I'm aware of a nudge at my waist. "I suspect there's more good in that man than we think," Jake says.

******

Evening

The hours before dinner drift in a muddled haze.

I refuse to sit. I don't know whether it is my feet that refuse, or my mind. Either way, I pace the length of the hall; a passenger on platform one waiting for the late arrival of the London Euston train. Bored of the endless walking, I stop and gesticulate with a guard. I ask why he didn't do anything. I ask how he'd feel if the roles were reversed. I stare into his soulless, unblinking eyes and shiver. The guard raises his vertical index finger to his mouth; he wants me to be silent, just like he is; like they all are.

Dylan takes my hand and guides me away. He grips me close enough for me to feel his warm breath on my cheek. "It wasn't your fault," he says. "What you did came from the heart, my friend. That's what counts. You get me? Sometimes these gestures backfire, that's all."

I grimace. "Why does it go horrendously wrong every time I try to help?"

Dylan arches his head to the side. He doesn't want to offload me with a bullshit response. "Sometimes things are out of your control, you know? And it makes zero sense to worry about things that are out of your control now, doesn't it? And other times you might think you've made a dog's dinner of things, but you don't realise they'd be a whole lot worse off if you'd done nothing."

I embrace my new friend (he *is* my new friend, isn't he?). Shortly afterwards, I join him for dinner. Sat next to Christian, a blushing, beaming Kim waves at me. I even exchange a nod with TJ, who – of course – sits on his own.

With dinner done and dusted, I sit on my own on the hard floor, with my head bowed low and my knees pressed to my chest. Rebecca hasn't made an appearance all day. That seems odd. They've just left us to our own devices. Why did I even pick teams yesterday? I daren't glance at the cameras. What must the world think of me? I've been skulking on my own for most of the afternoon, and the viewers at home won't even know why. If this is a popularity contest, like Dylan implied, then I'll be going home tomorrow. Despite what happened earlier, the thought of going home casts a bleak, black cloud over me.

"I know you've probably been told this a zillion times already, but it wasn't your fault."

Someone has joined me. It's *her*. I've only ever had fleeting interactions with her, but each one has impacted me more than it should have. And now she has (voluntarily, it seems) chosen to be with me in my moment of need.

She's mimicked my sitting position, with her long, slender legs tucked tight to her chest. The thick, shiny red hair covers part of her face. She blows a stray strand away from her mouth. "I've been watching you," she says.

"Like a stalker?" My laugh is high-pitched and ridiculous.

Not even a flicker of emotion crosses her face. "I did stalk somebody once."

I try to swallow the frog in my throat. "Really?"

She nods. "Yes. I was brought up by my mum in a little farming village where nothing much happened, and so it was kind of a big deal when I buggered off to university in Liverpool. I guess I hadn't had that much life experience. Mum fretted that I wouldn't fit in. You know what the funny thing was, though?"

Shaking my head, I wonder what could possibly be funny about a stalker story.

"I didn't actually *want* to fit in. People thought I lacked confidence, but that was bullshit. The problem was that I had too *much* confidence. I could easily have blended in with the cool crowd. Instead, I chose to pursue a man who didn't have an array of friends, who didn't have perfect teeth or a great physique, but who instead had this incredible mind. This man didn't want to fit in either. I've often pondered why I did what I did. I think I mainly wanted to prove I could have any man, and yet I didn't want a man any other typical university girl would go for. Do you know what the big problem with all of this was, though?"

I shrug my shoulders.

"The big problem was that this man wasn't interested in me. His reaction angered and fascinated me in equal measures. To be blunt, this man wasn't typical at all, and that enthralled me. It obsessed me. And I ended up stalking him for a few weeks, just to feel some semblance of control, just to get this intense sensation out of my system. And looking back, do you know what I think about all of this?"

Momentarily closing her eyes, she releases a sigh. "I think that I was an absolute twat. What I did was wrong, and I take responsibility for all the bad things I've done in my life. I was watching that guy for all the wrong reasons, you know?"

The woman tangles her fingers together. "I've been watching you for good reasons, though. I've been kind of worried about you. It wasn't nice what happened with that girl earlier. And whilst I take responsibility for all the bad things I've done, I sure as hell won't take responsibility for the things that weren't my fault. Life would be fucking unbearable. And you can't either. You really need to know that what happened wasn't your fault, and that you can't blame yourself."

I can't formulate the right words to say. My lips untangle into something resembling a smile.

She gazes in Kim's direction. "She is ecstatic.

Completely oblivious to what went on. What harm is there if she doesn't know?"

It crosses my mind that this is the kind of thing a bloke would think after sleeping with his girlfriend's sister. "You're right," I say.

"It's like they're conspiring against us."

"Who?"

"Them."

"You think?"

She turns to me. I feel like her green eyes are going to suck me in. "Like the whole world is, really. I think they have a vaccine, you know."

I try to restrain a sigh. "Right."

"Think about it. It's just a mutated variation of the flu. This is 2024. We have the greatest minds in the whole world working on it. Why wouldn't we have a vaccine?"

I don't want to argue with this woman, and it isn't *just* because she makes the hairs on my neck prickle, but because she has taken the time to look out for me. "If they have a vaccine, then why don't they release it?"

She slides her hands along her thighs – those undoubtedly smooth, delicious thighs – and stretches out her legs. I'm surprised just how far they stretch. "Their motive? Control. They want to change the human mindset first. They want us to believe that freedom is no longer our right. They want us to feel in their debt when they release the restrictions."

I swivel my buttocks so I angle towards her. "Why are you telling me all of this?"

She laughs. "You think I'm insane, don't you?"

I hurriedly tell her that – no – of course I don't.

"It's just you aren't wrong to think that," she says.

"I actually *was* certified insane before."

My eyes scan her face, seeking traces that she is joking. Her pale skin remains unlined.

"But I'm sure I'm on to something with this. It's up to you whether you believe me. I won't take offence either way. Anyway, I think they're going to release it in the next few weeks. The time has come. They want us to think they've saved the world just in time for Christmas. I guess you heard that they were looking to cancel that, too?"

I nod. "Why are you here? What reward did you choose?"

She looks away. "I wish I could say I chose something deep and meaningful, but I didn't. I chose Fortune. I haven't worked for a few years, and I'm skint."

Smiling, I tell her that I'm not here to judge.

"But it is more than that," she says. "I would have joined the show even if there was no reward. I don't find much reason to get up in the mornings. I am trapped in my poky little flat. Even the spiders have a name. Every day is a repeat of the previous day. I don't have many – if any – real friends. I've always thought that I don't like people, but now I am so lonely I feel like I want to break into tears all the time."

I tell her that I know exactly how that feels.

"I presume you chose Freedom. I can't see you possibly choosing anything else. I just wanted to make you aware before you jet off to the other side of the world, leaving your friends and family behind."

I raise my eyebrows. This is ludicrous. It is insane. And yet – and *yet* – clearly she believes it, and she cares enough to tell me. "Thank you. It's all kind of irrelevant though. I'm not going to win."

She smiles. "You're in my Top 5."

What? Why?

She presses her hands against the floor. Her flowing, loose hair tickles my cheeks as she kisses my forehead. "Just remember what I said about it not being your fault. I'm Sofia, by the way."

I call to her back that I'm Andrew.

Seconds – or minutes – later, Jake idles over. "She's as mad as a hatter."

Smiling, I tell him that I know.

"She is right about one thing though."

"What?"

"It really *wasn't* your fault, Andrew."

DAY THREE

Contestants eliminated: 0
Contestants remaining: 50

Morning

Sitting in the corner of the room on my own, I reflect on the night, on the morning.

I didn't get much sleep during the night. For hours I sat upright on my bed, with my door open, gazing through the window as my fellow contestants partied until the early hours. Some of them really didn't want the party to end. At some point, each and every one of them returned to their rooms. This was my opportunity.

At about four in the morning I left my bedroom and tiptoed into the main hall. With only a handful of guards patrolling the area – presumably just for show – I savoured the solitude and the quietness of the hall. I pressed my forehead against the glass window and peered into the pitch-black night. The overgrown grass, the shrubbery and the trees were merely shapes and outlines shimmying in the light win.

Something – or *someone* - outside moved.

I pulled my forehead away from the window. My wide-eyed reflection stared me down.

Edging closer, the hot air from my mouth smudged the glass like a giant thumbprint.

What was it? *Who* was it?

Narrowing my eyes into something resembling a squint, my body lightened. The fox stared back at me, his green eyes almost luminous. Wildlife has flourished during the pandemic; these days, foxes stand their ground, seemingly fancying their chances. With a wry smile, I turned my back and retreated to my bedroom, where I think I managed an hour's sleep.

I spent an hour or so before breakfast chatting with Dylan about his two little girls. The youngest is called Natalie, and the eldest is Tia.

"I'd take Natalie to gymnastics five times a week, you know? Natalie is the one who lives each day as it comes. Tia is the one who plans everything. Natalie doesn't have any ambitions to become an Olympian or anything. She just puts in the hours because she loves it. Or, at least, she used to."

"Before the pandemic, you mean?" I asked.

Dylan nodded. "They moved the sessions online, and Natalie just wasn't interested anymore. I mean, they were restricted with what they could do without the apparatus anyway, but it wasn't just that. Natalie loved to get out of the house. Tia is more studious and was quite content to bury herself in a book. But Natalie adored meeting up with her friends. She sulked and said it wasn't fair that she couldn't go to gymnastics anymore."

I pulled a pained face. "It wasn't fair, mate. But what could you do about it?"

"Nothing," Dylan replied. "But it was heartbreaking to see my little girl upset like that. Like I said, she normally has this intense love for life. Her whole world has been shattered, and in so many ways."

Breakfast, and showering, was less eventful this morning. We knew what to expect, and we dealt with it. I wasn't with Duncan this time, so I have no idea how he behaved. I wonder how many other men would have stood up to him like Dylan did? TJ would have, for sure. But how many others would have?

And now, in my distorted mind, I'm in the Naughty Corner. Sitting in this corner soothes my conscience somewhat, like I'm getting punished for my wrongdoing. Thoughts rebound, bouncing off the corners of my mind. I want to disappear within the fabric of the sofa. Looking up, my heart sinks even deeper within the pit of my stomach. Taking the seat opposite me, Kim greets me with a beaming smile.

It is like we exist in parallel universes.

She shares a smile that is intended only for me. After all, we share a secret. The real secret is that everyone apart from her shares a secret. In reality, she is Truman in this show.

Kim raises her eyes to the camera; but this is merely instinct, or habit. Waving her hand, she theatrically dismisses the camera. Oh God, I think, at least it was 'privacy' hour, and the viewing public didn't witness the travesty. Unless somebody says something then they will be none the wiser, just like Kim.

"There is something I want to tell you, Andrew."

I stare at my upturned hands, resisting the urge to sink my head into them. She wanted to tell me something yesterday; look how *that* ended up.

"You don't have to if you don't feel you want to."

"I just *told* you I wanted to," she says.

Kim's face brightens in response to my cracked smile. "There is a reason I don't drink."

"I know."

I tell her that there is always a reason.

Kim crinkles her nose. "The drinking. The virginity. It is all linked, darling. And not in a good way, let me tell you. I don't drink because I am terrified of losing control, of letting down my guard, of doing something I don't want to."

"Sounds similar to me. Have you ever drunk?"

"Never, Andrew. Don't get me wrong, I have really wanted to. Sometimes it feels like everyone else in the world but me drinks and has an absolutely fantastic time doing so..."

"You're not. And they don't. I know it feels that way, though. I haven't had a single drink in my life either, Kim."

Cupping my chin in my palms, I lean forward a few inches, like Parkinson trying to engage with an awkward interviewee. I shuffle back a few inches. I am interested, but I don't want to appear *too* interested.

"I can trust you, Andrew."

I glance away. My cheeks burn red. I am a husband who has returned to the welcoming embrace of his wife after secretly visiting his mistress.

"I told you about my cousin..."

I nod. "I can tell that she is an important part of your life, Kim. She sounds great."

Kim examines her nails. It feels like an awkward silence on a first date.

"*Everyone* liked her, Andrew. Well that's the thing. She appeared to be an angel, but appearances can be deceptive, can't they? I should know that better than anyone. Sure, they'll help a granny cross the road on a busy street. But how many of them would help a granny cross the road if nobody was there to witness it?"

I shrug my shoulders. I've had the same thought about the cameras. Take them away; how would the contestants in this place act?

"I idolised her. She was everything I wanted to be. She was everything I wasn't. But you know what, Andrew?"

"What?"

Kim sucks in air. She glances around. Her eyes can't help but glance at the camera. She doesn't want to, I can tell, but the lure is just too strong

"She looked like an angel sent down from heaven. But she was more like the fucking devil. She was evil. She was an evil little bitch."

My eyes widen. "Kim, you realise that we're on TV? Are you sure you want to be saying this?"

Kim mechanically jerks her head to the side. Unblinking, she stares straight at the camera. "Yes, I fucking do. Maybe the cameras are one of the reasons I *do* need to say something."

Reaching forward, I squeeze my friend's hand. I have already made one monumental mistake with this girl. I really don't want to make another. "Maybe it is best that you don't say anymore, though. You might get upset."

"She used to babysit me. Let's think. Yes. She was about fourteen and I was eleven. She was my best friend the first few times. I was on top of the world hanging out with her. After all, she was the most popular girl in the school, and she was my cousin. You need to remember that I was still this gawky, pimply little thing that nobody ever noticed.

She made me feel like the most important kid in the whole world."

Kim pulls away her hand to wipe a tear from her cheek.

"You don't need to say any-"

"And then this one time, when we were watching TV, she asked me to come and sit down on the sofa with her..."

Kim purses her lips, like she is desperately trying to draw enough oxygen to continue talking. Her grip tightens. Her hand shakes.

"I'm serious now, Kim. You really don't have to-"

"I fucking told you; I *want* to tell you this."

Her pitch is high. Her tone issues a warning, like a barking dog with bared teeth.

"She patted a space on the sofa for me to sit down. It was a tiny space, between her legs. It sounds dreadful when I say the words now. Believe me, the words have sounded dreadful in my mind for the last seventeen years, or whatever it is. But then, why wouldn't I sit there? After all, this was my cousin. It wasn't my creepy uncle with wandering eyes and hands. Sure, it felt a bit strange, but I was relaxed with her."

Kim squeezes her eyes shut.

"When her hand stroked my thigh, I thought that she was just playing. It sounds weird, but I thought she was tickling me. I really didn't want to say or do anything that would upset her. I was a young eleven, if you know what I mean, and I didn't know if this was normal or not. You've *got* to believe me, Andrew..."

Squeezing her hand tighter, I tell her that I believe her.

"And then when her hand kept rising higher – all

the way to the top – and she pulled my pants aside and – well, you know *what* – I just froze. She did it for a long time – I swear it was a long time – and I just sat there, not knowing what I was supposed to do, not daring to protest. I just let her do it. I didn't try to stop her. I am really not sure why I didn't try to stop her, Andrew. And that's when it all went horribly wrong-"

"What? *Now* it went horribly wrong?"

Kim uses her index fingers to rub a tear from her red-rimmed eyes. "Yes, *now* it went terribly wrong. She pulled her fingers out, pushed me off her and started shouting at me. You know what she said? Do you know what she fucking said, Andrew?"

Shaking my head, I desperately try to keep my eyes glued to hers.

"She said her fingers were wet. She said she was just testing me. She said I was a little pervert. It was the way that she looked at me that made me feel disgusting. And I've felt disgusting ever since, like I'm lying to people, like I'm pretending to be a nice person when really I'm just this disgusting..."

I pull her close to me now. My hand pats her shaking back.

"I ran to my room crying, and I didn't come out till the next morning, not even when my parents came back from the pub."

"That sounds awful, Kim. Did it happen again? Did you talk about it? Did you tell anyone?"

Pulling away, Kim shoots me a look so powerful that the hairs on my neck prickle. "It never happened again and we never talked about it. But when we were in a room on our own – which I tried to make sure hardly *ever* happened – she just put her index finger to her lips-"

"She didn't want you to tell anyone what happened?"

"No. It wasn't that. It was her way of saying that she had a hold over me, that so long as I was good she wouldn't tell anyone about *my* dirty little secret. She made it clear that I didn't have anything to say. It was *her* who could expose me."

The blood flows through my veins. Tongue-tied, I'm not sure how to put the words in the right order.

"That's absurd. That's outrageous. You are the victim. You really need to know that."

"I know that now, Andrew. I think I've always known the truth. But this place has just made me feel strong enough to say it out loud. And for the first time in my life I feel certain that I'm not disgusting. I don't care what other people think of me. I can strip away the mask and let people see me for who I really am. And you know what? It doesn't really matter if they like me. It doesn't matter if they approve of me. I like me, and that's all that matters."

Kim releases my grip on her hand. She stands up and sticks her face just a few inches from the camera. Her smile widens. "I would like the whole world to know that Danielle Parks sexually abused me as a child."

Sitting back down, Kim releases a long sigh and then uses her sleeve to wipe her forehead. The sleeve darkens. Tangling her long fingers together, Kim straightens her back. "Oh my fucking god, it feels so good to get that shit off my chest." She looks at me, smirking. "I know there has just got to be a good reason you don't drink, Andrew. Maybe you should consider getting that off your chest, too..."

I hold up my palms. "I'm just a big, crazy alcoholic, Kim."

Kim playfully slaps my knee. "Anyway, I just wanted to say thank you."

My smile disappears, like a raindrop in the ocean. Oh God, she is going to go there, isn't she? "Why? What on earth do you have to thank me for?"

Her smile widens. "You know, Andrew."

I look away.

"It was *wonderful*. I don't care if I only met him the day before. I don't care what people think. It was love at first sight. It was absolutely the right thing to do, in the right place, and at the right time. But I am such a little baby. I would never have been brave enough on my own..."

"Kim, are you sure you want to say these things? Remember, the cameras were turned off. Nobody needs to know. Do you really want viewers to work it out?"

Kim smiles. "I don't want any secrets. I can't cope with them anymore, darling. It is literally exhausting to keep secrets. The whole world can know, for all I care. It will still be a wonderful moment between just two of us. But I do have you to thank for making it happen."

"I'm sure that it would-"

"No, Andrew. I told you. I'm a coward. I've always been the lion in the *Wizard of Oz*. Did I tell you that is my favourite film in the whole world? I would never have done it were it not for your encouragement..."

Rocking back and forth in the chair, this time I can't resist the urge; I sink my head into my upturned hands. Sometimes the world is a kinder place when you can't see it. If you ignore reality for long enough then somehow – momentarily – it ceases to exist. I hid under my bed sheet for hours when Frances had her traumatic times, and then during the longer period when that just became normality.

"Andrew? What is it? Are you okay? Is there something you're not telling me?"

Maybe she is right? Maybe it *is* best not to keep any secrets?

Removing my hands from my eyes, the room feels much brighter, like I've removed my sunglasses. Maybe it is the anticipation that I can release this weight from my shoulders, that I can ease my heavy conscience, just like Kim has. It likely resembles the relief of quitting a job you can't stand, the honeymoon period before reality hits and you can't afford to pay the mortgage.

"There *is* something I have to..."

Kim leans forward. I can smell the minty fragrance of her toothpaste. Her wide, upturned eyes are those of a puppy. This girl is so sweet and innocent; she needs to know the truth.

"Don't tell her, Andrew."

I jerk my head over my shoulder. Blinking furiously, I take a second look. Jake looms over me like a dark shadow. His smile could melt an ice cap. He whispers to me. "Are you doing this for her, or for you? Are you doing this merely to ease your conscience?"

Kim crosses a leg over her thigh. "What is it Andrew? What's wrong?"

I slide my hand through my hair. "It's just...it's just...I'm worried that I influenced you. I put the idea in your head. That seems wrong."

The colour returns to Kim's cheeks. She reaches

forward and cups my hands. "Oh, you silly little sausage, Andrew. Don't worry about that. It was the most wonderful thing I've ever done in all my life."

I'm grateful when the middle door at the back of the hall flings open.

******

Rising to our feet, we stand to attention like kids in an assembly; we are the pupils, and Rebecca is our headmistress. Rebecca stands at the front of the hall, facing her audience. We gather in straight lines, hanging on her words.

"Oh, my little darlings, it looks like you have been having so much fun. I am delighted you've all been getting along so very well."

Maybe I'm paranoid, but I feel like Rebecca holds Kim's eyes for just a moment too long.

"Our intention was to make you feel as relaxed and as comfortable as possible, to ease you in. You may or may not have noticed I didn't grace you with my presence yesterday? But alas, all good things have to come to an end. Put simply, the viewers get bored of you being happy for too long. To be blunt, my sweethearts, you are all getting frightfully dull."

Rebecca puts her hand to her lips, before dangling a finger in the air. She points at TJ.

Trying to conceal my smirk, I think that it couldn't have chosen a nicer person. TJ paces up and down the hall (imitating me from yesterday afternoon), his long arms dangling in a straight line down by his side, resembling a drawing of an ape before it evolved into man.

Rebecca shares a reassuring smile. "Calm down,

TJ. How do you know that getting chosen isn't a good thing?"

TJ snorts. "How do I know this isn't a *bad* thing?"

"I can tell you are a jar half empty type of guy, TJ. You may want to change your mindset. Did you know that optimists, on average, tend to live longer than pessimists?"

"Just tell me what I have got to do. *Please.* Put me out of this misery."

Rebecca doesn't say anything. She merely turns to a security guard who carries three square glass boxes, each about a foot wide. The guard places the boxes on a table at the front of the room. A folded sheet of white paper sits at the bottom of each box. Rebecca instructs TJ to choose a box.

TJ's hand disappears inside the middle one. His eyes narrow as he stares at the paper. He swipes his arm across his forehead.

"Don't keep us in suspense, TJ," Rebecca says. "Can you please read what is on the card?"

He looks around. The eyes appear dead.

Rebecca purses her lips sympathetically. "You *can* read, can't you, sweetheart?"

"*Yes*, I can fucking read."

"Well then. *Read.* There's a good boy."

TJ's throat contracts. "This is Truth Card number two. The Truth Card says that one of the contestants in the show is a plant. They work for the show. They are not here to win, and they *cannot* win."

A gasp echoes around the room. We all analyse each and every other contestant.

I am not sure whether the paranoia is growing, but it feels like more than one pair of eyes fixate on me.

******

Afternoon

As the afternoon progresses, it feels like the contestants look up and see dark clouds gathering in the sky after a beautiful summer's day; they know that a storm is brewing.

The sullen atmosphere is a stark reminder of when things changed for the worse in our household. Sure, it was strained for a long time and yes, it happened gradually, but there was a specific moment when I realised the stench was permanent, that it couldn't just be camouflaged with spray.

Looking back, I guess I must have been about twelve. It was a drizzly Saturday afternoon, and Dad and Frances zipped up their coats and headed to the park, leaving me to pass the hours with square eyes and a numb bottom in front of the TV. As one cartoon followed another, a loud bang from the bedroom pulled me out of my trance. If I was left home alone then I would have suspected intruders and run out of the house. But I wasn't alone. There was one other person in the house.

I sprung to my feet, skipping a step as I climbed the stairs. I vividly recall stumbling as I reached the top; my lips were close enough to kiss the furry carpet. The door was closed. The door was *always* closed. I knocked. Nothing. I didn't hang around. I pulled the handle down and pushed the door open.

The smell, like fish had been left to rot, hit me like a punch to the face. Stepping over discarded clothes on the floor, I sprung open a window. The damp air from outside swept into the room. I turned and tripped, my outstretched arms pressing against the bed to prevent my fall.

I looked down. "Mum?"

My mum lay naked on the floor, her yellowed body tarnished with purple bruises. Gripping her chin with my hand, I turned her face upwards. Dried spittle outlined her lips. Her open mouth exposed mousy, yellowing teeth. Heavy eyelids struggled to open.

This was the same woman the dad's lusted after just years before.

"Andrew?"

For a brief moment, creases formed around her lips and colour returned to her faded cheeks. Both vanished as quickly as they appeared; it was too much effort to maintain. I reached down to hold her hand, but her long, icy fingers were curled in a ball. Untangling them, I prised a plastic bottle from her grip. I released a relieved sigh; the bottle was still full. I lifted my mother onto the bed. Although she was just bone and saggy skin, she felt heavy, like a dead, decaying body. I planted a kiss on her forehead, told her that I loved her.

Closing the door, and shutting away the misery, I stopped dead in my tracks in the hallway. My dad stood with his arm around Frances's shoulder, waiting for me. They both appeared forlorn, their heads bowed. My dad moved forward with outstretched arms. I inhaled the scent that was becoming more and more familiar those days.

"We need to stop making excuses for her, son," he whispered. "Just look how it is affecting Frances."

Frances's cheeks flushed, and her eyes watered. My dad didn't say as much, but clearly he was giving me an ultimatum – choose him and my sister, or choose my mother.

To this day, I still don't know whether I made the right decision.

The familiar desperation in the pit of my stomach returns; the black clouds suck any remnants of joy from my body. Raising my head to take in the scene, I see that contestants still huddle together in small groups, talking and laughing, and yet it is like the volume on the remote control is turned down a few notches. With the straight, ramrod back and the mechanically rotating heads, I'm reminded of meerkats searching for predators in the desert. One of us is a plant, which means one of us is the enemy.

One of the contestants wants to hunt the rest of us down.

Of course, I'm no different from anybody else. A thought besieges my mind. If I were the plant, how would *I* behave right now? Would I pretend to be analysing others, searching for the culprit? Or maybe – just *maybe* – the plant is the one who is trying just a little bit too hard?

I glance at TJ, who busily gnaws at his nails.

What will the newspapers make of all of this? Maybe they are taking odds on the winners and the losers. This could be a great scheme to grip the nation.

I know and everybody else in the room knows that there is more to this than just the plant, though. Rebecca's words deliberately struck a chord. They have lingered in my mind like an uninvited guest at the door.

She said that all good things had to end. What did that mean? What did she have planned?

The announcement distracts my mind, focuses my thoughts.

"Ladies and gentlemen, can we have your attention please? It is now time to vote for who you want to stay in the competition. You can only nominate a contestant from your team. Write your nomination on the card and put the card in the box. You have sixty seconds to vote. The sixty seconds commence at the end of this announcement. Anybody who fails to nominate a contestant within this time will automatically be eliminated."

My upturned head gazes at the clock on the wall, flashing with neon aggressiveness.

60. 59. 58.

Kim cups my cheek. "*Seriously?* It isn't that bad, Andrew. What is the worst that can happen? One of us gets kicked off and then we return to our old life. Nothing ventured and nothing gained. But that's not true, is it? If I lose, then at least I've met you. I'm a lucky, lucky girl."

My upturned lips shiver. She is right, and I need to show her that she is right. Looking at Dylan, his pensive brow suggests that he has doubts too, though. It worries me when Dylan isn't sure about something, because he *always* seems to know something we don't.

Kim's face appears numb for a few seconds, before she jumps to her feet. This feels like a race. Everyone runs around like headless chickens, like the supermarkets are running low on toilet paper. I glance at Dylan. Amongst the hysteria, he seems to be moving in slow motion. But then, at least he *is* moving.

The white cards are laid out on tables in a neat

pile. I reach out to grab a card, but it disappears from my sight. I glance to the next table. The final card vanishes. My heart pumps faster. I look to a security guard. With his hands balled behind his back, he stares straight ahead. I could light a match and he wouldn't flinch.

"There is no card left. How am I supposed to vote if there is no fucking card left?"

I spin in a circle. I blink away a droplet of sweat from my eye. / I raise my voice. "There are no cards left. Somebody help me, please!"

Somebody moves towards me with an outstretched hand. The steps are fast but measured. The head is bowed. I don't see her face. "I'm sorry. I took two by mistake. I have mad moments." And then she vanishes, leaving a trail of flaming red hair and me clasping the piece of card. Sofia.

I glance at the clock.

41 seconds.

My sigh is deep. Realisation hits that everything is going to be alright after all.

I find a space on a table and instinctively scribble, just to make sure the black biro works.

I don't even need to think about the nomination.

Dylan.

I fold the card in half, dangling it between finger and thumb. With my shoulders pulled back, I stride towards the box.

Midstride, I catch Kim's eyes. I'm hit by how beautiful they are; blue with flecks of grey and green. Have I even properly looked at her before? The smile seems so natural. Unusually relaxed. She nods, like she is acknowledging me walking past her on the street.

I'm completely motionless for just a moment. My thoughts, however, rebound off each other; a pinball machine in overdrive. Does Dylan want to win this as much as the other contestants? He told me it was all about his family, didn't he? He doesn't need to win the show to win their approval, does he? If I were his wife and kids, watching at home, then I'd be proud of Dad. Kim, on the other hand, well this place has made her happier than she's ever been. She *needs* this place...

I turn on my heel and return to the table. I strike a line through the name. I scribble a new name.

Kim.

I take a cursory look at the clock.

10. 9...

The piece of card disappears into the slot, like a Christmas card slipped through a letterbox.

Closing my eyes, I count the final seconds in my mind.

"My darlings, I'm delighted to confirm that you all managed to put in your vote. Admittedly, the task did appear more *challenging* for some contestants than others. As they say, every vote counts. Please give us a moment whilst we count the votes."

None of us return to our seats. It is like we've all taken a hit of caffeine after a long, lazy lunch. Our eyes follow the movements of a security guard as he picks up the box and empties the cards onto a table. Two different guards take it in turns to count the votes. One writes (presumably) two names; the other nods his agreement. Both guards disappear into the room behind the middle door.

I don't make eye contact with anyone. I can't help but think of Frances. This would have been a nightmare for her; it was, in effect, a popularity contest. She would have dreaded the concept that somebody might not like her. She would assume that something was dreadfully wrong with her, that not only did they not like her, but they hated her. She would seek out reasons, identify negative connotations. Am I boring? Do I talk about myself too much?

Or do they think I'm fat?

The middle door opens at the rear of the room. I don't even need to look up to know that Rebecca has returned to the hall. I'm sure she only left so she could make a grand reappearance. Her heels click on the tiled floor. Her perfume sweeps flamboyantly across the room.

"I have fantastic news, everybody," she says. "The votes are in."

******

Rebecca waves her hands in the air like she is conducting an orchestra. She has utilised the time by applying an extra layer of foundation. A stylish handbag dangles from her slender shoulder. Is this for our benefit, or for the millions of viewers watching at home? With a tinge of guilt, it crosses my mind that Rebecca looks attractive.

Rebecca claps her hands together. I exchange a look with Dylan. His smirk confirms he is thinking the same thing: how extreme is this? I manage a laugh. I feel surprisingly at ease now that I have cast my vote. Dylan doesn't care whether he stays or goes. Dylan doesn't care whether people approve of him or not. Initially I made a mistake, but I reconsidered my decision and took appropriate rectifying action. Whatever happens, I've done the right thing.

"This does remind me of the Eurovision song contest. Isn't it funny that however well the UK does, we always seem to get nil points from some of our European neighbours?"

Heads turn to TJ's raised hand. Rebecca does not attempt to restrain a sigh. "TJ?"

"Becky, any chance you could hurry this along please, darling?"

I lower my head, hiding my giggles. I am not the only one. I do not dare to look up, for I know my eyes are watery red.

"It is Rebecca, as you well know."

"Any chance you could hurry this along, *Rebecca*?"

Rebecca plants her hand on her hip, resembling a teapot. "Are you in a rush, TJ? Do you have some place to go?"

This silences the room.

"It is my great honour to announce that the contestant from group A with the most votes is Max..."

My face remains neutral. Max is a guy in his early thirties with a blonde, straggly beard and sky-blue eyes. He seems personable enough; I've just never spoken to him. I could easily imagine him in an Abba tribute band. I notice two dark patches under his armpits as he raises his arms in the air, Rocky-style. I clap my hands together to make sure I don't stand out as the only one who doesn't.

"Well done, Max," Rebecca says. "You have truly proved yourself a popular and valued member of your team. That is something you can be proud of, whatever happens next."

Group A moves away from the rest of the contestants, leaving Group B to huddle together, like outcasts at school. Kim reaches out and joins hands with the girl next to her, who in turn holds out her hand, and before we know it, we have formed a chain. Normally this would feel ridiculous, particularly with the eyes of the nation glued to our every move. Now, however, it feels natural.

"It is my great honour to announce that the contestant from group B with the most votes is..."

The woman to my right squeezes my hand. Is it Sofia? I want to take a glance; it would be too obvious.

"Kim!"

We bounce up and down; this is a shared success. Contestants queue up to give Kim a hug. I lag behind, waiting for the rush to die down, like I'm playing it tactical before boarding a flight. It is a good move, for I can savour the embrace without worrying about anybody waiting behind me. She tightens her grip around my body. Her lips are moist against my ear. "Oh my God, Andrew. People actually like me for who I am. Without the mask. Can you fucking believe it...?"

The noise subsides. I feel like I am at the theatre waiting for the curtains to draw for the second half of the production. After all, this was just the warm up act. We are waiting for the real show now. The announcement that *really* matters. I could be going home. Rebecca stands at the front of the room though, resembling a wax model.

I'm feeling brave. I'm feeling high. Maybe I'm pushing forward my own demise? "So Rebecca, congratulations to both Max and Kim, but when are you going to make the *big* announcements?"

Rebecca jerks her head, like she's been woken from her sleep. Her tilted head looks at me with vacant eyes. "Whatever do you mean, dear?"

I stifle an embarrassed laugh. I have an opportunity to have a dig at her, to play to the crowd. Something tells me that this isn't a good move, that it wouldn't end well. "You've announced the winners. But what about the losers? When are you going to announce the contestants who had the least votes?"

Rebecca's body seems to visibly loosen. "Oh I see what you mean, Andrew. I understand why you would be asking that, considering we failed to explain the change in rules-"

"Change in rules?"

"That's what I said, dear. At this point I can only apologise. We have conveniently put it down to an administrative oversight, darling." Rebecca shrugs her heavily-padded shoulders. "These things happen. All we can possibly do is to use it as a learning lesson for next time, to make sure it doesn't happen again."

TJ moves forward a few paces, so that his heavily-muscled back faces the rest of the contestants. I can imagine it is the move he makes when an opposition supporter taunts his football team. "What are you talking about? *What* change of rules?"

Rebecca inspects her nails for a few moments before looking up. "We need to make things *interesting*, TJ. We need viewers to keep this show going. You are all so terribly happy and friendly, aren't you? It is about as exciting as watching paint dry. So we mixed it up a bit. You didn't vote for who you wanted to stay in the contest. You just voted for who you wanted to be eliminated..."

******

It takes me a few seconds to absorb the revelation, to link the cause and the consequence. It has all kicked off by the time I do.

TJ stands out amongst the mayhem. Stabbing his middle finger in the direction of Rebecca, he shouts, "This is bullshit! Bullshit! You've taken the piss out of our votes. I voted for that girl to stay, not to leave!"

Four security guards rush out in a coordinated line, using their pumped chests as a barricade; like police standing up to protesters. One of them catches my gaze. His black eyes belong to a shark. His mouth flickers, just for a moment, but it vanishes, leaving me to wonder if I imagined it.

A pang of guilt hits me. Whatever Dylan, Sofia and Jake told me just isn't true; everything I do *does* turn to disaster. She needed to stay. I voted for her to leave. I'm ruining Kim's life just like I ruined my sister's. TJ thrusts into action whilst I stand and stare into space, feet cemented to the floor.

My feet start moving. With the security guards backed off, I stand side by side with TJ. Dylan is to my left. I am desperate to do something, to make up for my wrongdoing. "I second TJ. You are taking the piss," I say. "I forfeit my place on the show. I give my place to Kim..."

My words have impact. The room quietens. The contestants move apart. We all want to view Rebecca. Her face twists into an exaggerated look of sympathy, like she is passing a homeless man with no legs, but she isn't going to give any money anyway.

"I must say, that is an honourable proposal, Andrew. You are just the type of man this country needs in a war. Winston Churchill would have lapped you up, sweetheart. But alas, it is all wasted energy really, because this isn't a war. Let's not get carried away with our own importance, darlings. This is merely a reality show, and rules need to be followed. It would be unfair if we allowed you to forfeit your place..."

A voice emits from beside me. I feel stronger when Dylan is by my side. "Rules need to be followed? Can you hear yourself? The whole issue has been caused because you changed the rules. Change them again..."

Rebecca shrugs her padded shoulders. "Fair point, Dylan, and it is only reasonable that I address it. There was a clause in the conditions of the game which allowed us to change *those* rules, Dylan. There is no clause for this rule. I appreciate your apparent frustration, but frankly there is nothing I can do to rectify your concerns."

It feels like she should be giving us a telephone number to call customer services.

"You are a fucking cunt!" Dylan shouts, raising his fist in the air. Thirty heads jerk in his direction. So much for fucking diplomacy. And this is the relaxed, the reasoned guy? What hope is there for the rest of us?

Rebecca releases a deep sigh. She appears tired and irritated, like she just can't seem to swat that damn fly. Straightening her back, she stretches herself back to her five foot nothing. "It seems we are not progressing anywhere fast with this. Can the winner of the first vote, Max, please come to the front?"

Everyone stops talking, stops protesting. All eyes turn to Max. There is nothing mad about this Max. He appears calm and content, like a contestant who has accepted his fate when he is fired on *The Apprentice.* With slumped shoulders, he walks in a straight line to the front. He stops a few yards away from Rebecca.

"I want you to remember that your fellow contestants voted for you because they like and respect you, Max. Can you acknowledge that?"

He looks around, almost apologetically.

"I do know that. It means a lot. It wasn't their fault...."

"Which makes this an extremely difficult task. I am stuck between a rock and a hard place here, Max. But I am sure you have had to do difficult things in your life that you haven't wanted to?"

Nodding, Max smiles. I bite my lip. He should be throwing his toys out of the pram. He is too nice for this fate.

I release a sigh. I try to change my perspective. Why am I getting so worked up if he doesn't give a shit? At least the guy can leave the show knowing that he has achieved something. The other contestants voted for him because they wanted him to stay. The viewers at home will be on his side. The British public love a victim. We'll talk about him as one of the good guys.

In truth, I'm not really thinking about Max. I don't really know him. He isn't one of mine. I want to press the fast forward button. We all know what is going to happen next. The doors to the outside world are going to open. Max will hug his friends in here. We will all clap him as he leaves the show. I am bracing myself for what will happen after he leaves.

I am waiting for Rebecca to call the next name.

We watch as Rebecca's hand disappears within her black *Armani* handbag, like she is searching for mints. She pulls out a pistol. A girl releases a scream.

We watch as Rebecca pulls back the gun and shoots the winner of the Group A vote, Max, in the head...

******

For a few seconds, silence fills the room. It feels like hands are clasped around my throat, the grip gradually tightening. My lips move, but my words – if I do actually speak any – are soundless. My eyes fix on the crimson, sticky pool on the tiled floor. The circle of blood expands and spreads.

The guards work as a team. I have never seen them so ruthlessly efficient. Angled black shoes step around the blood. One guard grips under the armpits. Another guard takes hold of the ankles. After a wordless count of three and a nod of the head, they lift the dead body from the floor. They take it away, like they are removing the trash, putting out the bins. Another two guards stand ready with a mop and bucket. They work at a frantic pace, ebbing the flow of the blood. Within seconds the floor is wiped clean, making me wonder whether I imagined it all.

Did everybody else see what I just did?

The stunned silence is replaced by high-pitched

screams, piercing my eardrums.

It seems that they did.

Mayhem erupts around me. I stand still, my feet glued to the floor. I want to press my hands to my ears. I want to snap my eyes tight. I want to blank the rest of the world out. I want, I want, I want....

In the seconds before she blew a man's brain out, Rebecca had held the gun like a felt-tip pen, a mechanism to create and share wonderful ideas, and not a weapon of mass destruction. Her eyes displayed no ill-intent, no desire to hurt.

I snap out of my trance; I am suddenly Johnny Rotten up on stage, delirious and angry. I wave my arms above my head. "You won't get away with this! Have you forgotten that we are on the TV? What you just did was watched by millions, you psycho bitch!"

Rebecca casually slants a single eyebrow. This unnerves me more than anything.

Really?

The contestants split into two groups: those who choose to fight, and those who choose to flight. The second group act like they are hiding from terrorists; they lunge under the nearest table or behind the closest chair.

I want to join them. I want to hide.

I manage to pull myself into the middle of the room, joining the other fighters. I long to tell them to hide. I long to tell them that we are an easy target.

Instead I mimic their movements; I pace up and down, up and down.

Rebecca ignores us and instead chooses to reach out to the hiders. "Oh, darlings," she says, "there is no need to hide, you poor things. I thought I made my intention perfectly clear. I have no intention to hurt you."

"Why did you shoot him? What possessed you?" Dylan asks.

Rebecca looks out of the corner of her eye, nonplussed, like she doesn't even understand our confusion. "I explained the rule change, Dylan; quite clearly, I felt. Did you want me to put it in writing? I explained that the winner of the vote would be eliminated-"

"*Eliminated*?" I thrust my neck forward. "*Eliminated? I* thought we would be sent home! Not-"

"Sent home, Andrew? This isn't kindergarten. He didn't wet his pants. Oh come on now. You are a clever guy. We did exactly as we said we would. We did exactly as it said on the tin. We eliminated him. This is the world of show business, sweetheart. Where is the entertainment in sending him home?"

"*Show business?*"

"Yes, show business, darling. Each show needs to be that little bit more outrageous than the competition just to stay ahead. These types of shows are everywhere these days. We need a unique selling point. We have to stand out from the crowd, give them something they actually care about, sweetheart..."

Blowing out hot air, I turn my back on Rebecca and lower myself into a squat. I can't deal with it right now. I scan beneath the tables, in all the nooks and crannies, all the possible hiding places. I draw a blank.

"Looking for me?"

With her lustrous blonde hair swept behind her shoulders, she appears angelic. Has heaven already taken hold of her and welcomed her into the kingdom?

I reach out and squeeze so tight; hastily, I loosen my grip, afraid I will break her bones. She plants her lips to my ear. "I've worked things out, Andrew. I'm not as silly as I look."

Pulling away, my face distorts into protest. "*Silly?* Whoever said you were silly?"

Kim presses her finger to my lips, silencing me. "You saw me, didn't you? You *all* saw me. You saw me with Christian..."

My body lightens. My lips move, but then I decide against saying anything. I long to protest my innocence; but I'm *not* innocent. Lowering my head, I nod. Smooth, soft fingertips cup my cheek. "It's fine, Andrew. I understand. Everything is absolutely fine."

I glance over my shoulder. "Can the winner of the first vote for group B – Kim - please make her way to the front of the room?"

My body tenses. I look for Dylan. I look for Jake. I even look for TJ. There has to be something we can do? If we all work together? I squeeze Kim's hands. I need to make her believe. "We can form a barricade so they get nowhere near you..."

Her angled smile confuses me. She should be fighting. She should be protesting.

"I repeat. Can the winner of the first vote for group B – Kim – please make her way to the front of the room?"

Kim's feet remain fixed to the floor. A handful of security guards pace towards us from the left. TJ and Dylan pace towards us from the right. Both parties are ready to collide in the middle.

"No, Andrew. Don't you see? This is my time. For the first time in my life, I feel content. This is how I want to go."

I shake my head. "You are too young to go, Kim. You have too much to offer-"

"For me, Andrew. Please."

I shake my head.

"*Please*. Tell them to stop..."

I don't need to tell them. Everybody stops midstride.

"This is how I am going to go. I don't want a struggle. I want to go with dignity. I want to go happy, Andrew."

"Andy."

"Huh?"

"Andy. Call me Andy."

Kim releases my hands. "Bye, Andy."

Her feet start moving. She strolls like she is out for an evening walk in the park. I have never seen her slender shoulders appear so relaxed. She stops to embrace Christian. Kim was right; he *was* her first and last man. She releases his hold. Christian's damp, reddened face disappears within his hands.

Literally, Kim is the walking dead, and yet never has anybody walked with such grace. She stops just in front of Rebecca and smiles.

Rebecca's painted face brightens. This has proven much easier than she anticipated. "I want you to remember that your fellow contestants voted for you because they like and respect you, Kim. Can you acknowledge that?"

Kim turns and gives us all a flirty wave. Her eyes linger on Christian. Despite the situation, a few contestants can't help but laugh. "I acknowledge that. I love and respect them all. It means the world to me..."

Rebecca pulls back the gun.

"Oh Rebecca, can I say one last thing?"

"Yes, sweetheart. What is it?"

Kim speaks clearly and concisely. "I just wanted to say one final thing to you, Rebecca. *Fuck* you, and *fuck* your mother, and *fuck* your mother's mother, too..."

Rebecca constructs a slightly distorted face in the moment just before she pulls the trigger, in the moment just before Kim's face splatters all over the tiled floor....

******

Are you anything like me?

Let's see.

If you're anything like me, then you often get a sense – an inkling - that things aren't quite right in your life. You don't have anything concrete to work with, and you're unable to express your concerns in words but still – *you* know it is there – like a lingering smell that nobody else in the room has yet noticed. But then, this voice in your head – and fuck it, I don't care what anybody else says, it is *definitely* a voice – starts talking to you.

Let me tell you about this voice, just in case it isn't already your friend. Because it is a friend and, if you are like me, then you'd be lost without it. Only, it is the type of friend that would throw you in front of a bus and then laugh. Nevertheless, if you *are* like me then the voice is probably not just your friend, but it is your best friend, because it is always there for you, both in your moments of glory and your times of despair. The voice never leaves your side even though – quite frankly, dear – you'd often like it to fuck right off.

The voice is warm and syrupy and deliciously manipulative. If you are an alcoholic, for example, the voice will tell you that everybody deserves a drink once in a while, especially you. The voice will cheer encouragement as you walk to the bar for your second, third and fourth drink. It will tell you that life is short, that nobody likes a boring cunt, that the other punters love this version of you. And then, when you are lying in the gutter, and your wife is stepping over you with her suitcase in her hand, the voice will helpfully tell you that you really shouldn't listen to a word they say, you silly old bastard.

Would you agree that you are like me?

The voice started whispering words to me when I thought there wasn't something quite right with Frances. The voice told me that we live in an imperfect world, that even my beautiful little sister wasn't perfect all of the time. Who was I to judge? The voice told me to ignore it. Nobody else had noticed; what made me so special?

It was because of the voice in my head that I allowed things to drift, to let a tiny freckle turn into a cancerous mole.

I remember the day I realised that things were far from right, that – yet again – the voice was talking utter shit.

It was a Saturday afternoon, and neither of us had work. I gazed up at the clear blue spring sky before entering the coffee shop. I glanced at my wrist; I was a good ten minutes early. Knowing my little sister, I knew I could be waiting for ten minutes, or I could be waiting for thirty or forty minutes.

Smirking, I realised I didn't really care. I tended to organise my Saturdays filling the long, sleepy hours between breakfast, lunch and then dinner.

Sitting at a round table by the window, I glanced up from my newspaper every time I spotted shoes or heels walk through the entrance. Over and over, I kept returning to my newspaper. And then my smile widened. I pulled myself up from the chair.

"Frances!"

Only, I hadn't managed to open my mouth. Somebody, on their way out, got there before me. My sister embraced the woman with the big hair, a big smile and (doubtless) a big personality, with kisses on both cheeks. The woman was equally as expressive. "Oh you do look amazing, Frances."

My sister beamed. "Really, Maisie? You don't think this dress makes me look frumpy? You don't think it makes me look fat?"

Maisie reassured Frances that the dress most *definitely* didn't make her look frumpy and – of course – it didn't make her look fat. Sat on a wooden chair by the window, I listened to the two women reassure each other that they both absolutely, most definitely, looked beautiful. Moments passed until it became awkward, just watching and listening, and I returned to my newspaper.

After leaving a smudge of pink lipstick on both of my cheeks, Frances joined me at the table. I was theatrically generous. "Leave your purse in your handbag; Frances, these coffees are on me. What can I get you?"

She pursed her lips. "I'm alright, Big Brother. Thank you, though. You really are a sweetheart."

My smile became less angled, more awkward.

"Don't be silly, I said these drinks are on me!"

She nestled herself on the chair, angled so that she could glance at her reflection in the window. She sucked in her cheeks. "The caffeine makes me jittery, Andy. You go right ahead and sort yourself out."

"Caffeine? I have a solution, sis. Have a decaffeinated coffee. Do you want your favourite? Cappuccino?"

"I am fine. Do not worry about me. Truth be told, I am feeling a bit nauseated. I am here for your wonderful company, not for the overpriced drinks."

"Oh come on-"

"I said no."

Queuing at the counter for my drink, my cheeks prickled with heat.

The next hour or so passed blissfully. Feeling the unexpected coins jingle in my pocket, I treated myself to a second coffee. Maybe the voice told me I should? Frances eagerly shared gossip about the bitches in her office, how the men were all creeps and how she needed to get out. She said this about every place she worked at; I didn't care. I smiled so much that my cheeks hurt.

Frances lived out of town, in an idyllic Hansel and Gretel village, and the rural roads to her house curled like a Cumberland sausage. The hedges passed in a blur. I knew the roads like the back of my hand. Pressing my foot against the accelerator, the words to *Born to Be Wild* played in my mind. My thumb tapped the curve of the steering wheel. Taking a corner, I steered the car over the painted white lines and into the middle of the road.

My heart skipped a beat. I slammed my foot down onto the brake.

I blew air from my plumped cheeks. Sitting in silence, I didn't need to glance at Frances to know that she had a smile on her face even wider than mine. There were nine of them. The ducks crossed the road in an orderly straight line, without a care in the world. They were oblivious to us. Time was no object. My eyes flickered. A car grew bigger in my rear mirror. The music in my head changed to *Sitting on the Dock*.

I jerked my head to my right as the car overtook us. I thrust my neck forward and stared through the windscreen. I blinked my stinging eyes as the ducks disappeared beneath the car.

Neither of us spoke for the rest of the journey home. I thought about saying something, but what could I possibly say? But then, why didn't Frances mention it? Maybe she felt the same way as me. But then I was struck by another thought. Maybe I imagined it? Maybe the car didn't really hit any of the ducks?

Shutting the front door to Frances's home behind me, I followed my younger sister down the narrow hallway. The pulled curtains blanked out the sunlight, draining my already low mood. She barely left the living room before flinging her cardigan on the sofa. My jaw dropped at her straw arms, at the blue veins which popped out of her skin. Spinning on the spot, she pummelled her fists against my chest.

"How could anybody do such a thing? What is wrong with this fucking world? Why did they need to run the ducks over? Does nobody give a flying fuck about anything else anymore?"

Taking her in my outstretched arms, I made sure I didn't squeeze too hard; I was worried I would crush her. I let her go when she stopped sobbing.

And then she collapsed on the carpeted floor.

It was when I knelt over my unconscious sister – who was just a bag of bones – I realised that I should have ignored that voice in my head a long, long time ago.

The voice in my head – my best friend – had been telling me that things were absolutely fine, that I was merely being paranoid, when – clearly – things were definitely fucking not alright.

******

And now, just like with Frances all those years ago, I realise that the voice has been talking to me ever since I stepped foot in this place. I knew something was wrong. He told me that I was imagining it, that nobody else had a problem and so why should I? And now, after two dead bodies have been carried out of the hall by mute security guards, it is too late to do anything about it.

With Rebecca banished from the death scene, the room resembles a war zone. Contestants slump in chairs. Others lie motionless on the floor. TJ stands toe to toe with three guards. Each and every guard returned from behind the middle door armed with guns. I realise that they'll carry them at all times now.

"Shoot me. Go on! I fucking dare you." TJ says. "We are on TV. I am prepared to die. Are you prepared to go to prison for murder? They would destroy you inside. You would be somebody's little bitch..."

The voice in my head starts calling me a stupid

idiot. The laugh is loud and mocking.

The realisation hits me. There is no show. This is real. We are the *Truman Show* in reverse.

Grabbing Dylan's arm, I drag him to the centre of the room. There is no longer three of us; he is more important than ever to me now. I need him by my side. Please, Dylan – *please* oh God – be thinking the same as me. Let me be the sane one for once in my life. I know I am about to throw a grenade into the war zone. I know that all hell could be set loose. I need to do this with as little hysteria as possible, but whatever happens, I need them to listen, and I need them to understand the truth.

I speak loud enough for the whole room to hear me. "There is no show."

Contestants raise the back of their heads from the hard, unforgiving floor. Others appear from underneath the tables. Their reddened eyes portray bemusement and fear; there is only so much they can take in one day. Amongst the madness, amongst the noise, they realise that somebody has said something significant, something they should listen to; perhaps their biggest surprise is that the words came from me. I have banished my cloak of invisibility.

TJ turns his back to the guards. He opens up his hand; I am relieved that his fists are open. Within seconds he makes up the ground between us. I feel his hot breath on my cheeks. His eyes are a brilliant white. I bunch my hands behind my back. TJ wipes his mouth with the back of his arm. "What do you mean there is no show? Wake up. Are you blind? Look at all the cameras. The crazy woman keeps talking about show business, for fuck's sake. We *are* the show."

I shake my head. I open my mouth to speak.

"Andrew is right." Dylan's face is a crumpled cardboard box.

"What about the cameras?" TJ's voice shakes.

Dylan takes a step forward. "The cameras aren't on, TJ. Think about it. How long has it been since they shot Kim and Max?"

We all look at the clock, but it doesn't provide any answers. Time is generally meaningless in this place.

There is a voice from the back of the hall. "It has been over half an hour since they shot Max, I know that for sure."

Grimacing, Dylan manages to hold TJ's eye. "I'm no expert, but I know that if this show was being watched by millions of people in their homes then the police would have surrounded this place armed with guns by now. I'm right, aren't I?"

TJ goes to speak, but instead he releases an almighty moan and then walks away.

Silence fills the hall for God knows how long. It feels like minutes, but it is probably only seconds. I think we all have enough respect for each other to allow the brutal truth to sink in. When I envisage that sufficient time has passed, I look up at the cameras. I think back to the shower scene, to Duncan's act of depravity. I had my doubts then, didn't I? "And I thought the cameras were our enemy, that they took away our freedom. In reality, they were our protectors. They were our greatest friends..."

"Okay, cut the philosophical bullshit," TJ says, putting his hand up to me. "Where does all of this leave us now?"

Bodies start moving towards us from the cracks

and crevices of the room. Somebody speaks. "I didn't tell anybody I was coming on the show. They told me not to. They said that I would be eliminated. They said it again and again, didn't they?"

Another joins in. "I didn't tell anyone, either. I assumed the organisers of the show would know if I did, that they would be spying on me. I wanted to tell somebody, but I was too scared to. Nobody knows where I am."

"Me neither."

TJ speaks up. "You were all too terrified to break the rules..."

"Did you tell anyone, TJ?" Sofia asks.

TJ shakes his head.

"Cut the bullshit then, if you don't mind?" Sofia says.

Dylan silences the room. "Did anyone tell anyone where they were?"

I am aware that everyone around me is saying that they didn't tell a single soul. The memory of calling Frances invades my mind. The sound of her voice. I speak to her every day. I tell her my news. I had to tell her. She doesn't count; does she? It was just one person. She won't tell anyone.

I shake my head, along with everyone else.

I try to make logical sense of it all, but I suspect I'm likely to add fuel to a fire. Sometimes the truth doesn't care about feelings. "Even if a contestant *did* tell somebody they were going on the show, then they couldn't have told them where they were actually going-"

"Because we have no fucking idea where we are, that's why," TJ says. "Has anybody been able to work out where we are? Maybe from the helicopter ride?"

His question is met with silence.

"Okay," TJ says. "I repeat the question I asked Andrew a moment ago. Where does that leave us now?"

He looks to me for an answer. I want to put it in technical terms, but I'm not sure how to put the words in the right order. "It seems that it leaves us a bit fucked, TJ..."

This doesn't seem to be the answer TJ is looking for. I feel the full weight of his muscled frame as he bundles me to the floor. I could fight back, but I don't want to. He deserves to release his inner torment. His knee digs into my throat. I watch as he pulls back his arm. The fist doesn't reach my face. Flailing bodies wrestle TJ to the floor. I get to my feet before he has the chance to snake free. I make sure I walk far enough away for it not to kick off again.

I am relieved when Sofia speaks. "We are asking the wrong question. We shouldn't be asking where that leaves us. We should be asking what we do next."

Eyes turn to different faces, but none offer any answers. I turn to Dylan. He turns to the guards.

"Rebecca said that this wasn't a war," Dylan says. "She was wrong. This is a war. Everyone who isn't a contestant is our enemy. It is us against them."

******

How would the human race react if there were no rules and no laws and no lawmakers?

Would it be anarchy?

In reality, the group is too bewildered or frustrated or confused to take any meaningful action in the minutes and hours that follow the shootings.

We circle the motionless, soundless guards, like hungry wolves hunting down their prey. Only, the guards aren't sheep. They are the wolves, not us; they are wolves dressed as sheep. Only they've dared to bare their teeth. They expose the guns in their pockets; shiny, metallic deterrents visible for all to see. Their heads remain fixed straight ahead, their faces completely creaseless, devoid of any expression.

I've never even considered the guards as people before. I just thought they were faceless props, playing their part in the game. But now I know they are part of something much more sinister. They didn't flinch when Max and Kim were shot in the head; they must have known that was the plan. What sort of people are they to be part of this? What is their motive? Is it money?

Their indifference unnerves me.

We stop circling the guards. We find it more productive to bicker and argue and disagree. Who is our enemy? Is it Rebecca? Or is she just a puppet? If so, who is the puppeteer? Who control the guards? Are the guards in control? Between forty-eight of us, we formulate endless intelligent and sensible questions. Between forty-eight of us, we agree on zero intelligent and sensible answers. Throughout, Duncan thrusts his head forward and smirks, a blue vein pulsating at the side of his temple, goading the troops.

We all look up in synchronisation as the warm, syrupy male voice echoes around the hall.

"This is an announcement for all remaining contestants. We would like to remind you that the reward for winning this contest is fame, freedom or fortune. You chose your reward before you arrived. We would like to reassure you, in light of recent, unexpected developments for contestants, that this prize is still in place..."

I sink my head into my hands. What value is their reassurance now? And who in their right mind would believe a word these people – whoever they are - say?

"However, you are now aware of the stakes if you are eliminated from the contest. There will only be one winner. On the basis of fairness, we now give the opportunity for contestants to voluntarily leave the contest. If you do so, you will return to your previous, unsatisfactory life. You have sixty seconds to take the opportunity to leave..."

My head jerks to the door to the outside world, which thrusts open. It is like a light at the end of the longest tunnel in the world. A fresh, moist breeze sweeps into the hall. I look up at the clock.

60.

59.

******

For the first few seconds, I stare open-mouthed as a handful of contestants run out of the door, light on their feet, their knees high and fists pumping. The sky outside is cloudless; a perfect, serene blue. I long to walk barefoot on the grass, to reach out and touch the overhanging trees. I imagine the warmth of the sun against my skin. I can hear Frances's voice on the phone...

I run towards the door.

My legs pump, but I don't get any closer to the door. Somebody has grabbed my sleeve. The grip is strong. Glancing down, the white knuckles are strained.

"I am with you. I do whatever you decide to do. But let's talk about this first..."

My jaw drops as I stare deep into TJ's steely glare. What is wrong with him? Why would you possibly want to stay in this hellhole? And more to the point, why does he rely on my decision so much?

"Me too. Don't go anywhere until we've spoken about this."

Sofia's languid, fluid strides and curved smile make me want to pinch myself to check this isn't a dream.

"Oh for fuck's sake," I mutter.

I glance up at the clock, taunting me, calling my name.

44. 43.

"Nobody seems to believe me in this place, but I'm as mad as they come. I trust your decision more than I trust mine," Sofia says.

"Why would you want to stay?"

Sofia shrugs her shoulders. "What do I have to lose? I nearly killed myself before I came in here. What is to say I won't kill myself when I get out? For some reason, in here I'm desperate to stay alive..."

Jake whispers to me that this is the most important decision I'll ever make, that I should lead with my heart, and not my head. He asks me to consider what lured me into the show in the first place.

Dylan joins our little circle. "I am with you. We do this together..."

I stab my finger in the air. "How can we trust anything they say? We already said Rebecca might be a psycho bitch..."

Dylan shakes his head. "Andrew's right. We don't know we can trust a word they say..."

The clock ticks from 24, 23...

"Exactly," Sofia says.

Our heads turn to her for answers, the self-proclaimed nutcase.

She purses her lips and sighs. She really doesn't have time to explain things to us simpletons. "If we can't trust them, then how can we trust that they are actually going to let us return to our old life...?"

TJ pumps out his chest. "She's right! We witnessed two savage murders. What do you do with witnesses? You kill them, so they don't grass..."

I look to Dylan. I trust his instinct more than anyone else in here, much more than my own. "They could very well line up those that leave and shoot them. Maybe we are safer staying here?"

13. 12...

With a deep sigh, I say, "So we are staying?"

They all say the same thing, at the same time. "Staying."

We grip hands and stand and face the glass door.

7. 6...

We all stare at the door. One of the men who spoke to me on the helicopter emerges from the other side. It confuses me for a moment; my instinct is to tell him he's going the wrong way. It hits me that he has changed his mind. He *was* going to leave, but he has decided to stay.

Our heads turn as a figure flashes past us. A

woman has decided to leave. The seconds are passing and she needs to get to the door. My heart sinks. The woman stumbles, losing her balance; she lands flat on the floor. She crawls on her hands and knees.

2. 1...

The door to the outside world slams shut. The woman remains on her knees, just inches from the closed door. She lowers her head, before releasing a wild shriek that echoes around the room.

******

There was one time trouble knocked at my door that, at first, I *didn't* call Frances.

Autumn greeted me with darkness and a heavy mist, both to the sky and to my head. It had been absent without leave for quite a while and it *did* feel like an old friend. Drizzle followed me wherever I walked, which seemed to be a whole lot of places; I needed to keep my body active to numb my mind. The sadness weighed me down, it tired me out. The thought of getting up out of bed in the morning depressed me; the thought of *staying* in bed depressed me even more.

I am not sure how I got there, but when I looked up, I realised I was at the train station. The pitch-black night brought out the stars. With my hands bunched in my pockets, I blew steam from my mouth. Something told me it was cold, and yet a film of sweat coated my forehead. I looked up and down the platform. It was deserted. I was alone. My feet were sticky against the tarmac. Gazing down at the track, weeds poked through the pebbles. Familiar thoughts invaded my mind, the ones that always reappeared whenever the light faded and the darkness appeared.

What was the point?

Who would actually miss me?

Would it mean we would be together again?

The rumbling built momentum as the train moved closer, with lights like round saucers. The train called my name, offered me a way out. I took a step closer, and then another, until I balanced on the balls of my feet, my toes dangling over the edge. How far down was it? Was it six feet? Maybe it was eight? They always said to mind the gap, didn't they? But then, the gap wasn't the issue. It wasn't the gap that would crush me, that would leave my bloodied body in pieces.

As the horn beeped, I closed my eyes.

Would it hurt me?

I blinked the thought from my mind. Again, that wasn't the issue, was it? Any physical pain would be brief, it would be momentary. What would happen after I died? That is what people really feared, wasn't it? Would I go up, or would I go down, or would I remain in eternal nothingness? These thoughts didn't frighten me, either. After all, it couldn't be any worse than the lingering pain I endured every day I remained alive, that I remained on this planet.

The breeze ruffled my hair as the train shook and shuddered and rattled past me.

I took a conscious, deliberate step backwards.

Turning, I continued walking along the platform. Despite not *really* caring if I lived or died, I still navigated around the yellow spittle and the flecks of bird shit on the ground. The further I walked, the further I moved away from any possible sign of life.

The edge neared, and still I kept walking. This is how I always imagined doing it – if I ever *was* to do it - just walking and walking into the sea until the waves took me away.

I stopped right at the edge. Bouncing on my toes, I realised that – fuck yes – it really *was* cold. I stared at the poster on the lamp post. Despite myself, I started chuckling, just like a kid high on additives. The chuckling turned into a roar of laughter. They really had envisaged this eventuality, hadn't they? I was their target audience – somebody who kept walking along the platform and wondered whether this world was really worth it.

The poster was torn and yellowed from the rain. Apparently I wasn't alone. There were people out there who I could speak to. I took one of the cards, turned and started walking back down the platform.

Pulling my phone from my pocket, I flicked through my contacts.

I continued flicking, before looking down at the number on the card. Exhaling, I typed in the number.

The number began ringing.

******

The contestants who chose to leave disappear around the corner, out of sight.

I close my eyes. I start counting in my mind. I consider counting sheep, like my mum told me to when I couldn't sleep as a kid. I want to do whatever I can to dampen the thoughts in my mind, to make sure the seconds pass quickly. What is the next thing I am going to hear?

Will it be the sound of gunshot, of lives ending?

I try to picture what is happening outside the four walls of the hall. Inevitably, my mind creates the worst possible scenario. I imagine the men and women, clad in their dour, black outfits, lined up against a crumbling brick wall. The overgrowing nettles claw at their ankles. By this point, they know their fate. They kick out, and they scream. Their protests get swept away with the icy, autumn breeze. The guards raise their guns; they end their torrid little lives with no trace of emotion. It is a bloodbath.

The sound of gunshot would be tragic, a travesty. It would mean the loss of ten or fifteen lives, depending on how many decided to flee the game. I don't know how many left; I'm too afraid to count.

On the other hand, if the men and women were lined up outside the hall and shot, then it would mean that I made the right decision to stay in the game.

I blink open my eyes. That sound is familiar. It isn't gunshot; that is certain. Where have I heard that sound before? I search my brain, like I'm trying to remember where I've seen an actress in a film before. Of course; I know. For God's sake, it was only a few days ago, although it was a different world. I was stood in the wide, open field at the crack of dawn, ready to make what was, at the time, the biggest decision of my life.

I focus on Dylan. His eyes are open, too. Maybe he never closed them? He is a picture of contentment. He nods his head and smiles.

The volume increases. I glance up, look through the glass ceiling. The helicopter looms above us, like a massive floating ship. It casts a giant shadow over the whole hall. It hovers for a few moments, like it wants to say a final farewell, like it wants to leave us in no doubt that it is transporting the contestants back to their old lives, like it wants to gloat and mock us for staying.

Sofia stretches her arms around my shoulders, brushing her lips against my neck. Despite everything that is going on in my world right now, I can't prevent a tinge of desire. "They are alive," she says. "They didn't kill them. This is a good thing, Andrew..."

I nod my head, perhaps just a little bit too rigorously. Am I a monster for having these thoughts? We've already accumulated two dead bodies today. One of them was my friend, a girl who reminded me of my little sister. Why would I want any more dead bodies? "I know. It is. They let them go. They did a good thing. And maybe – just maybe – we can trust them a little more than we thought..."

My eyes fix on TJ. Rubbing his hands across his face, he catches me looking at him. It is as though he is reading my mind. "At least they weren't killed," he says.

My attention is diverted. Right by the corner of the room, two bodies cling together. They shudder. I am sure I hear them sobbing.

For a moment I wonder who they are, and then I realise one is the man who decided to come back, and the other is the woman who slipped and fell, just inches from freedom...

******

Evening

The middle door at the rear of the hall flings open maybe half an hour or so after the helicopter left the scene. Outside, the light has faded.

Rebecca waited until we were drained of energy, until we had no more fight left to give. She counts the heads with her middle, painted finger; a teacher dutifully taking the register at morning assembly. She beams, evidently delighted with the afternoon's progress. "Ah, there are thirty-two of you. Maths was never my favourite subject at school. But we started with fifty, we subtracted two and now we are left with thirty-two. By my calculations, that means sixteen left," she says. "That *is* less than I expected. I thought you would be mice escaping down a hole in the wall, running away from the cat. You little darlings surpassed my expectations. They *will* be pleased."

Instinctively, I jerk my head towards Dylan. There is a flicker in his eyes. Is he thinking the same thing?

"I just wanted to congratulate you on making the brave decision to stay in the competition, ladies and gentlemen-"

"Congratulations? We made the decision to die, while they made the decision to live. Why do you think this is worthy of congratulations, Rebecca?"

Turning her head, Rebecca blows air through her pursed lips. Is this really so tiring for her? "Now that is a very narrow-minded way of looking at things, isn't it, Dylan? The winner of this competition will be one of you in this very room. Those who left took the cowardly option. I have no respect for them. Do *you?* They may be alive, but so are all of *you*, and none of *them* will ever be a winner."

"We are all alive for now," Dylan says. "But for how long?" His voice is monotone, devoid of any emotion.

Rebecca doesn't seem to listen; she turns on her

heels and leaves the hall.

An hour or so later, Jake breaks my solitude. He appears from nowhere, a budgie perched on my shoulder. I shudder, like he'd appeared from the darkness of a piss-stained alley late at night.

Smiling, Jake holds out his upturned hands. "Sorry to startle you, Andrew. Although – who knows – maybe that was my intention?"

"What do you want?" I don't mean to be so blunt; maybe my mind is frazzled.

"I know this has been a traumatic afternoon for you. I wouldn't raise this now unless I felt I absolutely had to. Something has been playing on my mind, and I think we need to discuss it now, before it is too late..."

I arch my eyebrow.

"Your friend-"

"Which one?"

"Your best friend. Dylan. Sometimes it is those who make no noise who go under the radar until the damage has already been done."

What is he talking about? All of us witnessed the murder of two innocent contestants. We are all traumatised. We are *all* holding on by a thread. Why is he singling out Dylan?

"We both know he is hiding something," Jake says.

Is he trying to get inside my head? There are enough games taking place in this place without him adding to them. "We are *all* hiding something, Jake."

"I wholeheartedly agree with that statement, Andrew. After all, I am hiding more than anyone."

"What does that mean?"

Thumbing the underside of his chin, Jake's eyes

rotate the circumference of my face. "I think we both know what I mean, Andrew."

I slap my hand against my thigh.

"The thing is, Andrew, I think he is calling out for help. I think he desperately wants to tell you what he is hiding, what he is struggling with, but he hasn't yet found the courage to do anything about it."

"How do you know that?"

Jake's lips curl at one corner. "I told you; I observe and listen to people. You know that better than anyone."

I nod. "Okay. Guide me. What should I do?"

"Talk to him. Away from anyone else. Ask him questions."

"What if he doesn't want to talk? What if you've got it wrong?"

"Then he won't say anything. And you'll be in exactly the same position as you are now, only with a clear conscience. And sometimes it's heartening to know that people care. Would you agree with that?"

Jake moves to disappear, like he always does, but I grab his shirt. "Thanks, yeah. For looking out for me."

His smile reminds me of Mum's, before she got sick. "Don't thank me. Thank yourself," he says.

******

It is like a free bar at a wedding; everybody drinks copious amounts of alcohol just because they can, because it would feel wrong if they let the opportunity go to waste. I don't drink, and yet I don't blame them for doing so. On the previous nights the contestants drank for fun, they drank to be social. If the phones hadn't been taken away then their social media status would say it was wine o'clock time.

Now it is different. Now they drink to cloud the dark reality.

Kim's words taunt me. Sometimes I crave a drink, too. She said that she wanted to discover what it was like. Like me, though, I'm sure part of her longed to see if it clouded memories from her past.

I was maybe thirteen. It was a school night, and it was past my bedtime. I was still up though, probably because nobody was around to tell me to go to bed. Dad came home from the pub after closing time. He snuck into the room, gentle on his feet, and sunk his body into the sofa. I kept looking at the television screen.

"I love you, son."

I looked up and forced my face into a smile. Considering he had been in the pub all night, he smelt fresh. I suspect he'd planted a mint in his mouth and plastered his body with Brut. I lowered the sound on the TV. His slurred voice was the only evidence of his drinking; that, his bloodshot eyes and the smile that spread across his face. In those days, I always wondered what was wrong when he smiled.

"Love you too."

I mumbled my words. I wanted to say the words again, to utter them clearly.

Dad pointed his middle finger at me. "I love that little girl asleep upstairs, too. She is my little angel. I am the luckiest man in the whole world to have you two in my life."

I wondered if Dad was going to ruin it, if he was going to say that a boy was special, but every dad wants a daughter, a little angel; he didn't say anything.

I glanced back at the TV, then at my lap. "What about Mum?"

As the seconds passed, I longed to reel the words back in. "What do you mean?"

"You say you love me. You say you love Frances-"

"I don't just *say* it. I *do* love you."

"Do you love Mum?"

I didn't need to look at Dad to know blood flowed to his face. At the best of times his complexion had the pink glow of somebody left out in the cold for too long; at the worst of times his face turned positively purple. He fiddled with his hands. "Of course I love her. I married her, didn't I?"

I wanted to leave it there. I knew I *should* have left it there, but it felt like an itch I needed to scratch. "But the two of you don't act like you love each other. You don't treat each other like you love each other. You don't seem to make each other happy..."

"And who do you blame for that?"

I shrugged my shoulders.

"Come on, Andrew, don't be shy now. You seem to be the expert on every subject all of a sudden. It's a pretty simple question. Who do you blame? Do you blame your mum, or do you blame your dad?"

My mum wasn't there. She wasn't in the room. She was in the bedroom, either asleep or unconscious. My dad was there. My dad was sat six feet away from me. "It can't be easy for you, Dad..."

"Easy?" His laugh sounded bitter. "Do you blame me for having a little drink once in a while?"

"I never said anything about you having a drink-"

"She hides away in that room all day, drugged out

of her brain. She leaves me to look after you two. Easy? Don't make me laugh! But I am still here, aren't I? I haven't left her, and I haven't left you two. What does that tell you about how much I love her?"

His movements quickened; his voice rose. Every passing second was torture. My body tingled with embarrassment. I decided to go to bed without anyone telling me to.

"Night, Dad."

I reached over and hugged him. I realised that he wasn't so fresh, after all. Maybe the camouflage was fading? I inhaled the cocktail of stale beer and cheap aftershave. My dad hid his sobs within the depths of my shoulders.

Thirty-odd years later, and this is no usual free wedding bar. The guards worked hard in the late afternoon to create the kind of seedy, grotty setting fit for a stag weekend in Prague. Ravenous men throw monopoly money at gym-toned, scantily-clad women performing fantastic gymnastic feats from metallic poles. For the price of a fake ten pound note, the dancers lead the men to a tent at the back of the hall. Ten minutes later, the men reappear with reddened faces and prominent bulges in their trousers.

A young lady in a green bikini lowers her smooth buttocks onto Dylan's lap. Every inch of her sun-kissed body is smooth and toned. She turns to Dylan, close enough for him to inhale her (undoubtedly) minty breath. "I've been checking you out all night, darling," she drools. "Come for a private dance with me and I'll bring heaven to your living room."

Dylan doesn't dare hold her gaze. He cracks a polite smile. "I appreciate the kind offer," he says. "But I promised my wife I'd be good."

The lady pouts her lips. "Nothing turns me on more than a naughty husband. I think we both know that your wife isn't watching, sweetheart. This can be our little secret."

Dylan ignores the nimble fingers massaging his shoulders. His vacant eyes show no interest. The woman rises to her feet and walks away, unsteady on her (impossibly) high heels.

I don't have time to make a comment; I'm distracted by a figure approaching me. I'm sure I recognise him, that I know him from somewhere, but I can't quite put my finger on it.

"You not drinking?"

I hold up my hands. "I don't drink."

I shuffle my body along the sofa, like we are at the cinema. My leg presses against Dylan's. Opposite, Sofia raises her eyebrows, allows herself a wry smile. I'm conscious that she has effortlessly taken Kim's place. The man's hot, boozy breath blows against my cheek. "You seem like a good guy. Very popular. I like that."

"Thank you."

"Good guys don't usually do so well."

"Right."

"I think you like it in here. I think you have found your own little network. You probably didn't have that outside, in the real world?"

I don't say anything.

"Do you know what happened to me today?" he asks.

"Listen, I know it's been a tough day – for all of us - but-"

"That little bitch congratulated us for making the right decision. Well, I did make the right decision-"

"That's good. I'm pleased."

"I was out of this building. I felt the fucking fresh air on my cheeks. I didn't know it, but the helicopter was within touching distance. And do you know what I did?"

I know what he did. I know who he is now. I don't say anything. He is the guy who changed his mind. He left the hall and he decided to come back. The thing is, *he* decided to; nobody else made the decision for him. I remember where I recognise him from. I spoke to the guy briefly on the helicopter, didn't I? I recognise the tufts of hair outlining his temple. He questioned why I wasn't drinking on the helicopter, too. I didn't like him then, and I don't like him now.

"I came back! I made the right decision, and then I changed my mind. I made the decision to be a dead man walking, just like you and you and you. We are dead men and women walking!" He slides an empty glass across the table. "Take a drink with me."

"Like I said, I know it's been a tough day, but-"

"Today I made the decision to end my life, and you won't take a drink with me?"

I turn around to face him. I'm close enough to give him a kiss. I have faced this scenario countless times. Certain people have a real issue with other people not drinking. "Like I said, I appreciate you've had a difficult day. But you made the decision to come back, and not me. I've explained politely that I don't drink, but you still persist. We both now know that there are no viewers. And, like you said, we both know that, in all likelihood, we'll both be dead soon anyway. You made that perfectly clear, in your own charming way. So you really need to ask yourself whether I actually give a fuck right now. This allows us a certain jurisdiction to do things we wouldn't normally do in polite society..."

"Polite fucking-"

"And so if you keep asking me to take a drink, and if you continue to speak to me in that – quite frankly – aggressive tone, then I will take that glass and I will smash it over your head. Do you have any questions about this?"

His eyes widen. He glances at Sofia, who stares back at him with upturned, expressionless eyes. "You are fucking crazy," he says.

"Maybe I am. Maybe that is why you really should take me seriously right now."

The man turns his back. He raises his middle finger over his shoulder. The finger gets smaller and smaller as he joins his little group of friends.

Sofia starts roaring with laughter as soon as he is out of earshot.

"Fuck me, Andrew, that was *really* scary."

"It was all pretence," I say.

"Was it?"

I look away. Sometimes I don't know what is, and what isn't, pretence anymore. Sometimes I don't know when I am wearing the mask, and when I have taken it off. Now that *is* really scary.

I decide to change the subject. I have been thinking about this all night. "We didn't really get anywhere earlier, did we? I think we have brushed it under the carpet. What do you think our options are? In this place, I mean?"

"We can't trust anything they say, but we need to work on the most likely outcome," Sofia says. "The most likely outcome is that they are doing this for a reason. There has to be some sort of reason for all of this. There is some sort of game plan."

Dylan thumbs his chin. "And if there is a game plan, and we are contestants in the game, then what should we do?"

"I've seen nothing that suggests that there will be more than one winner. Which means that only one contestant will leave here alive. And so in answer to your question, Dylan, I think the only option is to do everything we can to win this fucking game."

We both nod our heads.

"But that means one thing." Dylan looks at Sofia before holding my eye. "Do you value your own life over everyone else's?"

******

As usual, I retire to bed ahead of a host of other contestants, even with significantly diminished numbers. As usual, I leave my door open. As usual, I can't sleep, however hard I try.

It's probably about four in the morning when I decide to join the solitary figure on the sofa. He diverts his gaze. I cough into my hand.

Dylan smirks. "I know you are there, mate."

"I need to talk to you," I say.

"Need? That is a powerful word that shouldn't be used flippantly. And what if I don't need to talk to you?"

"I get the impression you need to talk to *somebody*. And I don't see anybody else volunteering their ears."

Dylan runs his hands along his thighs, cupping his knees. "You need to stop looking up to me, Andrew."

I smile. "Need is a strong word, Dylan. So tell me. Why do I need to do that?"

Dylan scrapes at his middle nail. His eyes meet with mine. "Because," he says, "everything you think you know about me is a lie."

Minutes pass without us uttering a word. I feel like I am in an endless queue. I don't know where to focus my eyes. I long to dig inside my pocket and pull out my phone. Occasionally, I glance at Dylan. His eyelids are shut. I watch the gentle, rhythmic rising and falling of his stomach. There isn't a flicker of emotion on his creaseless face. To the outside world he appears the epiphany of calm. And yet I just know his mind is overflowing with tormenting thoughts.

I flinch as his eyes flip open.

"Remind me, Andrew. I mean, I'm pretty damn sure I know what it is, but please humour me. What is your F-Word?"

"Freedom. I want freedom."

Nodding, Dylan purses his lips. "I am different from everyone in this place. Everyone has an F-Word. Freedom. Fame. Fortune. It's pretty simple, isn't it? And yet..."

"And yet?"

"I don't have one."

My eyes narrow. "You must have."

"I don't."

"But what did you say when they asked?"

"I told them I wanted to enter the game, but I didn't want a reward."

I don't want to challenge what my friend says. I just want him to share what is on his mind. "Fair enough. But why did you say that?"

Dylan tangles and untangles his fingers. I could

just imagine him lighting up a cigarette at this moment were we in the outside world, free of the metaphorical chains. "If you performed a fantastic deed – maybe you gave me a monumental wedge of cash – then wouldn't you want to shout from the rooftops, so the rest of the world knows just how wonderful you are?"

My shrug tells him all he needs to know.

"I would, too, with every inch of my body. Who wouldn't? And yet – in my simple way of looking at things – surely it'd be a greater deed if I did it to help people, and nothing else?"

"I agree, but what..."

His raised middle finger silences me. "I wanted my wife and kids to know that I was in here to win them back, to see that I was an honest man. A *good* man. I needed them to know that I wasn't here for any other reason. I wasn't here to win some superficial prize."

My heart sinks. Win them back? I long to ask him what he means, but it feels like I would just be pouring petrol on a fire. But, but – I need to be saying *something.*

"You are no longer together, Dylan?"

He shakes his head. Looking up, his watery, reddened eyes fix on mine. "I had the perfect life, mate. My wife was my best friend. I fucking idolised my two kids. And I lost it all. And do you know what for?"

I divert my gaze.

"Excitement. I gave up real love and togetherness for excitement, Andrew. Like Adam and Eve in the Garden of Eden, I was enchanted by the serpent. My temptation was the temptation of flesh. And I gave in again and again until my wife gave me a final ultimatum. I thought our love was so strong that she would forgive me even if I kept messing up. But I was wrong."

"Dylan, I am so sorry..."

"And now I live in a bleak, one bedroom flat on my own. Sure, I get to see the kids every so often. But you know what? You know what really gets me? I get the distinct impression that they don't want to see me. Not really."

"I don't see that. They love their dad. I don't know much, but I do know that."

Dylan gazes out of the window. I am certain I spot a smile. "They do love me. But they love their mum too, with all their hearts. And they can't forgive me for upsetting Mummy. And why the fuck should they?"

I want to know why he didn't tell us this, why he came into the show as a charade, but I guess I know the answer; I guess he couldn't face the shame, he couldn't face the humiliation. Sometimes I struggle to look at my own face in the mirror, let alone hold it up for the rest of the world to watch and observe and judge. A light switches on in my mind. The rest of the world isn't watching, is it? The cameras are just for show. And if the cameras are for show, and the rest of the world isn't watching, then...

"Exactly," Dylan says, seemingly reading my thoughts. His wide smile exposes his meticulous white teeth. He smiles at the ridiculousness of his situation. "And if they aren't watching, then the whole purpose of me being in this show no longer exists."

My mind searches from every conceivable angle for something positive to say. I shift forward on the sofa. My knees brush against his. "You need to win this show, Dylan. And in the process, you need to start loving yourself. And then when you get out of here, you can win them back. There's a reason for you."

He shakes his head. And then he stops. He furrows his brow, like he is taking in my words. He slants his face to one side. "You think that could work? You think I could do that?"

I inhale a big bubble of air before speaking. "I know you can. And besides, what other choice do you have?"

DAY FOUR

Candidates eliminated: 18
Candidates remaining: 32

Morning

The middle door at the rear of the hall pushes open straight after our showers. Clearly, they're on a schedule.

Not for the first time in this place, I'm tempted to pinch my arm just to make sure this isn't a dream. Rebecca appears from behind the door in a purple princess outfit, the sort you'd dress your five-year-old in at a fancy dress party. Cinderella would be envious of her sparkling silver shoes (plus, she has two of them). White silk stockings cling to surprisingly lithe, lightly-muscled legs. The hem of the dress rises as Rebecca performs a twirl. I turn to Sofia; she places her hand over her mouth, *possibly* to stifle a yawn, *probably* to stifle a laugh.

Surveying her audience, Rebecca's demeanour is even sunnier than usual. I need to put my sunglasses on to tone down the light. "My darlings, it looked like you had a simply marvelous time last night. You really let your hair down after – how can I put this – quite a challenging day."

Somebody shouts out. "What happened to the

people that left? Are they alive?"

Rebecca's hands move to her hips. "Do you *want* them to be alive?"

There is muffled chatter as we all turn to each other. Which of us are liars? Which of us are hypocrites? And that doesn't even take into account the plant, the Judas amongst us. We tell her that, of course, we want them to be alive.

Rebecca points to two guards; immediately they move towards the back office. The guards return with a huge monitor, which they lower onto a table. Another guard passes Rebecca a laptop. She presses a few buttons on the laptop and then images appear on the monitor.

Gasps fill the hall. I don't know where to focus my eyes. It is like we are in a CCTV room. I move from left to right and then downwards. Most of the boxes are filled with figures relaxing in front of the TV. As my eyes rotate, they halt; the woman in this box is cloaked in a blue overall and she is surrounded by men in short-sleeved shirts who – and my eyes narrow to make sure I've got this right - appear to be restraining her. There are no handcuffs, though. I thrust my head forward.

The woman is in a mental hospital.

"As you can see, your fellow contestants are all alive."

This woman was one of us. She stood in this hall only yesterday. If she had made a different decision then she could be standing next to me right now, her own eyes scanning the monitor. And if I had made a different decision then it could have been *her* watching *me* in a mental hospital.

I shudder when another male contestant shouts

at the top of his voice. The shout comes from behind me; I don't know who the voice belongs to, but I imagine the man stabbing his middle finger viciously in the air. "Look! That one there! He is at the police station. You are done for now, Rebecca. He will tell the police everything there is to know."

Even I grimace; it is like when your dad tells a bad joke at a party. Is this the level of intellect we are working with? If so then we are doomed. Rebecca can't help but emit a chuckle. "Oh yes," she says, "I'm sure we are all frightfully worried, darling. What exactly do you think the contestant will be telling the police? And do you really think the police will consider him a reliable witness? We have seen this type of situation before-"

"Before?-"

"You think it is a coincidence we chose you as contestants? Think again. I am no Nostradamus, but I predict the next time we see this contestant he'll be with the female contestant at the mental institution."

A male contestant steps forward. "So they are alive then. We *did* make the wrong decision."

Rebecca's sigh would have blown the straw house down. "So you keep saying, darlings. You are beginning to become a broken record."

"Sorry if we are boring you, Rebecca," Dylan says.

"Oh you are. You really are. And frankly, I really struggle with people who bore me. I only want people here who actually want to be here with me. We all want to be loved, don't we? It is one of the laws of nature, like eating before you get eaten. We need to collaborate. I need to feel your love."

Rebecca types away again on her keyboard. Her

fingers are dainty and light. Fleetingly, I wonder how many words per minute she can type. Rebecca looks up at the digital clock. She presses return and the doors to the outside world slide open. The cool daytime breeze sweeps into the hall.

Rebecca addresses her audience, like Hitler to the masses. "I am feeling particularly generous this morning. I really don't know what has come over me. This is last chance saloon, contestants. I give you one more opportunity. If you *really* think it is a good idea to leave this competition, then you have sixty seconds to do so. I won't be asking you again."

My eyes are glued to the clock.

60.

59.

Seemingly, it takes a few seconds for the other contestants to absorb the scenario, too. And then – just like that – it is like a shopping centre on Black Friday. A figure whizzes past me. I can tell by the nape of the neck that it is the man I threatened to glass last night, the man who changed his mind about leaving yesterday. He disappears through the open doors with a hop, skip and a fucking jump. I count to three and the woman who tripped and fell to her knees just feet from the door joins him as a free woman in the outside world. I keep staring at the exit. Another handful of people join them.

A wise man once said that he didn't regret the things he'd done, but the things he hadn't done. With my feet planted to the floor, I have no idea whether I will regret not running out of the door, or whether I will regret not having the courage to stay and fight in this competition.

48. 47.

Somebody wraps their arm around my waist. A group of us huddle in a circle, a rugby scrum discussing tactics. I don't know who does it first, but we join hands, creating a chain.

"What do we think?" Sofia asks.

Jake whispers, "Why did you come in here in the first place Andrew? Do you really think those people out there are living? Or do you think they are dying slowly?"

A second or two passes. We don't have many of these to waste. Hot sweat prickles my skin. I blink salty moisture from my eyes. "This could be a trick," I say. "It's all too easy. We can't trust them."

"So what do you suggest we do?" Dylan asks.

Jake turns to me. "Are you content to return to your old life?"

"I'm staying." There is not a trace of a smile on Sofia's face, not a trace of a grimace.

"I'm staying, too." TJ reminds me of a boxer jumping into the ring knowing he's going to knock out his opponent.

"Me too."

"And me."

Breaking hands, we count down the seconds on the clock, count down the seconds until the doors to the outside world, and – potentially – to our freedom, shut.

And then they *do* slam shut. I have no idea if they'll ever open for me again.

The remaining contestants turn to the front of the hall, turn to a beaming Rebecca who busily counts heads. It doesn't take so long this time. "Glorious," she says. "It feels like we are separating the wheat from the chaff now, doesn't it? I am really beginning to become fond of you guys, and normally I don't allow emotions to mix with business. But something tells me that we think alike."

"Don't insult us."

It takes me a few seconds to realise that the words came from my mouth. I'm shocked. When did I grow some balls? What is this place *doing* to me? Rebecca doesn't seem offended, though. She merely displays more teeth, long and straight and perfect like keys on a piano. "And you, Andrew, are one of my favourites."

Heat flows to my cheeks. Jesus Christ, what is wrong with me? Sometimes I think I'd be flattered if Fred West chose me as one of his victims.

Two guards roll a wooden table into the hall. What is that? I squint. A roulette wheel sits on top of the table. What is this all about?

Of course. Roulette. It is the ultimate game of chance. It dawns on me what is happening. I'd been too tired, too preoccupied to care about anything other than what was right in front of my nose.

I swipe my arm across my forehead. Momentarily, I'd forgotten about the contestants outside, about the contestants who decided to leave. Just like yesterday, they ushered them around the corner, out of sight.

I turn to the person I rely on most for reassurance. His body language doesn't offer the reassurance I crave. Dylan's hands are balled together behind his back. I don't want to alert panic in anyone else, and so I whisper my words. "I haven't heard the helicopter."

His crumpled face reminds me of a piece of paper rolled into a ball and thrown into the waste basket.

A man in an immaculate black suit appears from behind the middle door. Standing at ease next to Rebecca, he reminds me of the MC at the boxing; I half expect him to open up his hands and announce, "Ladies and gentlemen, let's get ready to rumble!"

Curtseying (for whatever reason I have no idea), Rebecca says, "I would like you to give a warm welcome to our special guest for this evening. This is Adam, our croupier." Adam's smile widens; his pearly whites would make a tiger hide behind a tree. A few people start clapping behind me, and then we are all compelled to join in, until a polite round of applause fills the hall.

Buoyed by this reaction, Rebecca points her middle finger at us, one by one. She would be fantastic at a kid's perfect party, or as a children's TV presenter. "Eeny, meeny, miny, moe, catch a tiger by the toe, if he hollers, let him go, eeny, meeny, miny, moe..."

Her finger lands on Sofia. "Darling, can you please come and join us at the roulette table?"

Is Sofia deluded? Does she just not care? Either way, she gushes like she's won Best Actress at the Oscars.

"Madam, would you like to play some roulette with us tonight?" Adam asks.

"That would be just grand, thank you."

"Roulette is a game of luck," Adam says. "Or is it a game of daring? For this evening's proceedings we are participating in a simplified version of the game. Please take a look at the wheel. Each number is either a black or a red. There is an equal number of each colour. Please place the plastic coin on a red or a black. I will spin the wheel. If the ball lands on your colour then you win. If the ball lands on the other colour then you lose. All clear?"

Smiling, Sofia nods. I expect her to turn around and ask us what we think, to share the burden, to place some responsibility on us. She doesn't. She places her finger to her mouth, contemplating the choice. Almost in unison the contestants take two steps forward, moving closer to the action. I would choose black. I don't know why, but I would.

Sofia places the plastic coin on red.

Turning to face the rest of us, her mesmerising eyes fix on mine. For the first time, I wish they wouldn't. I long to glance away, but I can't. Sofia shrugs her delicate shoulders and smiles. My lips quiver.

Adam spins the roulette wheel with such grace it is like he was born to perform the role. Mozart was born to create music, Picasso was born to paint, and Adam was born to spin the roulette wheel. Gasps emit from our group as he does so, as though we expect a different result (God knows what we expected. Did we think he'd spin the wheel anti-clockwise or something?). Our eyes flick to the monitor on the wall; the camera zooms in on the table. The ball teases us with its movements. It is a proper attention seeker. It bounces and rebounds, rebounds and bounces, before eventually landing.

On black.

The gasps echoing around the room are louder this time.

"Bad luck, madam," Adam says, baring his teeth. I imagine the tiger purring like a pussycat behind the tree. "Like I said, this is a game of chance, and lady luck didn't land on you tonight. Better luck next time."

Smiling, Sofia rests her hand on Adam's arm. She is gracious in defeat, like a boxer who embraces his opponent after telling him in the build up to the fight that he would kill him and eat his children.

"You really shouldn't feel any guilt for your decision, madam," Adam says.

Sofia's smile vanishes.

We take the same three steps back that we took forward, allowing space for Sofia to rejoin us. Standing next to me, her red hair appears even longer, even more lustrous. Sometimes I imagine sinking my face into her hair and sniffing it; this is not something I plan to tell her or anybody else.

"What did he mean?" she asks.

I am only able to arch a single eyebrow. My lips quiver.

A few lines appear around her eyes. "When he said I shouldn't feel any guilt; what did he mean? Is this bad news, Andrew? What do you think they'll have planned for us now?"

I try not to look too concerned. "I'm not sure that this has anything to do with us, Sofia."

At first her face is bemused, and then her jaw drops. Saliva glistens on her teeth.

"I would just like to take this opportunity to reiterate what Adam said," Rebecca announces. "You were very unlucky, Sofia, but then it isn't the winning that matters; it is the taking part. And wasn't she a fantastic contestant, ladies and gentlemen?"

We surely know that we are merely characters in this theatrical drama, but we feel we have no choice but to murmur, to nod our heads and clap.

Rebecca bows her head, like she is reading at

church. "Could we please have a few moments' silence to show our respect for those that have lost their lives?"

Contestants turn to each other. What lives? Who died? My face remains forward. I close my eyes. This show has made it blatantly clear to me that I am delusional – and self-obsessed – but even *I* know what lives she means.

Our confusion is short-lived.

The sound of gunfire from outside the building turns my blood cold. I press my palms against my ears; it does nothing to silence Sofia's anguished scream. I flinch every time the gun fires.

It does so eight more times.

As reality descends upon the hall, my damp, vibrating shoulders muffle Sofia's sobs. My fingers untangle the flame hair flowing down her back. Over her shoulder I can just about make out Rebecca telling the remaining contestants to please enjoy a few hour's relaxation, that it has been an emotional morning and we will to preserve our energy for what lies ahead.

******

Afternoon

Enjoy a few hours of relaxation? Rebecca must have a sick sense of humour.

I spend most of the morning locked away in my mind, fretting about Sofia. In a perverse way this brings some benefits; my mind is occupied, and I'm not thinking about myself. I scan her beautiful face for cracks, for signs, but I can't find any. She looks just as divine as she did before she made the wrong decision, before she effectively decided the fate of a handful of innocent people.

Just what is wrong with her?

"It wasn't my fault, Andrew."

Sofia must be scanning my face, too. The cracks must be showing.

"Those contestants chose to leave. They chose their own fate. I'm not responsible just because the ball landed on the wrong colour."

I hold my hands up. "I'm just worried about you, Sofia."

Her lips soften. "I know. But don't. It's fine."

When TJ joins us at the lunch table, he looks as bad as I feel. The shadows under his eyes remind me of colourless, upside down rainbows. His dark stubble appears sharp, like pointed thistles on a paintbrush. Stretching his legs, he folds his arms tight across his chest. Why has he decided to join us?

He must read the look I give him.

"The way I figure it, this game is going to get to the point where we all start killing each other," TJ says, stifling a yawn.

Sofia removes a slice of toast from her mouth. With a flick of her hand, she sweeps crumbs onto the floor. "Cheery thought. Thanks for joining us, TJ."

"Anyway, I thought I'd start hanging out with other contestants. You get me? Fair play, I'm never going to be the most popular guy in the room, mainly because I don't really like people. But it would be good if others choose not to shoot me first."

I exchange glances with Sofia and Dylan. Sofia leans forward. I sense conspiracy in her angled lips. After all, she's already shown that she likes a good conspiracy. "So how is that going for you, TJ?"

His grunt reminds me of a hedgehog eating. Have you ever heard a hedgehog eating? Jesus, they're loud. His shrug is so elaborate it is like he is throwing an attacker off his back.

"You might want to take a different approach," Sofia says. "I would suggest you don't tell people that you are only being nice with them so they don't shoot you first. You should at least pretend to be authentic. I pretend to be authentic on a regular basis, and it really pays dividends."

TJ shoots her a look. "I didn't say I was going to be *nice* to people. I just said that I was going to start mingling with them. You need to cut me some slack here. This is a tough gig for me. I am something of a lone wolf in this world. I have trust issues. Like I said, I am not naturally a people person."

"No shit," Sofia says. "So imagine we're speed dating. You have a minute or so to impress. Tell us a little about yourself, TJ. Do you have any – lets think – hobbies and interests?"

TJ gives Sofia his best smile. "Well, I spend a lot of time in the gym. Obviously, you don't jut fall out of bed looking this good."

"Obviously."

"And I play table tennis. I'm not one to brag, but I'm quite good at table tennis. I've represented the county and everything."

Sofia's grin widens. "You play ping pong?"

TJ shakes his head. "No. I play table tennis."

"That's what I said. You play ping pong."

TJ blows air from his lips. "If you say so. Anyway, the crowd loves it when I play, because I get to wear a tight pair of shorts, if you know what I mean. Oh, and I'm a keen martial artist, and I box."

Even Sofia raises her eyebrows, seemingly impressed. "I do like a man who can protect himself, and those he is with. Any other interests?"

TJ leans back in his chair. "I like to do a little writing."

"With a pen, or with a crayon?" Dylan asks.

Smirking, TJ focuses on Sofia. "I write stories, of the erotic variety. The type of stories that get – how can I put this – a certain type of woman very hot and bothered."

Sofia sweeps her hair behind her ears. She rests her chin in an upturned hand. "Oh, aren't we the lucky ones? Tell us more, TJ."

TJ shuffles in his chair. "I wrote a story about an older lady; she was in her fifties. Still had plenty to offer. Bored, rich housewife; you know the type. Anyway, this young stud, not unlike myself, comes round to clean the pool-"

"Original storyline," Dylan says. "What was this young stud's name?"

"Derek."

We break into hysterics. "I think you need to change that name, darling," Sofia says. "So what reward did you choose?"

TJ doesn't even take a breath before replying. "Fame. I think the world deserves to see a little more of TJ. Don't you think?"

The door swings open before we can respond. My back straightens. On automatic pilot, we move to the centre of the hall. The guards circle us, sharks around blood.

Rebecca moves more fluidly than I remember, like she's just oiled her joints with WD40. "Hello my darlings," she says, flapping her hands. "I'm ever so sorry to cut your afternoon slumber short. You all may think you deserve to laze around like sea lions on the beach, but that's not the way it's going to be."

Our poker faces would put Lady Gaga to shame. "Oh you guys really *are* no fun. Never mind. Time for some excitement. I need a volunteer to pick the second Truth Card. Oh, I do so love the Truth Card game. It's one of my favourites."

Seconds pass in silence whilst we all wait for somebody (other than ourselves) to volunteer. Rebecca purses her lips. "If I don't have a volunteer then I'll be forced to choose somebody. And I really don't want to do that."

"I'll volunteer."

Our relieved heads turn to Melanie, the tall blonde woman. She exchanges a few pleasantries with Rebecca, before dipping her hand into one of the two remaining boxes and pulling out a card. She reads the card, but says nothing. Lines gather on her forehead.

"Hurry along, darling," Rebecca says.

Melanie turns her back to Rebecca. "The cameras are not real. You are not being filmed on TV."

Contestants roar like MP's in the House of Commons. "We know that already," one of them shouts. "What is the point of that card?"

We wait for the noise to die down. I decide to pipe up. My voice cackles. "Don't you see? If the card had been pulled out first then there would have been a point. It would have been a real revelation. The order we pull out the cards is important."

Rebecca's slow clap burns my cheeks. "Very good, Andrew. Very good. See, there are some brain cells in this room."

I feel eyes burning into me. Nobody likes a teacher's pet.

******

Rebecca returns within the hour, and this time she enters the hall on a white horse.

Standing over five feet tall, with an immaculate silky white coat, it is a beautiful creature. With her legs dangling from either side like a child's, Rebecca appears even tinier. A cowboy's hat sits atop of her head. Whilst I am sure it must be a genuine item, and knowing this place I am sure no expense would have been spared, she reminds me of the mother of the bride at a hen weekend. Exchanging a secret glance with Dylan, we both snigger.

"Howdy! Don't you ever want to be a cowboy entering a town for the first time?"

TJ stands with his hands on his hips. "Surprisingly not, Rebecca, mainly because I'm not fucking insane. You are one crazy bitch, you know."

Rebecca pulls a gun from her pocket, blows on it before spinning it in her hand. "I may very well be crazy, TJ, but I am the one with a gun in my hand, and not you. And what does that make you? Dumb. And do you know what Socrates said? No, of course you don't, you simpleton. Shall I educate you in relation to one of the world's greatest ever thinkers? Socrates said that it is better to be a human being dissatisfied than a pig satisfied. And in this instance, you are most definitely the pig."

TJ pushes his chin out. "Well, for all I know he may have been one of the greatest thinkers, but he is proper dead now isn't he-"

"Just a bit, TJ," Rebecca says.

"So who really gives a fuck what some dead old white guy thinks? I may be pork chops soon anyway, and so I'm happy to be the dumb pig. I sure as hell won't be getting on top of a horse, though."

"TJ, I have no idea what on earth you are talking about, but despite everything I've said, I do find your simple ways quite charming, darling."

Looking over my shoulder, I notice that the guards are putting in a hard shift (which makes a change) clearing tables and chairs, moving them to the corners of the hall.

"Right, that is quite enough of these charming pleasantries. To an innocent bystander with no responsibilities for arranging the logistics for this show, it may appear that we have all the time in the world, but the reality is quite different, my darlings; we actually have a tight schedule to keep."

She is wrong. I know they have a tight schedule to keep. Apart from one lucky winner, they need us all to be dead by day seven.

Pointing to each contestant in turn, Rebecca counts one and then two, one and then two. It crosses my mind that if she wanted to progress matters efficiently, avoiding unnecessary delays, then she should have considered not entering the hall on horseback, but there you go.

"Do I have your attention? Good. I have already indicated that, as much as I love you all, currently there are just too many of you remaining in the competition. We need to decrease the numbers quite significantly, and this game should really help achieve this objective-"

"Why don't you just shoot us and be done? That would be quick and efficient..."

I am not sure whether I am the only one who turns to TJ with daggers in my eyes, pleading with him to shut the fuck up.

Rebecca sighs. I get the distinct impression she doesn't appreciate the interruption. "Where would the fun in that be? No, that simply would not do. We are going to play a game. Most likely, you played a popular variation of this game in the playground at school, in the good old days before they banned every game that has any level of risk. This is a game of both physicality and mental prowess. It developed from the traditional chase games which originated in the 18th and 19th centuries, and I am extremely proud to add a further element to the game, whilst maintaining the traditional concepts..."

We turn to a guard pushing a trolley cloaked with a luxurious, thick white tablecloth, suitable for afternoon tea at the *Ritz*.

Dylan pipes up, "Anybody for sandwiches? Buy your sandwiches here..."

A few sniggering older men turn to Dylan. Their sniggers quickly turn to gasps, however, as Rebecca's fingers graze along the contours of the polished blade. I swear I catch her painted smile in the reflection. The blade must be three feet long.

"This sword is usually locked away in a safe; it is that valuable. You really must treat it with the care it deserves," Rebecca says, her eyes perfect saucers.

She stretches out her arm like a football referee. "If I chose you as a number two – pardon the pun - then can you please stand against the far wall, behind the white line which the guards have kindly drawn for you."

I try to keep my focus as I move towards the wall, but – hell – I always want to check who I'm with. I blow out warm air as Sofia joins me. The hairs on my arms stand to attention when she smiles at me. This is replaced by a stabbing pain right in the centre of my chest.

Is she on my side?

Or do I need to kill her to stay alive?

I glance over my shoulder. TJ has remained in the centre of the hall. This realisation does nothing to soothe the pain in my chest. If TJ is the competition, and this is a game of speed and strength, then I don't really fancy my chances. My eyes flicker. Oh no. Dylan stands next to TJ, with his head bowed. Either he is deep in thought, or he doesn't want to catch anybody's eye. I dig my fingernails into my palm.

Rebecca raises her voice so everyone in the hall can hear her. She addresses the other group. "This is a game of one-versus-one. Standing behind the white line in the middle of the hall, you'll each in turn choose an opposing player. As soon as you have chosen the player, you can move across the line and cover any patch of surface in the hall. Your mission is to use the sword to draw blood on your chosen opposing player. You can draw the blood from any part of their body. You must show the guards the blood on the sword. If you draw blood then you win. If you do not draw blood then you lose."

Rebecca silences the gasps with a wave of a hand, like a comedian quietening the laughing audience so they can continue with their next joke. Turning to our group, she takes about ten fluid steps forward, making sure we can hear her instructions.

"Your mission is to touch the wall on the other side of the hall without your opponent drawing your blood. You can start moving as soon as they call your name. Until then, one hand must remain touching the wall."

Rebecca turns her body sideways, like she is trying to navigate through a narrow gap. "Does everybody understand? It is imperative that you tell me now if you don't."

Bowing my head, I stare at the floor, but I'm aware that all around me heads reluctantly nod. They all understand, but they wish that they didn't. My fingertips touch the wall. I'm not sure whether I am using and abusing the wall to keep me standing up straight. I'm relieved that I'm definitely not competing against Sofia. I'm terrified that I may be up against Dylan.

Rebecca continues talking to our group. "Right, strip off your clothes to your pants. Ladies, I consider myself a feminist, and so I'll allow you to strip to your bra and pants. There is no need to thank me for this act of generosity. "

Rebecca releases a deep, heavy sigh. Maybe we all look at her like she is the pervert gym teacher at school sharing the communal shower with the kids. "We have to be certain that blood has been drawn," she says, with a smile. "These are human lives we are talking about, and we cannot be flippant."

Rebecca turns her back to us, to address the first group. I can't help but think that the first group are the lucky ones; they have the upper hand. For starters, they still have their clothes on; they haven't been stripped to their underwear. Secondly, they are the ones with the sword clutched in their hands.

"Right, TJ, you have been quite excitable this morning and as a reward, or a punishment – call it whatever you like, I really don't care - you can choose an opponent first."

******

All eyes fix on TJ, who paces up and down in the middle of the room; a hungry cat stalking a mouse.

"Can you please choose a player, TJ. Call their name so they hear it loud and clear. That is only fair," Rebecca says. She has moved away from the centre of the hall to join the players from TJ's group on the sidelines; they have their backs pressed against the wall, allowing as much space on the court as possible. "If you don't choose a player soon then I will be forced to choose one for you. And most likely I will choose one of your lovely new friends. You wouldn't want that now, would you, my sweetheart?"

The muscles in my body tighten. One of his lovely new friends? That can only be myself, Dylan and Sofia; for all his intentions to mingle, TJ barely grunts to any of the other contestants. Rebecca might choose me. TJ holds the sword so naturally it seems like an extension of his arm, like Edward Scissorhands and his metal blades. He'd slash my body to pieces with that weapon.

"Robert."

My mind draws a blank. *Robert?* Robert, Robert; who the *fuck* is Robert? I follow the heads twisting in the direction of a tired, middle-aged man with a weathered, leathery face. His freckled shoulders hunch forward. He carries a ring of soft fat around his midriff. Robert turns to the line of contestants with an open, almost apologetic face.

"It has been nice getting to know you guys," he says. "Sorry it had to end this way. Good luck with everything, yeah?"

Robert's freckled back shrinks smaller and smaller as he retreats away from us, heading towards TJ, each step taking him closer to his death. He reminds me of a mouse cornered by a snake with sharpened fangs. TJ stands with his legs slightly apart, both hands gripping the sword, biding his time, waiting to strike.

Robert changes direction and increases his pace. If he was a rugby player navigating through the opposing defence then he'd draw an appreciative gasp from the crowd. TJ moves sideways like a crab, cutting the angle, absorbing the space. Robert gets to within six feet and then stops; his approach is flawed. Turning, he runs back towards us, pumping his fists by his side. TJ senses an opportunity. He raises his sword above his head and then strikes down.

Of course, Robert's back is turned away from us. We can't see the result. His howl of pain tells us all we need to know, though. The sword connected with its chosen target. I imagine a raw, Harry Potter zigzagging line, like a bolt of lightning, shredding the delicate skin. Robert falls to the ground in a crumpled heap.

TJ drops the sword; it clatters on the hard floor. He lowers his head. He is a footballer who has scored the winning goal against his childhood team. Only, this isn't a game of football. He is responsible for the death of another human being. Two guards move towards the felled body. The inspection is fast and clinical. One of the guards raises his gun. I sense that I'm not the only one who turns to the wall, who can't bear to watch.

The bang of gunshot signals the end of a human life.

The guards studiously and meticulously mop the blood from the floor. They run a damp cloth over the contours of the blade. With a soundless count of three, they pick up the dead body, one gripping the ankles and the other holding the shoulders.

Rebecca moves to the middle of the room. "Congratulations, TJ; you have progressed to the next round of the game."

"Go fuck yourself, bitch."

"*Charming.*" Rebecca rubs her hands together. She rotates one hundred and eighty degrees, making sure that she addresses both teams. "What a great start to the game! I hope you all enjoyed that as much as I did?"

Most of us stare at the tiled floor. I'm sure others gaze through the glass ceiling to the heavens above.

"Let's move swiftly on, shall we? Terry, can you please come join me in the middle of the room?"

My mouth drops as Terry walks purposefully towards Rebecca, like the receptionist at the doctor's surgery has called his name. Again, I know his face, but we've barely exchanged pleasantries. His piercing blue eyes are often alight with mischief. Running his hands through his thick mop of silver hair, Terry gives Rebecca a broad smile. Her eyes widen.

"Don't be shy, Terry. Please go ahead and call one of the names. I appreciate that it can be a difficult choice. It might help if you consider which contestant you despise the most. Ask yourself which one you'd most like to be dead."

Does he even hear Rebecca's words? Standing with the sword at his feet and his hands dug into his pockets, Terry eyes the candidates like he is choosing a turkey from the supermarket. He picks up the sword.

"Sofia, please."

My heart drops to the floor with a thud.

Sofia spins on her heels. Sprinting towards the middle of the hall, her red hair flows behind her. It is, without doubt, one of the most beautiful sights I've ever witnessed. It all happens so quickly that I am left numb and open-mouthed.

Somebody next to me gasps. What the...?

Terry flings his sword on the hard floor in front of him, discards it like a dirty dish cloth. Bending his legs, he lowers himself to the floor and then stretches his arms in a downward dog yoga pose.

Sofia slows her sprint to a jog. Her long strides become awkward and almost embarrassed. She progresses within a few feet of Terry, and then she takes a backwards glance as she passes him. Sofia's hand touches the far wall. She does not celebrate her victory, though. It is like she hasn't won at all, and yet she has been fighting for her life. With her hands on her hips, she gives the deflated air of an athlete who finished fourth at the Olympics.

Terry remains in his yoga pose as the guards approach him. He appears blissfully at peace with the world as the guard presses the cold, hard barrel of the gun against his skull and then pulls the trigger.

The gasps spread like a fire through a forest. Surely most of us in this hellhole have become acclimatised to death? I suspect that most of us have accepted its inevitability. However, this is a different concept to grasp. We assumed we would fight to stay alive.

My emotions are torn. I can't help it. Dammit, another innocent human life has just needlessly been taken. But it wasn't the person I was close to. I didn't know the man who was shot in the head. He didn't die in vain. He kept Sofia alive.

The names continue to be called. Contestants continue to die. Momentarily, I'm relieved that Kim is no longer alive to witness a guard shooting Christian in the side of the head. If she *had* lived, then she would never have recovered from seeing that.

I am not sure whether it is a sign that I'm popular, unpopular or invisible, but when the names get called, one by one, mine isn't one of them. Naturally, my heart sinks when it is Dylan's turn to call a name. I don't fear he'll choose me (I may lack confidence, but it isn't quite *that* low) but I am sure as hell terrified that my friend could be dead within a few minutes. Just how good a friend is he? The thought of progressing in the contest without him seems impossible. The thought of continuing life without him seems impossible. I'm struck by the stark realisation of just how important he is to me.

It says something about his personality that Dylan ignores the older and more vulnerable contestants. He doesn't call the name of an easy target. Instead, he calls out the name of a young man with no visible disadvantages. Relief ebbs through my body when Dylan slashes his sword down against the young man's chest. *Yes!*

I'm sickened that I celebrate the death of another

human being.

Is this what it is like to kill your enemy when you are at war with them?

The bodies begin toppling like dominoes, until we are down to four. Duncan has a choice between me and another guy, a man of roughly the same age as me, of roughly the same build. I think his name is David. I long for Duncan to call my name. If I get to the other side, then my opponent dies. If I had a choice, then I'd like Duncan to die so that I stay alive.

"David."

My teeth dig into my upper lip. My blood always reminds me of battery acid. I don't want to delay the inevitable any longer. David starts moving and I realise that he is a dead man walking. The poor guy has an injury or a disability that he has kept hidden. He is unable to stretch his right leg out fully and, as a result, his movements are jerky and uncoordinated. He did well to survive in the contest this long. If the other contestants had known that he was easy prey then they would have chosen him earlier. Death is inevitable. The man is easy to hunt down, easy to slaughter.

Duncan corners him. His face distorts into an ugly shape as he pulls back his sword. He has the luxury of picking his target. Duncan sweeps down with his sword. The blade slashes David's neck. His head is nearly torn from his body. Blood gushes out like water from a hosepipe. The body collapses to the floor.

Hysterical, anguished screams fill the hall.

The guards move swiftly, stretching out their legs into a sprint. I'm sure it isn't to put the dying man out of his misery, but just to stop the gory mess from spreading. They know they'll need to mop up the blood from the floor, keep the hall to the hygiene standards Rebecca expects. As the sound of gunfire echoes around the hall, Duncan holds the sword above his head like it is a tennis racket and he is triumphant at Wimbledon.

"He died like a pig!" he shouts.

Gasps emit from both corners of the hall.

Now there are only two of us. My opponent moves to the centre of the hall, reaching out to take the sword from Duncan. Melanie's slim, athletic body strains and flexes beneath the shapeless outfit.

This is the woman who wants me dead.

Placing her feet just inches behind the white line, she straightens her back. I am sure I spot a smile creeping from the corner of her lips. My body shudders like somebody has scraped their fingernails down a blackboard.

Why would she smile at me? Why would you smile at the man you are about to kill?

"Andrew," she says.

This is my 100m Olympic final. Only, the stakes are higher. The losing Olympians live a life of regret, but they still live. This is literally life or death. If I get this wrong – if I fuck this up – then I'll end up six feet in the ground (if I'm lucky; maybe they'll just fling my body amongst the bushes) with a bullet hole in my skull.

My right foot crosses the white line as soon as Melanie calls my name. Everything disappears except for the moving shape in front of me. She is a shark fin skirting above the water in the deep blue ocean. I just need to keep her at arm's length. She comes within about six feet, with her sword raised, ready to strike, ready to draw blood.

Lowering my shoulder, I shimmy to my left. My opponent moves to my left. I shift my bodyweight to my right. My opponent stays fixed to the spot.

It feels like I'm looking down on the world from above. I pick up my pace as easily as pushing my foot down on the accelerator pedal. My cheeks hurt from my broadening smile. I move away from her. She isn't going to catch me.

I slap the palm of my hand against the far wall.

My knees rise close to my chest, like I've just scored the winning goal in the cup final. This wasn't a game of luck. This was a game of speed and courage and cunning. There was no place to hide. And I won.

I twist my head around. Colour flows to Sofia's face. She waves to me like she has seen me passing from the top floor of a bus. Dylan gives me a nod of the head, as if to say job well done. My body feels light, like I've stuffed two bags of sugar in my mouth and the rush has hit me.

I may be dead in a few days time. Who knows, I may be dead tomorrow. But at least I've achieved something on my way out.

"Look. I drew blood. I won..."

******

I heard the words. Subconsciously I know where and who they came from. I don't want them to sink in, though. My eyes remain fixed on Sofia. It is almost like somebody has turned down the brightness on the controller. The colour drains from Sofia's face. Next to her, Dylan's eyes drop to the floor. With the metaphorical click of a finger, I suddenly feel very alone.

The guards move towards the girl. Part of me wants to keep as far away from them as physically possible, to push my body against the wall; another part of me wants to move closer, to examine what the hell is going on. This is my life at stake. I decide to take a few steps forward, like a curious bystander who doesn't want to get told off by the police for getting too close to the crime scene. One of the guards glances at me as he progresses towards the girl. A cluster of lines appear around his eyes. Was that a flicker of emotion? It quickly vanishes before anyone else has the chance to notice.

My blonde femme fatale holds the sword up in the air like it is a lottery ticket and she wants them to confirm she has the winning numbers. "Look. I don't want to cause a scene, but there is definitely blood. Clear as day. I nicked him with the sword."

My world spins, like I need to hold onto something otherwise I'll collapse to the floor. Surely she didn't even get close to me? I kept her in the corner of my eye, in my line of vision; she was always at a distance, over there somewhere, rather than over here. But then, maybe I miscalculated the span of the sword? Maybe I didn't account for the sword at all? I was living in my own little bubble. My body was numbed. Would I have even felt the tip of the sword tearing open my skin?

I wish I had a paper bag to breathe into. I wish I had a black bin bag to hide my face underneath. I wish they could shoot me now, just to cut short the shame.

The bemused guards narrow their eyes. I dare to

look closer. What do I have to lose? I don't want to admit it, but there definitely seems to be *something* on the tip of the sword. It is like trying to ascertain whether the dark stain on the carpet that looks like shit and smells like shit really could *be* shit. The substance staining the tip of the sword is dark red. The guards look at each other. One nods. They both move their attention away from the sword. The sword is no longer of interest. They have a new subject of interest. The second guard raises his gun. The second guard starts walking towards me.

I'm too numb to speak. So this is where my life ends? I hold up my hands in protest, but then I put them down again. The image of Terry crouching down on the floor just minutes before, quietly giving over his life with dignity and respect, invades my mind. I stand still. I pump out my chest. If I am going to die then I am going to die with honour. I'm not going to beg for my life. The end of the barrel edges closer, to within touching distance. I hold my breath and then close my eyes.

"Stop!"

Heads jerk to the right.

Dylan sprints towards us, screaming for the guards to stop, for them not to shoot me. Thinking back to what Kim said, I do not want a long, painful and humiliating death either. If I am going to die then I want it to be fucking fast. I want to push him away. I don't want him to delay the inevitable. I view him as somebody trying to talk me down from the edge of a bridge – if I didn't want to do it then why would I be there? I am going to die, so let's not make a spectacle of it please.

"I swear on my mother's life that she didn't catch

him," he says. "And I am a man of honour. My mother brought me into this world. She is the most precious thing to me in the whole world. I don't utter these words lightly."

The guards hold Dylan's gaze. And then they turn to the tip of the sword. They never speak, but right now they don't need to. The evidence is all there. The blood is clearer now, or maybe I am daring to look more clearly. With curious interest, I observe that *my* blood is dark, like a splash of red wine.

"Just look at the sword, Dylan," I say.

Dylan rolls his eyes. "Whose side are you actually on?" he asks.

The familiar sound of heels clicking on the hard floor grows louder. I inhale the musky, exotic scent of her perfume. Her hands are upturned. "What exactly are you suggesting, Dylan? For all the fuss you have made, I do hope that it is something serious."

We all turn to Dylan. His eyelids flicker. I imagine a question mark forming on his forehead. Is he doubting himself? "I am not quite sure," he says. "But something isn't right, I am certain of that. This situation needs further investigation."

Rebecca sighs. "Further investigation?"

From the corner of my eye, I see that Melanie has turned her back to us. And it isn't just that. Discreetly, she has moved about six feet away from the group.

"You need to inspect her body," I say. "*Please*. Consider it a crime scene. This is my life we are talking about."

Rebecca closes her eyes for a moment as if she realises that this issue isn't going to go away unless she at least pretends to go through the motions. I am a popular contestant, and things could get messy if she doesn't give me a fair trial. My mindset changes, too. I am no longer convinced that I'm merely delaying the inevitable. Is there a miniscule chance that my fate here could change?

"Melanie, come here please," Rebecca says.

Melanie slowly turns, like we are searching for the person who emptied the cookie jar and she has the cookies hidden in her hands. Her measured steps remind me of someone walking a tightrope. She stops within about three feet. Rebecca tells the guards to inspect her clothes for any tears, for any rips. Their confused faces suggest they don't understand the reason for the command, but they start checking regardless, starting at the feet and working their way up. They reach the neckline and then turn and shrug their shoulders.

Rebecca purses her lips. What is going through her mind? "Melanie, strip off your clothes please."

Melanie's startled face is the epitome of an offended child. "What do you mean? That is a complete violation of my privacy," she says.

Rebecca blows air from inflated cheeks. "We are going around shooting people so – and please excuse my language, dear – you can go fuck your privacy where the sun doesn't shine. And besides, half of the people in this hall are already walking around in their pants. And just look at the state of some of them. Take off your overalls now before you really test my goodwill."

I can't resist a smirk as Melanie kicks off her shoes and steps out of her trousers. In different circumstances this would be wet dream material. Even now I can't help but notice her smooth skin, marvel at how impossibly far her slender legs stretch. Apart from a red scratch at her right ankle, she is flawless, like the type of woman a hormonal teenage boy would design on his computer at home.

Dylan points his finger like he has spotted a snake in the grass. "Look! There. Right there. The cut on her ankle-"

"Don't you see?" I say. "That is fresh blood. She has cut herself!"

My heart thumps hard again. This time it isn't through panic or desperation, but excitement.

Rebecca squats. She smooths two fingers along the cut. Her eyes narrow. She nods.

"She has," she says. "She has drawn her own blood."

Relief ebbs through my body. I *am* going to be okay. I *did* get across to the other side. Conflicting thoughts fight for my attention.

She cheated. She drew her own blood. Hold on, she cut herself so they'd shoot me dead. My relief turns to anger.

"You dirty little bitch!"

Melanie draws her arms up to her face. Does she think that I'm going to hit her? The guards take a step forward, blocking my path.

Rebecca turns to me. The scowl doesn't look too sympathetic. She looks at me like I've taken a leak on the roses in her garden. "Calm down, Snowflake," she says.

I'm bouncing on the spot now. "Calm down? That bitch nearly got me shot!"

The watching contestants roar with agreement; momentarily, I'd forgotten they were there.

Rebecca speaks with a level tone; she realises

she needs to take a different approach. "I understand your frustration, Andrew, especially as the stakes are so high. You are playing with the big boys and girls now, though. I agree that what Melanie did wasn't very sporting-"

"*Sporting?*"

"Yes, Prince Charming. Sporting."

My energy drains. "Listen, so long as you are going to shoot the little bitch then I am not going to cause a scene. I'm happy to just forget about this whole incident."

Rebecca's face reminds me of a referee contemplating whether to give a player a yellow or a red card for a two-footed challenge. She turns to Melanie. "What you did was, strictly speaking, outside the rules. You understand that, don't you?"

Melanie nods her bowed head.

"There are two ways of looking at this, however, and I am the kind of person who prefers to look at the positive in everything. The rules weren't very clear, were they?"

"No they weren't. I didn't find them clear."

"It would be reasonable to say that you used some initiative, that you bent the rules to your advantage-"

My voice is high-pitched and loud. "What *exactly* are you saying?"

Rebecca turns to me. "Melanie played dirty, Andrew, but I don't necessarily think that playing dirty is a bad thing. This isn't the type of place we give you a badge for taking part. It is dog against dog here, and none of you are poodles. Melanie showed she is a dog that bites first. In a way, I respect the fact that she did whatever it took to beat you."

My face distorts into an array of shapes. I feel my hands clenching into a fist.

"I am not going to shoot Melanie. She goes through to the next round. And I would prefer to be transparent with you, Andrew. Unless you calm down then I'll shoot you instead. We could really do with reducing the number of contestants in the show. After all, Melanie did draw blood. The rules on this matter weren't particularly clear. You could call it another learning lesson for us organisers. Do we have an understanding here?"

I've blown up a balloon and Rebecca has stuck a pin in it. I shrug my shrunken shoulders.

Heading towards the group of surviving contestants, I'm blissfully aware that I'm still alive. So why does my body feel so heavy? Why does it feel that my feet are treading through treacle?

Maybe it is because I can't shake the feeling that I am a dead man walking.

But then – for now – at least I'm still walking.

******

At the end of the game Rebecca turns on the charm like a flowing tap, praising us on doing fantastically well, for demonstrating our strength under pressure and our ability to maintain calm in difficult circumstances. It is as though we've participated in some team building exercise at a work Away Day. We've managed to eliminate nine contestants, bringing us down to twelve. That is right on target for day four, she says. We can finally see the wood from the trees. Stretching and pouting her lips, she opens the forum up to questions. She assures us that no question is a silly question.

"Do you wear underwear in bed?" TJ asks.

Rebecca waves away the laughter. "Okay, so maybe there *are* silly questions. TJ, you really do need to tone down this flirting of yours, otherwise the other men in the contest will be jealous-"

"I think I've just been sick in my mouth," TJ says.

I can't help but recall TJ's erotic fiction. Is Rebecca depicting the role of the cougar, and TJ the young stud? If so then that would make him Derek.

"There you go again, TJ. I guess you'll just need to find out whether I wear underwear in bed, you naughty young man."

I'm not sure that Rebecca's reply eases the rising bile in TJ's throat.

"How many games are there?" somebody asks.

"Now that *is* a good question. What makes you think it is all about playing games? That is just one element of the show. Now what is it they say? Oh yes. Variety is the spice of life. I do love to keep things varied, to stop life becoming predictable. Plus, we always need to have in mind that we need to stay one step ahead of the competition. I'm sure you understand. But rest assured that from now on at least one contestant will be eliminated every day, and probably a whole lot more."

"Shot?"

"I think you understand what we mean by eliminated, Dylan. Rest assured, we won't keep any contestant hanging around in here any longer than they need to. In the words of Queen, there is no time for losers. There will only be one winner. And the show will end on day seven."

The show continues to go through the pretence of

giving us an hour's personal time in the afternoon, even though there are no real cameras to turn off. I retreat to my bedroom and, as far as I can tell, I manage to get some sleep. Afterwards, I find the groups have disbanded. Contestants wanted time to gather their thoughts.

I sit cross-legged, my fingertips grazing the window to the outside world. Rain spits on the wet grass, flecks against the window. The greyness outside complements the darkness filling my mind. I don't like the way I've been thinking. People are dying. Their bodies are carted away. And yet, as the head count lowers, I can't help thinking that I'm closer to winning this thing.

My thoughts are just beginning to spiral when Sofia sits down next to me. I'm glad for the distraction. I don't even need to try to focus on her. Untangling her endlessly long legs, she sits in a Buddhist pose with her hands on her lap. She creases her brow. Clearly, she has something to say.

"You don't believe I'm mad, do you?"

I can't help but release a long sigh. People are dying all around me, including my friends. The best we can hope for is that one of us is still alive at the end of the seventh day, but the chances are that we'll both be dead. I can't cope with this conversation. "To be blunt with you, Sofia, your reaction to the roulette has made me wonder. I don't know if that was a normal reaction? Where was the emotion?"

Sofia raises a sculpted eyebrow. "What is normal? What benefit would there have been in getting emotional? What would have changed? Would it have brought them back from the dead?"

The hairs on my neck straighten. "How can you

talk about death so flippantly?"

Sofia's lips soften. "We all die, Andrew," she says. "Besides, you are trying to make sense of my reaction. I'm trying to tell you that it doesn't make sense. I'm mad."

I decide to lighten the mood. "Never before have I had to justify to someone that I think they're sane. You truly are unique, Sofia."

She pretends to throw something at me. Most likely, it is a fluffy pillow. The odds are high that it's a grenade, though. I pretend to catch the item. Sofia shuffles around, presumably getting settled. "Can I tell you a story? I think it might change your thinking about me."

Sofia tells me that she was a client manager in London. Her main role was to win new clients and then to keep them sweet.

"My natural instinct is to be a horrible little bitch, Andrew. It amuses me to be a horrible little bitch to unsuspecting people. When I can be bothered, or when it is in my interest to do so, I fight this urge. But you know what is weird?"

I purse my lips, like I'm posing for a photo to post on my social media feed (if I had one, of course).

"What is weird, *Andrew,* is that I find it a piece of piss to be amazingly charming, too-"

"There is no need to be humble around me, Sofia-"

"Not sure we have time for that sort of bullshit, do you? Every cloud has a silver lining, as they say, and the silver lining when you're hours away from dying is that you can cut the bullshit and tell it how it is."

I tell her she did well to find a silver lining in these circumstances.

"Right. Anyway. It is like I know exactly what people want to hear, and I'll say it. I'll behave just as they want me to behave."

"I dispute that. No offence, but you've got a whole load of backs up in this place. You've hardly endeared yourself to – let's think – Rebecca, and at times you've driven TJ up the wall. Even I can work out what the red-blooded TJ wants from you..."

Sofia dismisses my points with a wave of the hand. "Like I said, I knew what they wanted me to say, but I chose to do the opposite. I only bother to be charming when I want something."

I raise my eyebrows. I'm not sure if I'm impressed, or if I'm just a little scared. Significantly, I'm no longer sure whether this is the reaction Sofia is seeking. "So you're manipulative? You're a sociopath?"

Sofia looks to the ceiling. Her creaseless face shows no indication of offence. She is merely considering this. "I think it is fair to say I share many features common with a sociopath, Andrew. I accept that. But most of us do. I'm just more willing to embrace those traits. I think it is a symptom of my madness, but it doesn't define it."

Leaning back, I tell her that I still have no idea how any of this equates to her being mad. Sofia dutifully returns to her story. She tells me that she lured the clients (both men and women, their sex really wasn't relevant) like spiders to her web, and then she toyed with their emotions so they desperately and compulsively spent more and more money to spend time with her.

"They were," she says, "completely and utterly in love with me."

"And what did they mean to you?"

Narrowing her eyes, Sofia gnaws at a fingernail. "They were merely numbers on a spreadsheet."

My hands disappear behind my back. I don't want her to see the whites of my knuckles. "What am I to you, Sofia?"

I hold my breath as I wait for her answer. I lost a friend yesterday. I'm not ready to lose another one just yet. "I'm not quite decided yet," she says.

Blowing out air, I glance around at the remaining contestants, sat alone, doubtless struggling with their internal monologue. Right now, I'm not sure whether I'd prefer to be alone, too.

"I was winning all these awards and making all this money, and I was playing with so many lives that I felt special. I really had a god complex. Whilst I was able to recognise everybody else's limitations, I was completely oblivious to my own."

I pinch the skin coating my hip bone so hard that I grimace. "I'm not sure I want you to tell me anymore. If you want me to believe that you are mad, Sofia, then I'm all signed up."

It is as though she doesn't hear me. Either she doesn't really know what I want her to say, or she really doesn't care. "The thing is, I began to believe I had super powers-"

"You began to think you were Supergirl-"

"Pretty much. I didn't think I was human. I didn't think I was from this planet-"

"That really is nuts."

"Thank you."

My eyes flicker in all different directions, just to avoid fixing on Sofia.

"They thought I jumped off the bridge and into the

freezing cold river because I wanted to kill myself."

I squeeze her hand. It is warm and clammy.

"They were wrong. They thought I was depressed. I wasn't. I was delusional. Do you know why I jumped from the bridge?"

Sofia turns to me. I shake my head.

"I jumped off the bridge because I thought I would fly..."

Sofia continues to tell me that she often feels this way. She transforms into different personas with no awareness that she has done so.

The silence lingers in the air. I long to break it, but I don't know what to say. Sofia rests her chin in her upturned hands. "What are you thinking, Andrew? I really want to know what you are thinking."

Taking a deep breath, I glance over my shoulder, as if worried what people will think. "I'm just thinking that I'll have no idea when you have reverted to a persona, Sofia. And possibly more significantly, I'll have no idea whether you are merely using it to get exactly what you want."

A few lines appear on Sofia's forehead. "And how does that make you feel?"

I pause for just a moment. "It makes me feel absolutely terrified."

******

Evening

Not long after dinner, we all spring to our feet.

Is that a threat?

We can only see TJ's muscled, bull-like frame. "Why did you have to kill him like that? What kind of a monster are you?"

Gaining ground, I glance at the guards. They stand motionless in a straight line, their smirking, upturned heads gazing out of the glass ceiling. Breathlessly, I utter a few choice words that couldn't be aired before the 9pm watershed.

TJ holds his hands behind his back. Maybe this is an elaborate show to keep the guards off his case. Who is he talking to? I manage to get to him first. I stand side on, about six feet away, my shoulder pressed against the wall. Duncan. Who else? He stands, straight-backed, head jutting forward. TJ's forehead presses against Duncan's temple. TJ's spittle probably coats Duncan's cheeks.

"I have no idea what you mean, TJ. I thought that was the nature of the game?"

TJ takes a step back. The sinewy muscles in his neck tense. His jaw tightens. Judging from his whitened knuckles, he fights the urge to jab his finger in Duncan's chiselled chest, to pin him by his lapel and slam his head into the window. "Don't play clever with me, boy..."

"I could never outsmart you, TJ."

"You're a bully, and I fucking despise bullies. Tell me why you did it."

"Are you going to tone it down a bit first?" Duncan smiles. "You're frightening me ever so much. And you're causing such a scene. I'm really not one for attention."

TJ inhales deeply. He bides his time. "I'll be ever so nice to you, sweetheart, if it means you'll tell me the truth."

Duncan holds his hands up, making sure they don't touch TJ's chest. "I think I got carried away in the heat of the moment. I have a temper. I'm sure you've lost your temper before, TJ? I'm sorry, alright? But it didn't change anything."

TJ lowers his voice. "What do you mean it didn't change anything?"

"The practicalities, that's all. He died the same way everyone else did today. And every loss is tragic, there's no denying that. We just deal with it in different ways, don't we? But at the end of the day, the guard shot him in the head. It was the bullet that killed him. Not me."

TJ turns his back on Duncan. With his head lowered to the floor, he paces up and down. "Every other person used the sword to cut the body. You had the whole body to choose from. But what did you do? You slashed the poor guy's neck. You almost tore his head off. What does that say about you?"

Duncan holds TJ's stare. Maybe it is through bravado, or maybe it is because he really doesn't care. "What can I say? I have a few issues. I'm working on them. I thought you'd understand. You're supposed to be the tough guy in here."

TJ removes his hands from behind his back. He raises his balled fists to his chin. And then he runs his fingertips down Duncan's chest. "I'm keeping my eye on you."

"I'd expect nothing else."

With TJ's back turned, Duncan blows him a kiss. TJ remains oblivious to this gesture; I think we all know it is best it remains this way.

A few hours later my reflection stares back at me in the mirror behind the make-shift bar. I have caught glances of myself in pint glasses and windows over the last four days, but these were faded and distorted imitations of my real self, like filter in reverse, making me even uglier than I am. Am I *really* ugly? Nobody, apart from myself, has ever said I am. Mirrors in this place are isolated to the shower room and they are reserved for shaving, presumably and (ironically) just in case you cut yourself; I've decided that shaving is the least of my priorities, although I see the benefit in passing a few minutes in the morning.

"Your mind is away with the fairies, young man. So tell me, what will your tipple be tonight?"

A turquoise waistcoat complements the barman's crisp white shirt. The leather face suggests the man is comfortably into his fifties, but nobody has mentioned the passing years to his thick head of silver hair, pulled impressively into a bun. His measured and fluid movements defy his years. I order some drinks for the group, and a glass of water for me.

The barman smiles from the corner of his mouth. "Are you the designated driver this evening?" He takes pride in his job, I think, and then I consider that this concept is ridiculous – he has only been hired for tonight, and most likely he isn't even a real barman. So what does he do every other night of the week? Is he a homeless man, plucked from the streets on the promise of a shower and some food?

"Penny for your thoughts, sir?"

It is my turn to smile now. "You'd have to give me more than a penny for these thoughts," I say, collecting the drinks and returning to our table.

TJ has joined us again. I don't mind, but I do think his plan to appease the other contestants is flawed. He needs to spread his love more. And besides, our crew would still shoot him in the head first if it came down to it. It crosses my mind that secretly he enjoys our company, but he doesn't dare to say so.

TJ's smile broadens as I place his drink down on the table, exposing a row of teeth that – besides one notable absence - are generally straight and white. He has calmed down from a few hours ago. "This is the hottest place in town," he says.

I decide to ask him what he does for work.

TJ's smile disappears. He looks around the hall. "We have a jukebox and a pool table. It's like a party from a *Carlsberg* advert. All we need now are those strippers from last night."

"I could do you a deal on the striptease, TJ." Sofia displays a layer of saliva on her teeth; blood flows to my groin.

"So how come you changed the subject when Andrew asked what you do for work?" Dylan asks. "What's the secret, Big Man? Did you think we wouldn't notice your crafty ploy?"

TJ wipes foam from his upper lip. "What *don't* I do for work?"

Sofia kisses her teeth. "Well, you definitely don't have a job where you're expected to give a straight answer to a question. Are you a politician? A lawyer?"

Pumping out his chest, TJ's eyes linger momentarily on Sofia; during that moment she probably considers placing a restraining order against him. "I'm something of a builder. People hire my services when they need something – how do I say this? – when they need something *built*. When they have a job that needs both brains and muscle, then they give me a call."

Sofia's eyes sparkle with mischief. "And do you

then call somebody else who has brains?"

TJ seemingly ignores her. He stretches like a lion waking from an afternoon nap. "The women tend to hire me more than the men; especially the lonely housewives. Sometimes they'll slip me a few extra notes, and I'll slip them something extra in return. I tend to make a lot of women happy in my line of work and – you know – that makes me feel good."

Dylan clasps his hands together. The mischievous glint in his eye has returned. "What is their pet name for you? Derek?"

Sofia crosses her legs. She would be great at yoga. "That is so impressive, and so fucking *romantic,* TJ."

"Thanks," he says, folding his arms across his chest.

Without a moment's hesitation, Sofia reaches out and takes my hand. She takes Dylan's hand in her other hand. Before I know it, we are all joined (even TJ) forming a circle. "This shit has made us closer," Sofia says. "I'm sure it is how people felt during the war, all huddled together in a bomb shelter."

We all exchange smiles, sharing a moment.

"It does feel like we might be hit by a bomb any moment," I say. They know I am joking.

TJ nods. "You know what, I'm not one to share my emotions, but I do feel closer to you guys than I have with anyone for a long time. I'm going to feel proper bad if I have to shoot one of you tomorrow."

We break hands (but not our bond) to stifle our laughter.

******

Our round plastic table with chipped edges barely has enough space for the two of us. We are surrounded by other diners, leaning across their own tables chatting, engrossed in their own little worlds. I guess you could say we are the same; I imagine that we are enclosed in a bubble that just can't be popped.

"This is nice," I say.

"Yes, this is nice," she says.

Her smile stretches from one side of her face to the other. I take a moment to admire her creamy, flawless skin. Her sparkling eyes radiate happiness. I follow her spindly arms and legs as she retreats to the buffet. When she returns with a plate full of food, including rice and ribs and balls of various sizes, I think that this is a good start, that this is promising.

"So, how was your day?" I ask.

I am more than prepared for Frances to tell me all the wonderful things that were frightfully wrong with her day. It isn't immediately forthcoming, however. I smile as my sister holds up her finger to indicate just one second please, I'll be right with you. Her mouth opens like a dark tunnel. She scoops a spoonful of food into her mouth. Narrowing her eyes, she purses her lips, savouring the taste. I wait for her to finish chewing the food.

"Were you busy in work?" I ask.

Frances raises her finger again. She doesn't appear to actually chew her food. She scoops another spoonful into her open mouth.

"You still having difficulties with your team?" I ask.

Frances lowers her finger, but still she continues scooping food into her mouth.

My eyes widen and my smile fades. Patting my hair flat, I realise that the bubble has burst, and I'm smothered with soapy water. I wipe dark patches from my shoulders like they are coated with dandruff. I glance around to check if the other diners are still engrossed in their own conversations, to see if we are now much more of a spectacle, but I realise that now we are the only diners in the restaurant. The restaurant has emptied and the light has faded. Somebody has left the door open too, for a draught fills the hall, blowing dust and debris and crisp packets in from the pavement outside.

"Slow down, Frances," I say. "Let's just enjoy the food. And besides, it's not all about the food, is it? I am here with you. Enjoy the company."

Her face transforms into a snarl, reminding me of a wolf with sharpened teeth. She turns her finger around the other way, giving me the V-sign.

"Well *that's* not very nice, is it?" I say.

Frances doesn't seem to care whether it is very nice or not. She uses the back of her arm to wipe the sauce from her mouth. My head pulls back as she stabs her fork in my direction. "I just can't win with you, can I?"

"What do you mean?"

She blows out hot air. It smells foul, like rotting meat. "Did you not tell me that I needed to eat more?"

I feel like I have been forced into a corner and beaten with rolled-up paper. I want to raise my knees to protect my chest. "What?"

"Did you or did you not say that I needed to eat more?"

My sister speaks with such gusto that flecks of

spit coat my cheeks. "Well, Big Brother, now I am eating and still you are whining like a little bitch."

I hold up my hands. "Yes, but this isn't healthy..."

"All I ever heard from you was that I didn't eat enough, that I was too skinny. And you know what? It actually had nothing to do with you, did it? It is my body, not yours. Dad never said I was too skinny. And here I am eating, and guess what? You are still fucking moaning!"

Her bloated cheeks redden. I notice the skin under her arms sagging. The buttons on her blouse snap.

"Frances," I say, "you are growing..."

It takes me a moment to realise where I am. Dark shapes and shadows are all around me, but I recognise the dark shapes and shadows from my bedroom. It was a dream. Thank goodness it was a dream.

My knees vibrate together as I straighten my back and sit on the edge of the bed. It feels like the whole building is shaking; the giant from the beanstalk has picked us up like a ball to play with. Is this an earthquake? We don't experience earthquakes of any magnitude in the UK. Maybe we aren't even in our own country anymore? Just how far did we travel in that helicopter? God, we really have no idea where we are, do we?

My door is already ajar, just a few inches, of course. I push it open and slide my body outside. I expect to be joined by others, desperate to know what is going on, frantic to know what the vibrations were. The hall is empty. They all sleep with their doors shut, don't they? I realise it wasn't just vibrations that woke me, it was noise. I lift my head upwards. All I see through the glass is the darkness of the night. Nobody else is aware, nobody else cares, and so why should I? We have enough to worry about, and besides, whatever it was has left us now. I take a few moments to regain my composure. Walking over to the window, I inhale deeply through my nose, before exhaling out of my mouth. My reflected eyes appear disproportionately large to the rest of my face. The bags under my eyes are heavy and dark. My lips move to within kissing distance of the window. The shimmying branches indicate that the wind has picked up outside.

I jump backwards. My whole body turns cold.

Blinking, I take a deep breath. I need to get some sleep. This place is driving me insane.

For a fleeting moment, I thought I saw a face outside, staring straight at me.

DAY FIVE

Contestants eliminated: 38
Contestants remaining: 12

Morning

Back home, the alarm woke me in the mornings. This morning, I'm woken by a scream.

I jump out of bed and scurry into the hall in just my underwear. Apart from a few straight-backed guards, the hall is empty. I must be dreaming again. This place is playing mind games with me. I no longer know what is real and what is a figment of my imagination. With a deep, embarrassed sigh, I turn on my heel.

What was that noise?

Jerking my head, I spot him in the corner of the hall. Duncan. Crouched forward, he presses his knees into the hard floor. I stand motionless for a moment, taking in the scene. What is he doing? Is he praying? I just my head forward. No, he isn't praying. Someone else is there, lying on their back next to Duncan's knees. Duncan has him pinned down. One hand grips the man's throat, the other hand digs into his temple. The man twists and writhes underneath him. He eyes stare at the ceiling, through the glass and straight at the sun.

Duncan is trying to blind him.

I sprint towards Duncan. I lunge at him from about three feet. The side of my shoe slams against his cheek. Duncan rolls over. I thrust my knee into his chest, pinning him down. I pull back my arm and pummel his face, again and again and...

The guards pull me back, dragging me away. I kick with my dangling legs. The guards twist my arms until I fear they'll snap. My body loosens. The guards release their grip.

Gingerly, Duncan rises to his feet. He wipes his sleeve across his bloodied lip. He smirks. "Is that all you've got, Andrew? You punch like a little boy."

I glance at the floor. His victim has vanished. He presumably disappeared back to his room. I have no idea who it was.

I turn to the guards, my face perspiring profusely. I hold out upturned hands. "So you pulled your fingers out when I defended the guy? Why didn't you do something when Duncan tried to burn a hole in his eyes?"

They shrug their shoulders.

I stab my middle finger at them. "You guys are a fucking joke, you know that?"

It seems that *I* am the joke, for the guards break into hysterics.

I consider telling TJ what happened, but I assume he'd kill Duncan with his bare hands. Right now I couldn't give a damn if Duncan ends up six feet underground. I'd dance on his grave. But what would they do to TJ? Would they shoot him in the head?

Instead, I tell Dylan, over breakfast. Dylan spits out a mouthful of granola. "Duncan is a psychopath," he says. "Pure and simple."

I nod. "It's almost like he is going out of his way to cause problems."

Dylan dangles his spoon in the air. "Do you think that's what it is?"

I raise my eyebrows.

"Going out of his way to cause havoc? I'd say Duncan has to be the plant," Dylan says.

By that logic, there are other contenders. Melanie springs to mind. And what about TJ?

We both swivel in our chairs. We have a front row seat. TJ scrapes a chair across the hard, polished floor. He may as well pick up the chair and throw it against a window, the amount of noise it makes. He abandons the chair like it is a shopping trolley in a car park. He grabs a brown roll in each hand. He strolls to the far corner of the room, like he is walking along the promenade on a Spanish beach holiday, absentmindedly searching the shops for a fridge magnet.

Sofia appears from nowhere. She leans on my chair. "What is he up to now? There is never a dull moment with TJ, is there?"

"I don't think he's just letting off steam," Jake whispers to me. "I think he is getting at something here. He is making a point about something."

TJ stops walking. Bending his legs and twisting his body at the waist, he throws a bread roll at a camera with the ferocity of a baseball pitcher. The roll rebounds off the glass lens. If he throws the roll any harder then he'll smash the glass. His next throw is harder, but it just misses the target.

We watch, open-mouthed, as TJ soundlessly walks back to the tables. It takes him about thirty seconds to walk from one end of the room to the other. This time he picks up as many rolls from the table as he can manage, like he is trying to make the most of the *Harvester* salad bar. He grips a roll under each armpit, for fuck's sake. He nestles a roll under his chin. Turning, he strolls back towards his chosen camera. He stops when he reaches his target and drops all but one of the rolls to the floor. One by one, he throws the rolls with serious intend at the camera.

The guards gather around. There are six of them. Their jerky bodies appear agitated. Does it really need six? They raise their guns. TJ opens up his arms to them. "What? What do you want? What is it?"

TJ kneels down and picks up another roll. It rebounds off the glass. His face reddens; it looks like it is going to explode. He turns to the contestants. "They told us that they're not filming us, yeah? They told us that we aren't on TV. Is that what they told us?"

He keeps standing, like a wrestler antagonising his opponent, waiting. "I'll repeat the question. Is that what they told us? Yes or no?"

Seconds pass. "Yes," one of us shouts.

TJ wipes his mouth with his sleeve. "Right. Well, I'm not the brightest person in this show. You might say I'm the dumbest. I don't care. But something is really troubling me. If they aren't filming us, then why does that little dwarf, Rebecca, keep talking about getting ahead of the competition? What competition? And why the fuck are these dumbass guards so pissed off when I throw bread rolls at the camera? Are they afraid I'll break it?"

TJ shrugs off the attention of the guards. It crosses my mind that maybe the guards just don't like TJ throwing things around the room, potentially damaging the property; I decide against mentioning this. TJ pulls out his chair and sits down. He picks up his knife and fork and starts digging into his food, completely calm, utterly content; it is as if he had never gotten out of his seat, as if he had never caused any fuss whatsoever.

Dylan's eyes widen. "Okay. I admit it. Maybe there are two contenders for the plant."

Jake interrupts my laughter. His face appears serious. He looks me straight in the eyes. "You mark my words," he says, tapping the side of his nose. "TJ is on to something."

I turn to Sofia. "Who knows? Maybe TJ is smarter than he looks?"

Sofia plants a playful punch into my rib. She whispers in my ear, "Well he couldn't be any *dumber* than he looks, could he?"

Not for the first time since I joined the competition, I struggle not to spit out my food.

******

Rebecca struts into the hall with her hands on her hips and her (by my uneducated estimation) 4-inch heels clipping on the polished floor. Soundlessly, we all gather in a circle, like poodles promised a dog biscuit. Wiping my crusted eyelids, I cover my mouth with the back of my hand. I wince; even I'm offended by my sour breath.

"You all know the dreary, recycled formula, darlings," Rebecca says. "At some point in *every* reality show the contestants read their letters from home. Surprisingly, most of their family actually miss them. I don't know about you, but it makes me grab for the nearest waste basket so I can vomit. Maybe it is just me, because my family were always a bit weird, and they became a whole lot weirder with me once I was – let me remember now – yes, once I was fourteen..."

Rebecca's words drift away, like a plume of cigarette smoke. One of the other contestants dares to put up his hand, to ask Rebecca what happened when she was fourteen.

Rebecca gazes into space before glancing up, her eyes perfect circles. "Something happened in our idyllic little village. They were always suspicious of me after that. I don't know why, because nobody else did. Maybe they were the only ones who knew what I'm truly like." Without a metaphorical click of the finger, Rebecca returns to the real world, or as real as it can get when you're trapped in a giant hall made of glass.

Our eyes follow a security guard carrying a red post box. His subtle, creased smile suggests he enjoys his role as Father Christmas. He places the box flat on the floor. Whilst the box is nearly as wide as the guard, it barely reaches his knee. I imagine it is made of cardboard.

Rebecca strides up and down in a straight line. We twist our heads from left to right and from right to left, like we're at the tennis. Stopping, she bends slightly at the knees. "I am not going into technicalities, but that formula won't work here. For starters, I'm not convinced your families actually *will* miss any of you lot but – and this is much more significant – they don't even know you're participating in this wonderful show. There is no point trying to fit a square peg into a round hole now, is there? So we have needed to think outside the box, haven't we? It reminds me of how Spielberg was forced to innovate when the expensive central prop stopped working during the filming of Jaws. And we all know what the result of that piece of innovation was, don't we?"

A voice behind me pipes up, "A lot of people got eaten by a gigantic motherfucking shark, that's what..."

"And so, just like Spielberg, we have needed to innovate, and as a result we have brought you something ground-breaking and original."

Lifting his knee to his chest, the guard slams his shoe down against the box. It flattens and folds. Rebecca pauses, possibly waiting for a gasp from the crowd. The gasp never materialises. Scooping up the box like dog muck from the pavement, the disappointed guard exits the hall.

Rebecca taps her nimble fingers on the laptop. We turn to the huge screen on the wall.

"I have a responsibility to set expectations," Rebecca says, smiling. "I need you to know that what you're watching isn't live."

"So when did you film it?" Who knows which one of us asks the question, but it is the question all of us want answered.

Rebecca's smile transforms into a smirk. "We have been secretly filming your family or close friends from the moment you arrived in the show. The irony isn't missed on me, contestants. We have picked out some of the highlights for you over the last few weeks."

A woman stifles a gasp with her hand. Tears flood from her eyes. I turn to the screen. Two teenage boys sit around a round kitchen table with an older man. In the background, I spot abandoned plastic cartons and dishes stacked in an uneven pile. The man clasps his hands together. "We have to accept the possibility that your mum is dead," he says.

I don't dare look at their mother. Somehow, it feels intrusive if I did. Her howls subside, not because they soften, but because she flees the group.

Following the same logic, I only glance occasionally at the screen. The sounds that emit from the hall tell me all I need to know as the film flicks from family to family. The contestants release shrieks of anguish, or cries of delight. There is no middle ground.

"Look at the screen," Jake whispers to me. "I'm positive that this is your turn."

I release a sigh. I don't want to look. The interviewer wasn't lying when she spoke about my family. With me no news is definitely good news.

"Just look," Jake says.

I turn with half-open lids. My jaw drops.

To the casual observer, an attractive lady in her early seventies idles in an armchair. Lustrous silver hair partly covers an angular face. Slim, delicate fingers trace the outskirts of the chair. She unfolds long, slender legs.

She seemingly speaks to nobody in particular. "Where is my Andy? I haven't seen my Andy for a long, long time. He is a good boy, my Andy."

I inhale a mouthful of air just to keep breathing. My whole face burns.

Mum remembered who I am.

******

Imagine returning to a patient waiting room when the specialist has just told you that you are free of cancer. You probably want to yell your wonderful news at the top of your voice. And yet – and yet you are probably surrounded by patients who are moments away from being told that their own cancer is terminal, that they have days or weeks or months left to live.

I have good news. Others will have bad news.

I stay silent. I remain respectful.

My mind tells me to look away from the screen, and yet I'm compelled to keep watching as another family appear on screen. Again, they sit at the dinner table. Two girls – I'd estimate that they're about ten and twelve – dig into a plateful of food. A beautiful black lady with high cheekbones and full, ruby lips pours orange juice into four glasses. The man, wearing a black short-sleeved top presumably designed to display his gym-toned arms, says something – I don't know what – and the two girls laugh. The woman turns to him and gives an encouraging nod of approval.

There is a flurry of activity next to me. The footsteps are quick and light.

"Go after him," Jake says to me. "If you do one thing today, make sure you go after him."

I follow Dylan's retreating back. My walk turns into a jog just to keep within touching distance of him. He keeps moving away from the group and away from the screen until he reaches the far wall, until there is nowhere else to go. I know that right now he longs more than ever to smash the glass window, to keep on walking and walking until his burning legs cannot take him a single step further.

He turns around. His wet face isn't surprised to see me. "Tell me you get it. For Christ's sake, tell me you understand what this means."

I nod. I *do* understand.

Dylan puts his hands on my shoulders. "You saw Natalie and Tia up on screen. You saw how happy they were. I can't win them back, Andrew," he says. "It is too late. They are already gone."

******

Afternoon

They cook us Sunday roast for dinner, and it isn't just any Sunday roast, it is the crème de la crème of Sunday roasts; it is lamb. Filling my plate with roast potatoes, lamb, stuffing, carrots, broccoli and sprouts, my food reminds me of a ski mountain. Of course, I drown the food in a thick smothering of gravy before licking my lips and tucking in.

When I left home for university, the weekends were the worst days of the week. I sporadically attended lectures during the week, contributing very little, but at least there was some reason to get out of bed in the mornings, or the early afternoons. On the weekends I lay in bed, staring at the cracked ceiling, faded yellow, with my knees high to my chest. Repeatedly I asked myself whether it would make any difference to anyone else's life if I stayed in bed all day, if I just started my life again on Monday.

Repeatedly I failed to find any reason to get out

of bed.

But I *did* drag myself out of bed. And, every Sunday, I ate lunch on my own in a cold and bleak house that had wafer-thin carpets and stained curtains, imagining all the other families in the world enjoying their food together. Or, more specifically, I imagined my family back home enjoying their food together.

There was a time when my family wasn't that much different from any other family. Once upon a time, Mum cooked roast every Sunday afternoon. We created our day around lunch, or dinner as we called it. Both Dad *and* Mum enjoyed the occasional glass of wine. Dad was funny when he had a few drinks. If we played football in the morning then we needed to be back for dinner; if we had a party in the afternoon then it had to wait until we had finished lunch and our food had time to settle. We waited for the ice cream man to park directly outside our house and then we put our feet up in front of the Grand Prix.

At that point in my life, Sundays were my favourite day of the week.

And now, as my heavy, tired body sinks into the sofa, a nagging thought irritates me. The thought isn't the typical type of itch; it reminds me of when I had chickenpox and I longed to scratch my raw spots so much that Mum slipped my hands inside a thick pair of socks to provide a protective layer from my sharpened fingernails. My mum warned me, with her familiar delightful smile, that I'd be left with scars if I scratched my spots. I've met many smiling assassins in my time, with Rebecca at the top of that list, but my mum wasn't one of them. Mum was flawed, she was damaged, but she didn't have a nasty bone in her body. God, I wanted to scratch those spots more than I wanted to devour a Big Mac, but I knew neither temptation would end well.

The realisation gnaws at me that these people have lulled us into a false sense of security. This isn't a new tactic. We have been caught out before, and yet, like a drinker who envisages they'll work off yet another hangover the next day, we blindly walk towards a fall. I glance at the other contestant as they scoop spoonfuls of ice cream into their open mouths, their drooping eyes suggesting that they're ready for an afternoon sleep in front of the TV. They're basking in the warm ocean, with the sun pinking their necks, unaware of the shark lurking in the distance, smelling blood, ready to attack when they are at their most vulnerable. I really should tell them about the shark.

Fighting the urge to close my eyes, I stifle a yawn and then push myself up from the sofa. Pacing up and down the hall, I sense eyes like lasers on me; like I'm the crazy person running a marathon in the stifling August heat.

I need to remain alert. I should tell Sofia and Dylan – my closest friends in this place, in *any* place – that they should remain alert, too. Sofia sits in a Buddha pose, with her legs crossed, her eyes barely flickering. And Dylan – well, I don't want to say anything that will unnerve Dylan. I've decided not to say anything to him at all after the video. What *can* I say? Dylan stares out of the window like he is sipping coffee in a Paris cafe, observing the passersby. To anyone else, he appears content and relaxed. I know that he is lost in a world of his own, thinking about his lost family.

The rear middle door pushes open and suddenly

everybody is splashing and screaming in the water.

Or, at least, the other contestants are on their feet with the click of a finger, rubbing the underside of their eyes, desperately trying to shake away their slumber.

Even I blink to make sure I'm not imagining things. Why do I do this? I've witnessed enough lunacy in this place to expect the unexpected. I've witnessed Rebecca entering the room on horseback, so why should anything that happens surprise me?

Two guards bend forward at the waist, straining like strongmen pulling a truck. Only, they aren't pulling, they are pushing, and there isn't a truck anywhere to be seen. The guards are pushing – and I narrow my eyes to make sure – yes, the two guards are pushing a Spin the Wheel apparatus. Standing at least seven feet tall and with a solid wooden base, it is the type of apparatus you'd find in a fairground or – at a push – a spectacular village fete.

Rebecca follows behind the straining, perspiring guards in a grey pinstripe suit. The top two buttons of her cream blouse are left unbuttoned. She has changed her glasses; the elaborate, round lenses span most of her cheeks. She looks like she is suited and booted for an important business meeting. In different circumstances - and maybe if I actually drank alcohol - then I'd possibly say that she'd mastered a sexy librarian look. The guards release a relieved sigh when she asks them to leave the wheel in the centre of the hall. When the apparatus stops moving, I'm not the only one in the room who edges forward, who takes a closer look. My initial thoughts are confirmed.

Our names are printed on the outskirts of the

wheel, like numbers on a clock.

A man with cotton wool grey hair and an open-collar linen shirt bursts onto the scene holding a microphone. Whilst he's probably in his sixties, his orange, stretched face and white teeth look like he's been dipping into his wallet to turn back the hand of time. Normally I'm sure his presence would hold anybody's gaze, but today our attention is short-lived. All of our heads twist to take in the two young, lithe women in white high heels and blue bikinis, who stretch out their long legs behind him, flashing sparkling smiles. A few of the men in the group wolf whistle.

TJ turns around with open hands and a pleading face. "Come on, guys, this isn't the eighties. Can you please show some respect and stop objectifying women?"

"I didn't object to them at all," Duncan says. "Far from it, TJ."

"Ah, look out, TJ the fucking feminist," another says.

TJ breaks into a smile. "I just respect women. Is that such a bad thing?"

Sofia takes a few steps forward. She stops within touching distance of TJ. She is a braver person than I am. I notice that her hand runs through her luscious red hair. What is that about? "Respect women? You've been staring at me with those big beady eyes for the last five days, TJ."

"I've just been respecting your beauty, Sofia."

"Respecting my beauty? You look like you've wanted to bend me over the canteen tables."

"Would you let me?"

"Not if you were the last man in the room."

TJ wipes his lips with his sleeve. "That might only be a few days away, Sofia. Are you giving me a definitive no?"

Sofia doesn't answer with words. Instead she plants a playful punch onto his chest.

Rebecca takes her time before interrupting. "Can you two please stop flirting? You are making me jealous."

TJ thrusts his pelvis forward. "I still have plenty of time available for you, Rebecca."

Rebecca's blue eyes flicker. Spreading her lips, she turns her gaze away from TJ. ""Who said you were the one I was jealous of, TJ?"

I'm not sure if I am relieved when I turn to Sofia and catch her face crumbling into a look of repulsion.

Rebecca paces up and down the imaginary stage. "Let's move things along, shall we? It is my privilege and honour to introduce you to our special guest. This fine specimen next to me is Anthony."

Anthony pulls the microphone to his mouth with the fluidity and gusto of Elvis Presley. His voice is suitably syrupy. He would be perfect for radio commercials. Despite my determination to focus, I'm distracted by the models parading either side of the wheel, rubbing their hands along the exterior of the Spin a Wheel like they're advertising a car. As TJ would say, I can't help but objectify the women.

I turn to Dylan. His eyes fix on Anthony. Within Dylan's world, it is as though the women don't exist. Maybe it is temptation like this that tore his world apart? I bite my upper lip. Clearly, Dylan is transformed. He is an addict who resists his drug of choice. And yet it is seemingly too late. He told me that – over and over and over again – just hours ago.

"We have an exciting show for you this afternoon, ladies and gentlemen," Anthony says. I *know* that his eyes scan the room, that they connect with all of the contestants, and yet – and yet it still feels like he is talking directly to me, like I am the only one here. "The winning prize is our biggest yet. Can you guess what it is?"

One of the contestants asks if it is a Ford Fiesta. Another suggests that it could be a speedboat. Anthony silences them with a wave of the hand. "Whilst those would indeed be fantastic prizes, the prize today is even more spectacular." He pauses for a moment and then pulls the microphone close to his lips, close enough to kiss it. "If you lose, then you die. If you win, then you stay alive."

A gasp emits from a stereo. In unison, we look open-mouthed to the ceiling like somebody has pointed at a hot air balloon in the sky. A round of applause replaces the exaggerated gasp.

"Our first game is straightforward. We need one of our contestants to please...."

Anthony looks into the distance and then raises his hands. From the radio speakers the audience shouts, "Spin the wheel!"

This time, Rebecca doesn't mess around; pointing to a young woman with bitten fingernails, she tells her to spin the wheel. The woman walks to the wheel like she has a gun to her head; thinking about it, I guess this isn't too much of a stretch of the imagination. She takes a quick glance over her shoulder. We all look away. Bending at the knees and twisting at the hips, the woman spins the wheel.

Our eyes glue to the arrow as it passes name after name. It completes a full rotation before it even begins to slow. Passing my name, my body lightens. There is no way it will come all the way around to me again. I scan for Sofia's name. It isn't going to reach her. Where is Dylan's name? It isn't going to reach him either. It dawns on me where the arrow is going to stop a few moments before it does so.

It lands on TJ.

TJ crosses his arms over his chest. I want to look away from him, but I can't manage it. I notice that one of his hands is trembling.

Rebecca isn't finished yet. She chooses another contestant to spin the wheel. This time she picks a guy in his twenties with a thick head of unkempt, curly hair and a beard that a wizard would be envious of; I imagine this guy would get quite a few crosses against his name if he ever tried Speed Dating. He doesn't waste any time before spinning the wheel with gusto.

Straight away I can tell that it is going to take longer to land on a name this time. The arrow begins to slow down. I count the names. How many until Sofia? Too many. How many until my name? I should be alright. How about...? No, please don't.

It lands on Dylan's name.

Dylan slides his fingertips through his hair. He transfers his weight to his left foot and then to his right foot. He glances at me. He pulls a face as if to say that this can't be fucking good, can it?

I shrug my shoulders. I wish I didn't. The gesture is intended to calm him, to tell him that it is probably no big deal. And yet, how ridiculous is that? I don't know what else to do, though. I have no idea what the appropriate alternative is. And, to be blunt, who knows if getting chosen *is* such a bad thing? In this place sometimes it *is* good to be the chosen one.

"I am so excited," Rebecca says. "I feel like the girl who has been asked on a date by the coolest boy in the class." The way she stares longingly into the distance suggests that the coolest boy in the class never *did* ask her on that date. "The game we are about to play was one of my favourites as a child. It might be difficult to imagine it now, but I was something of a tomboy growing up. This game was perfect for me. It gave me a chance to explore the darkest corners of the house, to hide away in some of the nooks and crannies that usually go unexplored. Can you guess what the game is?"

"Marbles," TJ says. His face remains expressionless. His tone is deadpan. "Of course we can guess what it is. It is Hide and Seek. Do you think we are six years old?"

Rebecca thrusts out her hips. "I don't think you are six years old, TJ. When you were six years old and the seeker found you – and knowing you, TJ, you probably hid behind the sofa or the curtain with your big, stupid head sticking out – then you probably had a little hissy sulk and a baby cry and then ran to your mummy. You are the seeker this time, TJ. If you find somebody in this game then they will get shot in the head. Is that grown-up enough for you, sweetheart?"

TJ doesn't say anything, and nor does anybody else. Smiling, Rebecca takes a yellow builder's hat and places it on TJ's head, tightening the strap at the back. She has the conscientious look of a tailor measuring a suit. She straps a watch to his wrist, and then goes through the same process with Dylan. I notice that she glides her manicured fingernails down the nape of Dylan's neck, probably trying to make him tingle. Clearly, she knows all about his urges.

"Right," Rebecca says, walking and talking, "I am going to explain the rules of the game, and so I need you all to listen carefully."

We nod.

"We have two seekers, Dylan and TJ. The rest of you are hiders. You will have sixty seconds to hide before Dylan and TJ are allowed to come and find you. Dylan and TJ have sixty minutes to find you. Any questions so far?"

A middle-aged man puts up his hand. Rebecca sighs. "Yes?"

He asks what the helmets are all about.

"Good question. If you look closely, there are cameras on the helmets. I know that cameras are a bit of a sore subject for you delicate flowers – please don't be offended by me saying that – and so I'll explain this in sensitive terms. Don't worry; there is no secret, malicious intent behind the cameras. They merely allow us to follow Dylan and TJ's movements. It will record when they have found a hider. We'll be able to watch events unfold from here. I'm sure you'll understand that, with so much at stake, the cameras are needed. All good?"

We remain silent.

"You will notice that our two adorable seekers, Dylan and TJ, are wearing watches. Again, I reassure you paranoid people that there is no sinister conspiracy behind this. The watch allows them to keep track of – wait for it – the time. Why reinvent the wheel? Like I said, they have sixty minutes to find you. If Dylan and TJ fail to find any contestant within sixty minutes then they are eliminated from the game, and so it is important they keep track of time. That is only fair, don't you think?"

A few contestants shrug their shoulders. Nobody says anything.

"A few more things. If a seeker does find a hider within the allocated sixty minutes, then that hider is eliminated from the game. A seeker is only allowed to find one hider, and so – whatever happens - only two people will be eliminated from this game. That is one silver lining we should all hang on to."

Rebecca's eyes scan the room, looking for questions. When none are offered, she glances to the clock.

60:00

Rebecca's face breaks into a warm smile. "Right then ladies and gentlemen, it seems like we are ready to get events under way. Hiders, you now officially have the right to hide."

The doors to the outside world thrust open. The seconds on the clock start counting down.

******

After days and nights captured inside that overgrown greenhouse – prisoners peeking at the outside world but never getting to touch, smell, taste and feel it – it is like discovering Narnia at the bottom of a dusty old wardrobe.

Stepping outside, it feels like I am experiencing the world for the first time; a toddler fascinated by the different colours and shapes and fragrances. I inhale deeply. My feet sink into the grass. Looking down, the grass is bright green and it flickers with moisture; this is the first day the drizzle hasn't fluttered against the glass windows. Is somebody shining a torch in my eyes? Flinching, I pull my arm to my face to shield my eyes from the blinding sun. The heat hitting my face reminds me of stepping off a plane in a tropical country. Daring to pull my arm away, I catch the contestants fleeing in various directions. Their movements are awkward and confused, like zombies in an apocalypse movie.

Stepping over nettles, my eyes focus on a rusty metal sign that has fallen to the ground. Crouching down, I pull away the overgrown grass. I know what I am looking for. The arrows on the sign point in an array of directions. The letters are painted in flaky, black paint, but I can just about read them.

Playground.

Apartments.

Funfair.

Reception.

I straighten my body. Picking up speed, I skip over the remains of a campfire and the shreds of a broken bottle. A realisation floods my mind.

For the last five, torturous days, we have been living at an abandoned holiday camp.

I'm aware of my heavy, sporadic breathing as I stretch out my legs. Turning the corner, the camp opens up in front of me. My eyes follow the narrow winding trail where, at 3pm on Fridays in the height of summer, the cars would have queued to check in; I picture children bouncing up and down in the back seats and panting dogs poking their heads out of the windows. Some of the punters probably arrived earlier (keen as mustard), their shoulders reddened from the sun, their cheeks hot from the warm, stale beer served in disposable plastic cups, melting ice cream coating their lips. The cars probably parked at outrageous angles on the expanse of tarmac outlining the grass verge, like an airport runway. For many, this would be the happiest moment of the year, an escape from the drudgery of everyday life.

My heart sinks, hit by the bleaker, more dismal reality of the situation. The monumental brick wall outlining the park must be fifteen feet tall. The sharp, menacing barbed wire on top of the wall is clearly intended to prevent intruders accessing the park. A cold shiver hits my body. It reminds me of a prison, of a deterrent to stop people escaping.

There is no way out of this place. Even though they released us from the hall, we are still prisoners. We are still captive. We cannot escape to the *real* outside world.

I'm struck by a jolt of guilt. What am I doing? The seconds are passing. I begin to run. With the gentle wind blowing through my hair, the spiralling three-storey building rapidly grows bigger. Under normal circumstances it is the type of building I'd run away from. It reminds me of a 1970's concrete metropolis you'd find in a decaying city centre suburb.

The image of the metal sign invades my mind. Is this my best option? I consider the fairground. There must be lots of nooks and crannies there, lots of dark places to hide. I look around, complete a full rotation. I have lost my bearings. The car park and overgrown grass stretches out in front of me. I can't locate the fairground. I don't have time to head back in the direction I came from. They could be heading straight towards me. They might be gaining ground on me as we speak.

They.

Dylan and TJ.

Unless Dylan finds one of us, unless he finds one of the contestants who are literally hiding to stay alive, then my best friend will be dead within the hour.

Blinking away the thought, I pick up my knees and continue heading towards the brick apartments.

I smile when I realise just how many apartments there are. And each room must have – what – three to five rooms? It will be like searching for a needle in a haystack. Sure, I want Dylan – and TJ, thinking about it – to find a contestant, but I don't want them to find me.

I reach out to grip the metal staircase, which is flecked with dried bird shit. I need to head upwards. After all, they are more likely to search the ground floor. They are fighting against the clock, and the ground floor is the first one they'll come across. The sole of my shoe massages the first step. Will they choose the ground floor? They will know that we will try and locate the best hiding place. Maybe the ground floor is too obvious?

I attempt to get into the minds of Dylan and TJ. Dylan will play it strategic, but TJ will just go with his gut. My mind drifts. The seconds pass. I turn my back to the blocks of apartments to gather my thoughts. My eyes wander. They fix at the group of trees. I stare at the carving on one of the trunks.

My jaw drops as I take in the words.

AM and FM were here. 1990.

******

Hidden under a bed in the second-floor apartment

bedroom, listening out for footsteps, I'm like a thwarted lover who's heard the shutting of the front door and the sound of the husband creeping up the stairs, out for revenge.

My heart sunk when I pulled down a metal door handle, and tried to push the door forward, only to meet resistance. Instinctively, I pulled the door towards me. It didn't open. Shuffling sideways like a crab, I moved to the next door along. I glanced over my shoulder, like a burglar completing a day shift, looking out for passing neighbours. I pushed the door. Nothing. I pulled the door. Nothing. My shoulders tensed. I moved to the next door, and then the next.

My plan was flawed. The doors were locked.

I eyed the wooden doors. They were paper thin, and the paper looked like it had been left in the rain overnight. I could easily kick it down. No problem. The leftover evidence in doing so, however, was a major fucking problem. It crossed my mind that the seekers wouldn't notice. They were up against the clock. I took another look at the doors, an estate agent evaluating a property. The chipped, worn doors reminded me of a bruised apple. The rotting wood was coated in debris, and yet – goddamn – the doors were still in place, with no evident holes or cracks. Sure, the seekers were up against the clock, but they would be hunting for clues, drawn to any signs like a shark to blood. They'd notice if I kicked down one of the doors.

I looked for an alternative entry route. Running my fingertips along a window frame, specks of white wood crumbled like sawdust. The zigzagging cracks made the windows resemble an ordinance survey map. And yet none of the windows were open, and there were no holes between the frames.

The seconds passed and yet – and yet – I still needed a moment to gather my thoughts. I sucked in a mouthful of air and then blew it back out. I turned my back to the apartments and gripped hold of the rusting metal barriers overlooking the rectangular grass forecourt. I'd already made too much ground and wasted too much time to change tact. The arcade or the funfair or the swimming pool and all the other glorious hiding places were no longer an option. I had to work with what I had and then rely on a great big dollop of luck. I had to leave some evidence. That was just collateral damage. It still left me with a chance. Otherwise I may as well hand in the white flag. I had to do *something*. And now.

Spinning around, I raised my knee and stretched out my leg. My foot went straight through the flimsy woodwork. I pulled it out. The hole was the size of a baby's head. The door itself hadn't moved. For fuck's sake. Leaning backwards, I located a higher target, much closer to the door handle. I rested the tip of my shoe against the door, and then I pushed.

The door thrust open.

It reminded me of an out-of-town cowboy making his entrance in the local salon. I disappeared inside the apartment. Shutting the door behind me, it hung precariously from the hinges. Evidence? It was like leaving a body in the middle of a busy city centre with a knife still plunged in the neck. The door stood out like a sore thumb from all the others, and that was before you took into account my great big foot imprint.

Shaking my head, I took in my environment. The

musty, damp stench made my eyes water. Had somebody died in here? Looking down at the torn brown carpet, I half expected to see the chalked outline of a body on the floor. Moss peppered the walls. Plants seeped through the concrete floor. I considered my hiding options. I guessed I could crouch behind the sofa. I could stand like a statue behind the shower curtain. Every option was a terrible option. It wasn't even as if there was much space to search. I knew that the seconds were counting down and TJ or Dylan could burst into the room at any moment. With my heart on the floor, I pulled open the door to the bedroom and then pushed it shut. The gap was just enough to squeeze my body in.

I rolled underneath the bed and kept on rolling until I could roll no more. My shoulder pressed against the flaking, painted wall.

And now, minutes later, as I lie hidden underneath the bed, I'm desperately trying to speed up rather than slow down the seconds. I want to slam my middle finger on the fast forward button of that remote control. Momentarily, I slam my eyes shut, trying to black out the awfulness of the situation. I try not to think back to my games of Hide and Seek as a kid. I know what the reality is, but I just don't want to face up to it. I know that one of the first places you look is under the fucking bed. My best hope is that they don't reach the apartments, that instead they find one of the other hiders somewhere else. I have a chance of staying alive, don't I? After all, there are plenty of other hiding places.

I can't control my breathing. It sounds like I have a plastic mask on. With my straightened arms pressed tight against my body, I know my arm is already locked. I focus on the spiralling cracks on the far wall, on the dust on the carpet, on the cobwebs clinging to the stubby legs of the bed. With nothing happening, and no watch to refer to, it is impossible to tell just how many seconds and minutes pass, how many seconds and minutes remain until the hour is up. But they *do* pass.

And then, just as I think that everything will be alright, just as I allow myself to believe that I'll make it to the other side of the sixty minutes alive, I hear something.

Of course, I try to convince myself that it isn't what I know it is. It could just be a mouse scurrying across the carpeted floor in the front room. But it isn't. The footsteps are too big and loud to belong to a mouse. Maybe a fox is rummaging through the bins? But then, a fox wouldn't scrape a chair across the floor or pull a sofa away from the wall.

However hard I try to convince myself that everything is still okay, I *know* that another person is in the apartment. Scrap that; I know that a seeker is in the room.

My heart doesn't beat any quicker as the bedroom door is pushed open. It doesn't feel like a fist is banging down hard against my chest as the black shoes make their way across the room. I feel calmer than ever, like I've finally confessed all of my sins and I have nothing else to hide. A sense of contentment flows through my body. I no longer need to worry about possibilities.

My fate is sealed.

I become curious more than anything about the movements of the scuffed black shoes. The movements appear languid and light, like they are not contending with a ticking clock, like they have all the time in the world. They stop moving just inches short of my bed, close enough for me to reach out and clasp an ankle, possibly drag the man to the floor. What size are they? Maybe a ten? Maybe an eleven? I try to imagine what size shoe TJ would be, what size shoe Dylan would be.

I wait for an upside-down head to appear underneath the bed, for a camera to flash in my face. I hold my breath and wait for the inevitable. I start counting. One. Two. Three. Nothing happens. And then the shoes turn in the opposite direction, so that the tips face away from me. My immediate world shrinks. There is less space underneath the bed.

I know what has happened, but I struggle to believe it.

The searcher has sat down on the bed.

******

It has to be TJ.

I had him right from the beginning. How did I allow him to convince me that he was alright? He doesn't want my death to be quick. He wants to prolong it, to torture me. He is going to give me hope, and then he is going to dash it literally at the last moment. He wants me to wait and to stew.

He thinks he is in control, but he isn't. He knows that the only way I can speed things up is to hand myself in. I'm not going to do that, because it would be suicide. He doesn't realise that I'm ready to die, that I'd prefer to die with dignity than to squirm and writhe for the last few seconds of my life. I'm going to tell him to go fuck himself. And then I'm going to pull myself out from underneath the bed and pummel his gloating face with my fists. Sure, he'll fight back, he'll overpower me, but it doesn't matter; I'll at least inflict a few bruises, a few dents to his pride before I die.

I open my mouth, ready to shout out. And then my mouth snaps shut.

A floppy hand dangles in the gap underneath the bed. It falls just short of the right ankle. I stare at the array of lines on the palm, at the long, delicate piano fingers. It isn't TJ's hand. It is Dylan's hand.

I know that the camera on his helmet is aimed at the far wall. Even though he is sat just inches from me, the video on the camera gives no indication that I'm even in the room, that I'm even in the apartment. Instinct takes over. Adjusting my body, I reach out with my right arm and squeeze the hand. His grip is strong. His grip is undeniably strong.

I've only known him a few days, and yet he is the greatest friend I've ever had. He wants to say goodbye to me before he is responsible for ending my life.

Dylan releases his grip on my hand.

I start rolling from underneath the bed. I want to embrace my friend before the guards come. There must surely be a handful of seconds before they'll be able to reach us. But as soon as I roll towards the shoes, they start moving away from me. I stretch out my hand to grab hold of them, to pull them back, but they keep walking. Sticking my head from underneath the bed, the black, scuffed shoes disappear out of the bedroom door.

My eyes follow his shoes as they disappear out of sight.

My fingertips tingle. There is hope, after all. Dylan has presumably heard another contestant. He knows where they are. He has chosen to find them over me. We are both going to stay alive, at least for another day. Within hours we will be reunited. We will share a secret. Of course, nobody else must know.

"Seekers, you have sixty seconds to find a contestant or you will be eliminated."

The announcement is louder than ever. There must be speakers positioned all over the park. It takes a few seconds for the announcement to sink in. When it does, it is like two hands grip my throat. Dylan doesn't know where another contestant is. He hasn't chosen them over me.

Crawling on bent hands and knees, I pull myself out from under the bed and run out of the room.

"Dylan!" I scream.

I run out of the bedroom, through the living room and then out of the apartment. He must have jumped over the railings and on to the patch of grass.

"Dylan! No!"

My screams are blown away with the gust of wind. Dylan walks with his shoulders back and his hands clasped behind his back. He holds his head up and looks straight ahead. He heads towards a single guard. The guard already has his gun raised.

"Seekers, you have ten seconds remaining to find a hider, or you will be eliminated."

Dylan merely picks up his pace, until he is twenty and then fifteen and then ten yards away from the guard.

"Seekers, your time has now elapsed. If you have not found another contestant then you will be eliminated from the competition."

My screams are drowned out by the sound of gunshot, by the sound of the guard shooting my best friend in the head.

******

In a perverse way, it's lucky that I've had my fair share of death in my life, and that's even before I came into this place. I know what works for me to pull me through, and what doesn't. I *want* to lie down and shut my eyes and soak up my own thoughts; however this will only lead to over-thinking, self-pity, regret and remorse. My numb body doesn't want to do *anything,* but my damaged mind just can't rest.

What I *need* to do is to keep busy, to do something – anything – even if it's the absolute last thing I feel like doing right now. That way, my brain will be too preoccupied with whatever is going on right in front of me to allow any unwanted thoughts to slip into my mind.

And so, that's my plan of action.

I don't want to go back into the hall. I'm not deluded; I know that the grounds to the holiday park gave us a false sense of freedom, that there was no way of escaping to the real outside world, but it felt magnificent to merely be free of the hall, to be outside. I know I need to return, though, and that if I show any sort of resistance the guards will shoot me. I merely take my time, dragging my soles on the saturated ground, my arms dangling by my side.

I only take a few steps inside before the doors slide shut behind me; I must be the last one to return. The coolness of the hall makes me wonder whether the yellow sun outside was stifling or whether the air conditioning inside is intense.

I don't need to keep occupied, to keep busy. Sofia rushes towards me with outstretched arms. With my head resting on her shoulder, my face disappears within her tangled hair. She plants a kiss on my cheek. "He's gone, hasn't he?"

I don't say anything. Pulling away, she dabs my tearstained cheek with her finger.

"He was a good man," Sofia says. "I really liked and respected him, you know."

I nod. "He was my best friend."

I long to tell her how he died, that he forfeited his own life for mine, that he died with dignity.

"You know he didn't die for nothing, he..."

I know I can't tell her. They will say that we broke the rules. They will shoot me. I am not sure I care about that anymore – not right now – but what was the point in Dylan giving up his life if I'm going to die anyway?

"He did what, Andrew?"

Sofia's angled face isn't curious. She isn't probing for information. She merely wants to make sure I'm okay.

Jake isn't here, but I know what he'd say. He still manages to converse with my mind. He tells me that there is no benefit telling Sofia what happened, that it would undermine the wonderful sacrifice Dylan made to keep me alive.

"He died with dignity. And there was a real point to his life. He brought two children into the world, didn't he? Natalie and Tia. One was ten and the other was twelve. He loved them, and I just know they loved him, too."

"They did, Andrew. Of course they did."

A shadow grows larger behind Sofia's shoulder.

"I'm sorry, Andrew."

With my frazzled brain, I must look confused.

"You know, about Dylan. I know you guys were close. Like brothers."

My eyes are drawn to a red indent on TJ's forehead. I presume this is a strap line where he removed his helmet. His eyes are reddened and watering. It doesn't look like it has been a great hour for TJ, either. At least he is alive.

I manage some sort of a smile. "Thank you. You made it then?"

TJ's eyes flick to the floor. "Yeah, I made it."

"I'm glad you did."

TJ holds my eyes. "You *are?*"

I think about this. There is no room for bullshit in this place anymore. I owe the other contestants more than to bullshit them. I think back to the game. I thought it was TJ sat on the bed. I thought TJ was torturing me by delaying the inevitable. I'm relieved that it wasn't. Under normal circumstances I'd probably feel guilty for thinking he'd do that. These aren't normal circumstances; any sign of guilt is drowned by remorse for Dylan.

I am never going to see him again.

His family are never going to see him again.

They don't even know he is dead.

"Yes," I say. "I am."

"So I've worked out who you found, TJ," Sofia says. She looks around the room. There aren't that many of us left. I don't have the energy to look around, to use my brain.

"Who did you find, mate?" I ask.

TJ blows out a deep breath. "God, I'll be honest, I

didn't think I was going to find anyone. It took me a long time. That place is big; there are so many hiding places. But I knew who I wanted, and I found her-"

"You wanted someone in particular?"

TJ bounces up and down on his feet. His face looks sheepish. He understands the undertone of the question. He wanted a specific contestant dead. "Yeah, to be honest. I wanted her dead for what she did to you-"

"Me?"

"Yeah. She cheated. I know it is dog eat dog in here, but that was out of order. She shouldn't have cut herself to get you eliminated. There are people I'd like to stay alive in this game, but she sure as hell wasn't one of them."

I shrug my shoulders. I don't know what to say.

"Sounds fair enough to me, TJ," Sofia says.

"Melanie is dead," TJ says.

I don't know why I do it, but I reach out and give TJ a hug.

******

As the afternoon hours drift away, Jake takes his opportunity to speak to me. "You did everything right by your friend. You only knew him five days, but you made a difference in that time, and he valued you. It would have ended differently if he didn't feel that way towards you."

I examine his face for any signs. Noticing me looking, he nods. "I know," he says.

I go to ask him how he knows, but how can I? Deep down, though, I think I know. I think I've known all along how he seems to understand everything about me.

Jake leans closer. "You've been pushing away your worst memories. They are painful. They are unwanted..."

"There are so many."

He nods. "There are. And each tragedy was horrific. But remember what I said a few days ago? I said that what doesn't kill you makes you stronger. You survived each tragedy. You are so strong, Andrew. Don't push the memories away. Embrace them, even if it is just for a short time..."

I bury my head in my hands. My fingers massage my oily, perspiring temple. I tried to help Frances, just like I tried to help Kim. Kim needed my help. Frances needed my help.

They *did* need my help, didn't they?

It was four years ago. The Saturday afternoon football results silently flickered on the TV in the background. Rocking back and forth, Frances nestled her dry forehead on my shoulder. Through a crack in the curtain, I observed crisp orange and red leaves blowing in the wind. It was grey, drizzling and overcast, with no prospect of sunshine. I couldn't quite tell if that was the forecast outside, or if the bleak outlook was confined to my mind.

She looked up; a baby longing for her dummy. "Thanks for being here for me, Andy. Everyone else in the world abandoned me. Mum, Dad-"

"Well, that isn't strictly true, is it, Frances?" I said. I wanted to divert the conversation. I didn't want to go there. "They can't control-"

"And that's just my family. They say you can't choose your family, so in a way it's just the luck of the draw. But I chose my friends, and they abandoned me too, didn't they?"

I rolled my finger along my sister's nose. It was always everybody else's fault. It never used to be like this. "I know it feels like that right now, Frances. You need to look at the big picture, though. Your friends tried to look out for you, but you kept ignoring them. They even contacted me to find out how you were, to try and work out what was wrong. You just didn't let them in..."

"Like I said, my friends abandoned me, just like Mum and Dad. But *you*, Andy; you are different. You have always been there for me."

I didn't want the plaudits. I couldn't cope with the adulation. I slanted my body so that Frances's forehead drifted away from my shoulder. "I'm your big brother. Of course I'm always going to be there. And you have always been there for me, too. Remember that time we were playing golf..."

My voice drifted. I was talking to myself; it felt pointless continuing. I glanced at the living room door. Slapping my hands down against my thighs, I decided to open the door. Just a few inches. Sinking back into the sofa, I wasn't sure whether Frances had even noticed me leave.

She stared at me with wide, intense eyes. "I'm going to do this, Andrew. *We* are going to do this. I am going to get healthy. I am going to eat three healthy meals a day."

Emitting a pained smile, I tapped my feet on the floor. "That's great, Frances," I said, leaning forward. "I stocked up the fridge in preparation. I'll cook something light for both of us. Something small. I know you haven't eaten for a while and your stomach won't be able to take it."

She tore at my sleeve. Her fingertips pinched my skin. "Tomorrow, Andy. I need to get a good night's sleep first. It is best to start afresh."

I muttered under my breath, "You said that yesterday."

Frances gripped my wrist. "What was that?"

"I said that tomorrow sounds good. Let's do it."

Her face broke into a wide smile. I cursed myself for noticing that her front two teeth were stained. They appeared brown and rotten. "I love you, Andrew."

My hands stroked her arms. I resisted the urge to look over her shoulder. "I love you too. With all my heart. Everything I do I do because I love you. You know that, don't you?"

Her eyes narrowed with apparent bewilderment. "What?"

"You know that everything I do I do because I love you, right? Even the things that I really don't want to do. I need you to know that, Frances. It is incredibly important."

I shuddered at the knock on the front door. Sensing the fear in her eyes, I kissed my sister on the top of her nose. "I'll get it. You just relax."

Moments later, I returned to the living room followed by three men holding up their badges. Frances looked up with panic in the whites of her eyes. The first man told my sister that he was obliged to detain her for her own safety.

Frances rose from the sofa as calmly as if her name had been called at the doctor's surgery. She paced towards me. Pulling back her head, she covered my face with phlegm.

"I had no choice, Frances," I said, wiping my face

with my sleeve. "You are killing yourself. This is the only way I can keep you alive."

The men pulled my sister away. She kicked and screamed and wailed. "You have just signed my death warrant. I am nothing without my freedom. You all fucking abandon me! I thought you were different, Andrew. You *are* different. You are even worse than the rest of them!"

The noise subsided as the men escorted Frances down the corridor.

The front door slammed shut, leaving me alone in my sister's damp, cold house.

Now, as I release my head from the depths of my hands and glance around, I realize that. Jake has gone.

******

Evening

I return to my bedroom straight after dinner, just to take a break. With my upturned head engulfed by my pillow, I gaze around the room, lost in my thoughts.

We have lost two people today, bringing the numbers down to ten. My main threats in this place are now Duncan, TJ and Sofia. Two of the three are my closest friends in here. When it comes down to it, I still need to decide whether I'd take their life to save my own.

Dylan never gave me the choice. He made it easy for me.

I never met his family, but I know they *did* love him; he just gave them no option but to take a different path. He was a good man, and I know he was a good father, regardless of his mistakes. I know they loved him.

And now – now they don't even know he is dead. When will they even find out? His wife will try to contact him at some point. When she can't get hold of him she'll file a report to the police. He will just be a missing person.

They'll never locate his body, which means that they'll never know for sure that he is dead. It is the same with Kim's family.

I sit up when there is a knock on the open door.

"Come in," I say.

Duncan takes a single step inside my bedroom. His thick hair sticks up at the temples. The side of his face is crumpled, like it's been plastered against a pillow. The bruises on his cheeks have turned blue.

"Get out."

"I just wanted to say sorry about this morning, mate."

"I'm not your mate."

"I was going to let him go. You must know that. I just wanted to teach him a lesson. He made a comment about my mum. You see, she is in a care home. She went a bit crazy, if you know what I mean? I just lost it. I'm very protective of my mum, maybe too much."

I straighten my back. "*Your* mum went crazy?"

He narrows his eyes. "Yeah."

I bite my tongue. "Okay."

Duncan's face brightens. "Okay? That's good. And I am sorry about Dylan. He was a good man."

I nod.

Duncan continues to stand in the doorway. He glances at the door like he's never seen one before.

"You always keep this door open?"

"Yeah."

"How come?"

I hold his gaze, but say nothing.

"Okay, see you around, Andrew."

******

For the first time since I've been here, I'm one of the last still up.

I sit with Sofia in what has become one of my favourite spots: on the hard floor, with my back pressed against the window, my knees pulled tight to my chest. Sofia's knee occasionally brushes against mine.

"You've had a whole lot of grief to deal with this week," Sofia says.

"True."

"How are you fixing up?"

I raise my eyes to the ceiling. "I guess I haven't got any option but to cope. None of this feels real. *If* I get out of here then it will probably hit me."

Sofia glances at me. "*If* you get out of here then you'll be mourning my loss, too."

"Thanks for that," I say, smiling.

"No problem, sweetheart. How are you feeling about getting out of here?"

I rub my thumb over my knees. "Honestly? I'm torn about the whole thing."

"How come?"

I kiss my teeth. "The deal is that I'll be flown off to a country where there is no virus. That has been my driving force throughout..."

"But?"

"Well, for starters...you told me that they might already have a vaccine."

Sofia smirks. "Don't ever listen to anything I say, Andrew."

I run my hand through my scalp. "It's not just that. You know the videos from this morning? My mum called my name. She remembered who I was. I visit her as much as possible, but she hasn't said my name for years. I began to think that it was pointless me going to visit her. But now..."

"But now you're not so sure."

"Exactly."

Sofia stretches out her legs before crossing one over the other. "It's great, though. That she remembers you. My mum is dead."

I squeeze her hand. "I'm so sorry. When? How?"

"Last year. She caught the virus."

I shake my head. I'm reminded – again – that I'm one of the lucky ones. I lost my liberties, but others lost their lives. Just how important is it for me to be free? "Who did they film for your video, Sofia?"

"My step-sister, Olivia. Bless her; they filmed her phoning friends and family, asking if they'd heard from me. She really cares. We have the same mum, but different dads. My dad died before I was born."

I stroke my thumb along Sofia's palm.

"My mum carried a picture of my dad in her purse at all times, you know. Her family said that he was a bad man, but my mum wouldn't have any of it. She always said that she loved him, that he had a good heart."

My eyes narrow. "Who do you believe?"

"I've always believed my mum."

I nod. "Sofia, do you really think you're mad?"

Her face brightens. "I know I *have* been mad, and I know at some point down the line I *will* be mad, but right now – well, right now I'm not too sure. I always thought it was hereditary. My grandparents always said my dad's mum was mad. Over the years I've realised that she wasn't. She just had mental health issues. I liked my nan. Right now it feels like the rest of the world might be crazy and I'm the only sane one left."

Laughing, I tell her that sounds about right. "Sofia, can I ask you a question?"

She tells me that of course I can.

"Is there a man in the show called Jake?"

She furrows her brow. "What do you mean?"

I shrug. "I mean exactly what I asked. Is there a man called Jake in the show?"

"Nope. There is nobody called Jake in this show."

I nod. I fix my eyes on Sofia, and then glance away.

Sofia's runs her fingers along my hand. "Andrew, what is it? What is wrong?"

I exhale. "In my mind there has been a man called Jake in the show."

Sofia stifles a laugh. "I'm sorry. What has he been doing?"

"He's been talking to me. He's been giving me guidance."

Sofia's face shows no trace of surprise. "Has he been looking out for you? Has his guidance helped you?"

I nod. "Yes. It has. I think I know why he's here, too. It's because I have been unable to speak to my sister since I've been in this place."

"Well then, what's the issue?"

I angle my lips. "Do you think I'm mad?"

Sofia breaks into hysterics. "You're asking *me* if I think you're mad?"

I wave away her laughter.

"I don't think you're mad. I just think you've used whatever it took to get through this ordeal."

Pushing her palms against the floor, Sofia plants a kiss on my forehead. She tells me that she is heading to bed.

A few minutes later, I gain the energy to head back to my room. A middle-aged Asian man, Gurpreet, hovers close to my door. We've only spoken a few times in this place. He's softly-spoken, and incredibly polite. He waves as I get close.

"Thanks for saving me earlier, Andrew," he says. "I owe you. I'd be blind if it wasn't for you."

So it was *him.* I shake his dangling hand.

He is just about to turn, to head to bed, when I pull him back. "Duncan said you offended his mum?"

Gurpreet's eyebrows meet in the middle. He pulls back his head. "His mum? Andrew, I would never say anything bad about anyone's mum. Our mothers bring us into this world. They look after us. They nurture us. They protect us. Offending somebody's mother goes against all of my values. Please tell me that you believe me."

I examine his eyes. "I believe you," I say.

******

It must be the middle of the night when my eyes flip open, for the hall is completely soundless, and in every direction I turn I'm surrounded by darkness.

Jerking my body straight, I use my wet arm to

wipe a thin layer of cold, salty sweat from my forehead. I'm reminded of my university days, when I frequently dried my glistening, showered body with a damp towel. My legs and arms are numb, like it is the morning after an intense workout.

A dream. I had one of my dreams again.

I can barely see six feet in front of me, but I can make out the gap of about seven inches where the door is ajar. The darkness outside reminds me of the deep ocean, where you have no idea what lurks beneath the crashing waves. Gripping the bed sheets, I commit to remaining still, just for a few seconds. The silence brings attention to my breathing; it is as though I am on a ventilator.

What was that?

I allow myself a smirk as my back connects with the bed. I push away the bed sheet to allow my body to cool down. I went through a paranoid phase back home, when I was forever alert to sounds downstairs in the middle of the night. Every night of the week I was convinced that an intruder lingered downstairs, rummaging through my private possessions, biding their time to creep up the stairs and pounce. And every morning I woke to an untouched, lonely house. At the end of the paranoid phase, I concluded that buildings just happen to make noises.

Lowering my eyelids, I place my hands against my belly. My hands rise, pause, and then begin a gradual, conscious descent. I don't try to force myself to sleep, because that just makes the resistance stronger, like trying to push away unwanted thoughts. It needs to come naturally. My mind just needs to focus, to not drift. I merely need to calm my rambling thoughts. My smile expands as the ascent and descent of my hands slows.

Maybe I *should* shut that door?

After all, I am sure I heard a noise outside and whilst buildings do make noises, I live alone at home and here I am surrounded by contestants who want to win this thing. Besides, I don't really know who they are and I'm not too keen on some of them and so is it more vigilant to shut the door. But then if I shut the door then I'm going to be terrified about getting trapped inside, and that is a real fear because I was trapped inside before and I couldn't get out and...

And I decide to tell my thoughts to shut the *fuck* up, and to keep the door open, just a little bit.

Maybe seconds pass, or maybe it is minutes, but my thoughts begin to tire and my eyelids feel like they are hooked to lead weights and...

My eyes snap open, and they stare straight into the dull eyes of another man.

A knee presses down against my ribcage with such force it feels like the barrel of a gun. I push the chest with both hands, but my arms merely shake, and I sense them weakening. I lunge for his neck, but it moves a few inches away. Out of reach. Two thumbs dig into my windpipe. The grip around my neck tightens. I throw frantic, upward punches, but it's like I'm treading water. My fists rebound from the chest, from the midriff. My legs stop kicking. My arms go limp. I stare up.

Duncan's frenzied smile angles at one corner. Spittle dangles from his foaming lips.

Reality sinks in. I stop fighting. Finally, after all this effort, my racing mind quietens. I look down at the hall, at the bedroom, as though I am observing it from space. My thinking becomes ordered; it becomes logical. This isn't the way I wanted to go. Nobody will know what happened to me, that I was murdered by a savage killer in the middle of the night whilst the rest of the world was sleeping. I knew I was going to die at some point, but I didn't want to be murdered in the middle of the night by this depraved bastard.

I keep staring into the whites of Duncan's eyes. He is going to take my life, but I'm not going to give him the satisfaction and pleasure of seeing me squirm and beg for mercy.

And then the bulging whites of his eyes shrink. They move away. The grip of his hands around my neck loosens. Strength returns to my arms and legs. Pressing my flat hands down against the bed, I straighten my back and then snap a left hook and then a straight right against his lip. Blood splatters from his mouth and onto my cheek. I pull back my head and slam it against his nose.

There are three of us in the room now, of course. I don't need to take a second look to know that the third man is TJ. The muscle in his right arm bulges. His choke hold appears unbreakable. He holds my gaze for just a millisecond, before nodding his head. The snap of Duncan's neck echoes around the room.

TJ puts a finger to his lips before dragging Duncan out of the room. I tiptoe behind him. He stops in the middle of the hall. Meticulously, he straightens Duncan's arms by his side and uses his two middle fingers to close his eyelids.

And then, soundlessly, without even gesturing to me, he disappears back to the comfort of his bedroom.

I'm aware that my heart is pounding against my chest, and that my thoughts are so rampant none of them can possibly make any sense. With a deep outward breath, I return to my room.

And this time, I decide to close my door.

DAY SIX

Contestants eliminated: 41
Contestants remaining: 9

Morning

With one day left, we are down to nine contestants. I have no idea how many of us will be left tomorrow. If I wake up in two days then I will have won the show, a free man living in a different country with no restrictions on my freedom. If I don't wake up in two days then it will be because I'm dead.

I won't be the first man from my family to die before their time. The last time I saw my dad alive was seven years ago.

The Saturday afternoon sunlight was fading. I rang the doorbell and then peered through the gap in the curtain. He lived alone by this time. I used my spare key to let myself in. I brushed aside the pile of yellowing letters on the doormat. I rubbed my hands together; outside a layer of snow coated the pavements, but inside it felt like the heating hadn't been turned on for days. I shouted my dad's name. Silence. I opened and closed doors. Nothing. I was just about to leave when I spotted him in the corner of the living room, his back pressed against the cold radiator, spaghetti arms hugging his bony knees. An empty vodka bottle lay by his feet. I sat down next to him.

"Where's the furniture, Dad?"

Dad sniffed. "Had to sell it."

I adjusted my backside on the hard, dusty floor. "Even the carpet? Who would want to buy your carpet?"

He shrugged his skeletal shoulders. He turned to me, fixing me with watery eyes. "She's finally beaten me, son."

I sighed. Steam emitted from my lips. "What do you think came first, Dad?"

His stare intensified. "What the fuck are you talking about?"

I clicked my wrists. "You blame Mum for everything, don't you? But why do you think she became sick? Was she sick before you started drinking and treating her that way?"

Dad stared absentmindedly into space. His lips trembled. A tear trickled down his cheek. "I'm sorry, son," he said.

I embraced my dad before pushing my hands against the floor and leaving his grotty, decaying home for the last time.

They call the first four contestants to shower, leaving five of us. Sofia and TJ sit opposite me. I follow Sofia's eyes as she scans the room, counting heads. "Nine?"

I shrug my shoulders.

Lines appear across her forehead. She crinkles her nose. "Where's Duncan?"

TJ rotates his head. Devoid of any hint of expression, the guy appears genuinely nonplussed. Only hours ago, in the early hours of the morning, he snapped another man's neck, killing him with his bare hands. Admittedly, it couldn't have happened to a more deserving bloke. But *still.* I expected his eyes to flicker with nerves, with guilt. I envisaged his hands trembling, like he'd opted for a large Costa coffee instead of his usual medium. But the guy looks exactly the same as he did last night. He thumbs his chin, like Plato contemplating the meaning of life. "Beats me," he says. "Maybe he struggled to get out of bed this morning?"

We barely have time to settle after our showers when the middle door swings open. Rebecca bounces into the hall like Tigger the fucking tiger after a morning snorting a line of coke. I release an audible moan. Shoot me now (no, I don't *mean* it!). Rubbing the underside of our eyes, all nine of us move to the centre of the room.

With her hands cupping her slender hips, Rebecca thrusts her left leg forward. Her face appears solemn, or at least what she imagines a solemn face looks like. "It is with great regret that I have some tragic news to share with you. We had a death in the night. Unfortunately, Duncan passed away."

"That's great news!" Gurpreet shouts, pumping his fist.

Quite a few of us smirk. "How did he die?" Sofia asks.

Without a trace of humour, Rebecca says that he passed of natural causes.

TJ thrusts forward his head. "I'm no medical expert, Rebecca. But is it usual for a guy in his thirties to die of natural causes? He's not the queen, for fuck's sake."

I wipe the smile from my face. Does TJ *want* them to probe further? TJ is playing with fire. He is dicing with death. But then, he has reached the same conclusion as me: they know exactly what happened to Duncan; they've just decided to do nothing about it.

Rebecca grins through gritted teeth. "Like you said, TJ; you are no medical expert, and so it is probably best you keep your opinions to yourself. The good news is that I am now in a position to announce that Duncan was the plant. So you don't need to trouble your pretty little heads working out who it is any longer."

"Every cloud has a silver lining, eh, Rebecca?" TJ says.

"Quite."

Rebecca releases a sigh. She has got the technicalities out of the way (like running through the evacuation procedures at the beginning of a meeting) and now she's ready to get onto the real business of the day. She stretches out her arms, gathering some energy.

"I've been told that there are still too many of you left for day six."

"Who told you?" I ask.

"I beg your pardon?"

"Somebody told you there are too many of us. I'm just wondering who? Who are your puppeteers, Rebecca?"

Rebecca pouts her lips. "It's just an *expression*, sweetheart. Gosh, I do need to be careful with my choice of words, don't I? You are so easily offended, aren't you?" She holds my eye until I look away. "Right. I have a question for you. Don't you think children spend too much time indoors these days? Parents just don't seem to appreciate the benefits of unsupervised outdoor play-"

"You'd probably let your kids play with traffic," TJ says.

Rebecca either doesn't hear him, or she chooses to ignore him. "I mean, it can't be healthy, can it, glued to their electronic devices all day? The human body craves natural sunlight. And if you are stuck indoors all day then that environment becomes your comfort zone, don't you think? I love to watch children playing-"

"Fucking pervert."

A flicker of a smile appears on Rebecca's lips. "Quite. Anyway, I was reminded of this when you – those of you who managed to stay alive – came back yesterday afternoon after your little adventure outdoors. You were like dogs – mongrels - let off the lead free to roam in the park. All of you came back rosy cheeked and bushy tailed-"

"I came back even more morbidly depressed than usual," I say, raising my voice higher than I intended. I'm frustrated by the cackle that I can't keep under control. "It might have something to do with the fact my best friend got shot in the head."

Seriously, though, her observation that we came back rosy cheeked and bushy tailed alone was enough to aggravate my temper. We came back like the walking dead. Even TJ tempered his boisterousness.

Rebecca purses her lips. She looks at me sympathetically, like I'd just been told my dog got run over by a Tesco delivery van. "I appreciate that you two were close, Andrew. From my perspective, it was simply wonderful to watch how your relationship blossomed. If I had my choice, it wouldn't have been Dylan who was eliminated yesterday..."

Rebecca's gaze wanders around the room. At this point I may be imagining things, but it felt like she kept eye contact with both Sofia and TJ for a moment too long.

"There's no need for any of us to die, Rebecca..."

Rebecca puts her middle finger to her lips. Perhaps I am too infuriated to keep talking. Either way, she manages to silence me. "Are you familiar with the serenity prayer, Andrew?"

"The serenity prayer? Yes, the AA thing. It-"

"God gave me the serenity to accept the things I cannot change, the courage to change the things I can, and the wisdom to know the difference."

Sofia takes a step forward. Colour rises to her cheeks. "Dare I ask what your point is, Rebecca?"

"The point is that Andrew – bless his little cotton socks – is worrying about the things that aren't going to change, darling. And you simply don't have enough energy left in the tank to do that. Whether he likes it or not, contestants will be eliminated. It's the name of the game. What you need to worry about is making sure that you aren't one of them."

Rebecca pauses to give us opportunity to say something. When we don't, she turns to me. "We can provide details of excellent bereavement counsellors who will be able to give you all the support you require. Of course, this is all dependent on whether you make it out of here alive. If you do survive, I want you to know that we will be here for you. Is that okay, darling?"

"Fuck off."

It crosses my mind (and not for the first time) that Rebecca might be a masochist. It isn't much of a stretch to imagine her in leather boots holding a whip in her hand. Knowing Dylan's sexual urges, he probably imagined this scenario, too. I allow myself a smile; Dylan would have found the funny side.

Rebecca stifles a yawn. "Enough of these ghastly pleasantries; it is time for the next game. You may have gathered from my introduction that today's game will also be played outdoors. I'm delighted to say that it is a wonderful day for it."

Our host turns to a guard pushing the trolley cloaked with the luxurious white tablecloth. "Impeccable timing, young man, impeccable timing. You would make an excellent stalker, appearing out of nowhere at just the right time."

We step forward to take a closer look. Three days ago I gasped when Rebecca pulled a gun from her handbag. Now it's as though she's merely picked up a security pass to enter an office building.

"I will keep the rules of the game straightforward. I find that works with you simpletons. Are you ready?"

I, for one, nod my head.

"You will each be given a gun. As you can imagine, these aren't toy guns from kindergarten. These guns are real-"

"No shit," someone shouts.

"Each gun has six bullets. You cannot obtain any more bullets. The doors will open and you *must* go outside and then vacate the vicinity. Throughout the duration of the game, you cannot under any circumstances return to the hall. If you do so then you will be eliminated. There will be a twenty second gap between each contestant leaving the hall. Once all of the contestants have vacated the hall, the countdown will officially start. The game will last for sixty minutes. Within that sixty minutes you must shoot at least one other contestant. You *can* shoot more than one other contestant, but it is surplus to requirements. If you don't shoot at least one other contestant then you will be eliminated from the contest. Understood?"

We turn to TJ's raised hand; a schoolboy asking if he can go to the toilet. "What if nobody shoots anybody?"

Rebecca rolls her eyes. "You really are a stupid boy, aren't you, TJ? If no contestant shoots any other contestant, then the game is over. You all lose. Losers."

"Is that fair?" TJ asks.

"Do I care if it is fair? What do you think this is: a kids' sports day? You don't get a certificate just for taking part."

With the nod of Rebecca's head, we all queue in an orderly line to collect a gun from the trolley. The guards stand to attention with their guns raised. Maybe they worry that one of the contestants could go berserk and start shooting everyone? To be fair, I had thought about doing so myself.

The metal feels cold against my warm hand. I can't help but swagger away from the trolley, feeling like a gangster with a gun in my hand.

Unprompted, I embrace each contestant in turn. I wish each of them good luck. Of course, I squeeze Sofia just that little bit tighter. I inhale the scent of her glorious hair. I brush my lips against her cheek.

Pulling away, I start to ask Rebecca a question – surely we must *all* be thinking this? – but she raises her hand to silence me. "One other thing," Rebecca says, "you *can* shoot anyone who isn't one of the other eight remaining contestants, but it won't count and so you'd only be wasting your bullets."

What does *that* mean?

I begin asking Rebecca, but the doors to the outside world slide open. Rebecca calls my name. I am the first contestant to leave the hall. Within seconds, I stand outside, ready to shoot or be shot, to kill or be killed...

******

Shielding my eyes with the back of my hand, my first thought is: Rebecca was right – it is a wonderful day for it. This is bucket and spades weather.

Is there such a thing as a wonderful day for a shootout?

The sun seeps through the cracks in the spiralling trees. Within seconds, a film of sweat covers my forehead. From the heat? Or the adrenaline? Fleetingly, it crosses my mind that I could stand a few feet from the door and shoot an unsuspecting contestant as they leave the hall. My conscience doesn't reject the concept. I reject the concept because Rebecca instructed us to leave the vicinity. They'll eliminate me from the contest if I shoot a contestant before they leave.

These twenty seconds are an advantage; I just don't know how to use them. Was it chance that she chose me first, or did I earn it from my previous performances? They really have no idea that Dylan found me in the last game. They have no idea he forfeited his own life for mine. If they did then I'd already be dead.

The aim of yesterday's game was to hide and not get found. Well, that didn't work out too well for me, did it? This game has added complexities. I need to address a second issue (you could call it the great big fucking elephant in the room) – I don't just need to find somebody, I need to shoot them, too. I am both the hider and the seeker, a boxer who needs to hit and not get hit. Not surprisingly, I've never shot anybody before. I struggle to piss straight in a urinal; what makes me think that I'm going to be able to shoot someone? But what about the other contestants in this place? Why were they chosen for the show? I still don't really know who they are, or what connects us. What are *their* dark secrets? Maybe they have shot and killed people? Maybe they were killers before they came into this place? Maybe I'm surrounded by killers?

Lifting my legs high, I navigate through the overgrown grass and stand at the crossroads; the car park stretches out in front of me. Dismissing the apartments as a viable option, I stretch my legs and head towards the funfair. Instinctively, I step over dark, unrecognisable items on the floor. My pace increases as I move in the direction of the bumper cars. The canopy provides some shelter; the dark shadow will hopefully hide me. I crouch down. My hand brushes a car's rubber trim. My knee digs into the dusty, plastic yellow frame. I am hidden, and yet – *still* - I have a good view of the fairground forecourt.

I can shoot without getting shot.

What are my motives for staying alive? I no longer know if I want to be deported to a foreign land with no restrictions. I long to see Mum, though. I want to hear her say my name. Andy. I'm desperate to hear Frances's voice, too. But it is more than that, now. I owe it to Dylan to at least do everything I possibly can to stay alive. Otherwise his wonderful gesture will be futile.

Without thinking, I check my wrist. They didn't *give* us watches. Psychologically, that is going to play with our minds. None of us have any idea of the time. We won't know if we have thirty minutes left in the game, or thirty seconds. Of the two, it is best to opt for thirty seconds, just in case. The others won't want to take any chances – they'll want to shoot, and kill, early. I need to act quickly, whilst remaining in control. Of course, this is easier said than done.

Adjusting my position so that my body doesn't cramp, I imagine that I am a sniper hidden in a grotty, darkened hotel room, with my gun pointing through a tiny window, biding my time, ready to strike at the exact right moment. My target is about 200 metres away, navigating past innocent civilians. If I pull the trigger a millisecond too early or a millisecond too late then I could blow a child's head off.

I slap my forehead with the back of my hand. Stop daydreaming. Stop living in a fantasy land. I am not a sniper; I can't shoot anybody from here. I have no idea if I can shoot a human life from two metres, let alone two hundred. I need to work out my strategy. What do I do if I spot a contestant on the forecourt? I need to get close to them, without them spotting me. I can do it slowly and subtly, or I can charge them, taking them by surprise.

I grip the gun in my right hand. I'm shocked how much it shakes. I swear I can hear my heart thumping. I try to slow my breathing, try to calm my nerves.

My feet nearly leave the ground when the bumper cars around me start moving.

******

What the hell is going on?

How did the contestants reach the bumper cars before me when I was the first one released from the hall? Did I dawdle for that long? Sliding both my knees backwards, I lie flat on my stomach and stretch my arms out in front of me, gripping the gun with both hands. Daring to flip one eye open, and then the other, my jaw drops almost to the floor.

You can shoot anyone who isn't one of the nine remaining contestants, but it won't count and so you'd only be wasting your bullets.

My scrambled brain knew something didn't make sense with this instruction. I have no idea who drives the cars, but it sure as hell isn't one of the other remaining eight contestants.

I count three heads. Two men and one woman. Their grins are wide. They drive in haphazard circles. One hand rests on the steering wheel. The other perches on the passenger seat. I eye their spare hand.

They don't have guns.

I know who they are. The realisation hits me like a slap to the face.

They fled from the hall – and the game – two days ago. They fled with gleeful smiles (and barely a backwards glance) and out through the open door. Minutes later it ended in tragedy. We all heard the gunshots. They lined them up outside and shot them in the head.

We *did* hear the gunshot, didn't we?

If we didn't, then I must be losing my mind.

If we did, then these people must be ghosts.

I know what happened. I didn't sleep well that night. I was certain I heard something in the middle of the night. I conned myself into believing I imagined it. I know what I heard. It was a helicopter, gaining bluster as it rose from the ground.

I did see a face through the glass window in the middle of the night. I imagined Jake. I *didn't* imagine that face.

More than three fled that morning, though. Are there any more of them out there, trying to kill me?

One of the men halts his car about six feet away from me. I know him. I don't like him, though. It is the man who dared to mock my lack of drinking. I threatened to glass him. There is no love lost between us.

He taps the steering wheel with his thumb. The other two follow suit, parking in an adjacent straight line, with just about enough space to slide a hand between the bumpers. Their eyes look like they are hanging from the sockets. Their broad grins are hysterical. The woman is foaming at the mouth, like a dog locked in a car on a hot day. They glance at each other. They exchange nods. They slam their feet on the pedals. The cars accelerate towards me.

Their cars slam against the car I'm hid behind. The car lifts off the floor and then slams down, almost toppling over. I peek over the wobbling car, with my gun at the ready. Should I shoot them? There are three of them, and I only have six bullets. What if I miss? Killing them won't save my life. I still need to shoot a remaining contestant.

I jump to my feet. I tiptoe on the balls of my feet, like I'm walking on hot coals. Reversing their cars, they grind to a halt. The bumper cars head towards me.

They want to snap my legs. They want to break me in half. They want me dead. Turning my back, I sprint towards the forecourt. I make about three or four steps. A bumper clips the heel of my shoe, sending me flying. My flattened hands break my fall. My lips kiss the dusty, filthy floor. I bite my lip. I cough and splutter as blood seeps down my throat. Daring to glance over my shoulder, I'm met by snarling, laughing faces, like rogue clowns at the circus.

The one I threatened (when I had my mates to back me up) pulls himself out of the car. He is bulkier than I remember. His hands are like shovels. I raise my arm too late. Lifting his knee, he pushes the sole of his shoe into the side of my face. "Get to your feet," he says.

Pulling myself up, my rubbery legs feel like I've just completed a marathon. Three of them face me, but my glazed eyes see at least five or six. I focus on the widest one. Snarling, he glances at my gun, still gripped in my right hand. "Throw the gun on the floor. Fight me like a real man. Just you and me, now your mates aren't here to help you."

Fuck this. I'm going to shoot all three of them. I raise the gun. My right hand trembles. If I shoot them then I waste at least three bullets. I'd sign my own death warrant. I drop the gun. It clatters and bounces on the hard floor. I sweep it along the floor with the underside of my shoe, making sure it is closer to me than to them. The three of them laugh hysterically.

What is wrong with them? Spittle flecks their yellowed teeth. They foam at the mouth. They aren't normal. They've drugged them, haven't they? The three ex-contestants who are out to kill me are all high on drugs.

I lunge at my opponent, swinging with my right fist. I punch thin air. His fists connects with my midriff. Losing my breath, I drop to my knee. Tugging my head down, his knee connects with my jaw. I spit out a mouthful of warm, claret blood. The sound of laughter rings in my ears. Kim's image invades my mind. They are playground bullies mocking and taunting their victim. He pulls back with his left fist, like a sling. It is the knockout blow.

I see it coming. I block the blow with my right hand. I twist his wrist. The man releases a yelp. I grip his throat with my outstretched left hand. His eyes widen as I thrust my face towards his cheek. My teeth dig into the skin, a Rottweiler attacking an intruder. I spit out a mouthful of bloodied flesh. The man collapses to the floor in a squealing, pitiful ball.

I turn to the other two with open hands. They eye the raw meat hanging from my teeth. "Fancy becoming dessert?" I ask.

They turn and flee.

Swiping the gun up from the floor, I vacate the track. Psychologically, I feel myself grow with every step. My shoulders widen. I look down on the rest of the planet. I spot a couple of other contestants in the forecourt – the real contestants – and yet they are just outlines on a map. I jog diagonally away from them.

I know I still have six bullets left, but I have no

idea how many seconds. How much time did I waste fighting off the former contestants? I no longer have any idea where I'm heading. Right now my sole objective is to stay away from imminent danger. And then, at the right moment, I need to *become* the danger.

Finding shelter, I bend at the waist, seeking to regain my breath. When my world stops spinning, I'm overcome by the darkness that surrounds me in every direction. My eyes are open, and yet everywhere there is blackness. I rub my hand against the side of my head, half expecting it to be leaking. Was I shot on my escape from the bumper cars? Maybe this is what death really is – just eternal nothingness.

I stretch out one arm. My hand slides against something resembling a metal bar. Catching a glimmer of light through a crack on the floor, I begin to gain my bearings.

With a sigh of what could possibly be relief, I realise that I am in the ghost train.

Unlike with the bumper cars, I don't jump when the train starts moving, rattling and shaking on the track. This time I expect the unexpected. I know eight contestants are out there, intent on taking a life.

Andrew, Andrew, Andrew...the name of the game isn't just to hide. I need to move. Time is passing. I won't shoot anyone hidden away in here. I either need to get out of the ghost train or (at the very least) get close to the exit so that I can peer outside and hunt down a passing target.

My body shudders at the sound of gunshot outside. Six bullets. For all I know, there could be seven dead bodies lying on the forecourt outside, or there could be none. Glancing up, I spot slivers of sunlight through the cracks in the ceiling.

My hand grazes against a nettle or a bramble. It wouldn't surprise me if I'm surrounded by rats scurrying around in the darkness. Did someone light a match? I glance around. If somebody *did* light a match, then this wooden hellhole could erupt in flames within seconds.

Where *was* that?

I jump back a couple of feet. A lit face appears just inches from my face. A tongue dangles from the mouth. The lips curl upwards, like the Joker. "Surprise!"

It is one of the drugged-up gang. How many left that day? How many of them are out there? He puckers his lips. "Give me a kiss, handsome!" Dazed, the man pulls back his head and then butts me on the nose. Two hands grip my neck. He squeezes my windpipe. "Will you be going up or down? Heaven, or hell?"

I take hold of his wrists. His vice-like grip tightens. The man arches his head to the side, like he is examining a piece of art. Leaning back, I raise my knee and push out with my foot. I connect with his midriff. The man – whoever or whatever it is – releases his grip. He stumbles backwards. I think he is bent over in pain, but no – he is bent over with laughter. My left fist connects with the side of his head. His legs buckle at the knees. He topples over onto the track. My eyes widen as the ghost train rattles around the corner. The train edges closer. The man remains motionless. Doesn't he see it coming? Or does he just not care? The train connects with his skull, pushing him off the track. I raise my gun – just to be ready – but the man pulls his legs to his waist and curls into a rocking ball. Prizing the match from his finger, I blow out the flame.

I think about putting him out of his misery, like a bird with a broken wing, but then I don't want to waste my bullet.

Blowing air from my mouth, I take a forward step, a step closer to getting off this goddamn ride. My foot doesn't reach the floor, though. A hand smothers my open mouth and jerks me backwards. I swipe behind me with my elbow, but I don't connect. I stab back with my foot, hitting a shin. The man grimaces, but the hold on my mouth tightens. Digging my teeth into the hand, I taste acidic blood and then raw flesh, but *still* the grip tightens. The other hand smothers my nose. I can't breathe. I'm going to suffocate. My body weakens. My head lightens. Drowsiness kicks in.

Running out of options, I pull my head backwards like a goat, butting the man's lips. Just for a millisecond, the hold loosens. Reaching down, I grab a handful of balls and I clench my fist. This time, the screams are not from a sound system. He is a wounded animal. Twisting around, my knuckle connects with this jaw. Through the darkness, I can just about see phlegm escape from the man's swollen mouth. Grabbing the neck, I pull the man to the floor. There is a dull wince as I dig my heel into his face.

I could snap his neck, just like TJ did with Duncan's. I could pummel his bloodied face with the underside of my shoe. I could make him beg for mercy. I don't. I leave his wounded body in a pitiful heap on the floor.

Time is running out. I need to stop hiding, and

start hunting. The light outside is blinding. It is like I've escaped from a lifetime trapped in the basement. Heat burns my cheeks and sweat prickles my skin. Glancing around, it takes a few seconds for my world to stop spinning. I can only see Sofia. Wandering around the forecourt with her gun raised in front of her; she's utterly disorientated. Sensing my movements, or perhaps noticing my looming shadow, she turns to me, ready to shoot. Realising it is me, a friend and not an enemy, she lowers the gun. She releases a defeated sigh. A smile flickers on her ruby lips.

Maybe she *does* have feelings for me?

We glance to the cloudless sky when we hear the announcement.

"Contestants, you have sixty seconds remaining. If you do not shoot one of the remaining contestants within this time then you will be eliminated."

Sofia's lithe body deflates. The anguished lines disappear from her forehead. The colour seeps from her cheeks. She is the epitome of beauty. She drops her gun to the floor.

What do you do when you are told you have sixty seconds left to live?

She seems content to die. She was probably ready to die before she entered the show. Accepting her fate, Sofia holds out her arms, seemingly seeking one final hug. I am privileged that this beautiful, wonderful woman longs to spend her last few seconds alive embracing me.

I take a few steps towards her, so that I am close enough to inhale her sensual fragrance.

And then, raising my gun, I pull the trigger and shoot her.

******

Falling to one knee, Sofia's unblinking eyes never leave mine. Her lower lip quivers and her eyes water. I can almost read the thoughts spiralling within her mind. She is recalling the brief moments we spent together, the late-night chats we shared. How many people in this world did she tell that her mother was dead? How many people in this world did she trust enough to do that?

Rebecca said that contestants get eliminated. It is the nature of the game.

"You decided to save yourself?" she asks. "I thought you cared about me?"

The words come out in a dull monotone. She dropped her gun when she spotted me. I chose to keep my gun raised. I decided to use one of my six bullets. She decided not to.

If anything, there is acceptance that she was right about human nature all along, that she was right to be cynical, to latch onto the conspiracies.

Lines appear around her eyes as I walk towards her. She doesn't want me anywhere near her, not now I've made my choice. My knee digs into the unforgiving forecourt. I pick up the gun. Sofia's eyes narrow. She clenches her fist.

"Open your hand," I say.

Her look is quizzical.

"Take the gun," I say.

Sofia shakes her head. "Go away. Leave me alone. Leave me to die."

I untangle her fingers. "Take the gun. I need you to shoot me. Just shoot me in the arm or the shoulder or the leg. Anywhere that won't kill me."

Her eyes fix on me now. The tendons in her neck tense. "Maybe I *want* to fucking kill you, you Judas bastard."

"That's your choice," I say.

She appears bewildered. I take her chin between my finger and my thumb. "I shot you in the arm, Sofia. Shoot me. I don't know if this is going to work, but it is our only chance."

Sofia's eyes widen as she takes in the damp red patch on her bicep. The expectation that she was about to die had overwhelmed any physical pain; she hadn't even considered what and where the pain emitted from.

"Contestants, you have ten seconds remaining."

I close my eyes and clench my teeth. I leave my fate in Sofia's hands. I start counting down from ten.

10.

9.

8.

7.

I release a dull moan as the sound of gunshot fills the air.

******

Exchanging confused shrugs, the guards clearly don't know what to do with us. The narrowed eyes indicate that they are contemplating shooting both of us. It seems a viable option.

"It's like getting your haircut, gentlemen," I say, holding my thigh. "There is nothing you can do if you cut too much off. But if you play it sensible then you can always come back and cut it shorter. What do you say?"

Of course, they don't *say* anything. I don't know if they understand my point. They clearly don't like the idea of explaining to Rebecca that they shot two contestants who didn't break the rules, though. They aren't going to be able to bring us back to life, but they'll happily shoot us in the head if Rebecca gives them the green light to do so.

"Good decision," I say, as they take us by the arm and lead us back to the hall.

I break into a furious sweat as the doors slam behind us. Maybe it was colder outside than I realised. It is either that or the bullet lodged in my thigh making me sweat. I decide to bark before I'm bitten. "How come those lunatics were out there? They left the contest. You shot them."

Rebecca peruses me through half-open eyes. "You heard gunshot, Andrew. You assumed we shot them." She turns to Sofia. "I thought that you, with your wild theories, would have been suspicious."

Holding her arm, Sofia merely whimpers.

"We gave them a choice. We offered them a hundred grand if they stayed in the show, and stayed alive. A couple left in the helicopter. I believe you heard it leave the other night, Andrew? Most stayed. A couple of them are still out there. We'll pay them, don't worry."

Rebecca's lips curl as she eyes the bullet wounds, as she eyes the seeping, spreading blood. "Is this a coincidence, or are you both horrendous shots?"

Sofia shrugs her slight shoulders.

Rebecca turns to the guards. "Why are they both alive?"

They exchange glances. I spot their lips moving. Are they tempted to speak?

They stay silent.

"This outcome isn't the idea of the game," Rebecca says.

Despite the throbbing pain, I muster some bravado. "I've begun to see you as something of a mentor, Rebecca. I absorb and I act on what you say. I recall that tall, blonde girl. Was her name Melanie? Regardless, tragically she is recently deceased, and I try not to speak ill of the dead. Anyway, when that dead little slut cut herself to try and get me shot, you said that she demonstrated initiative. And so, I've tried to follow her exemplary example. Can you please remind me of the rules of the game, Rebecca?"

Rebecca outlines her lips with the tip of her tongue. Clearly, she is thinking. I do some thinking of my own. I decide that I should tone down my bravado so that I don't piss her off too much. Our fate is still in her hands. It is them, and not us, who now hold the guns.

"You were supposed to eliminate another contestant," she says.

I go to speak, but Sofia gets in there before me. "You said that we had to shoot a contestant, not that we had to kill them..."

Rebecca waves a dismissive hand. "That was an oversight-"

"We took a risk. We used some initiative. We shot each other."

Rebecca turns her back to us. She paces up and down the hall. Unexpectedly, she turns to one of the guards. Is she seeking his input? Does she give a damn what they think? The guard puts his hand to his ear, and then he nods his head.

"Frankly, Andrew, I think you have taken the proverbial out of me. However, I'm always one for giving the benefit of the doubt. I view myself a reasonable person in an unreasonable world..."

"I couldn't agree more," I say, hopefully limiting the sarcasm.

"The underlying fact is that the game eliminated six contestants, regardless of this – how shall I put this diplomatically? – this little fiasco. We still have a day left. If we keep you in the show then we still have three remaining contestants. Ideally we'd like to begin the final day with two of you remaining. And so, as I said, we've decided to give you the benefit of the doubt."

"Sounds like the right decision," I say, grimacing. "After all, showbiz comes first, doesn't it?"

"Three contestants?" Sofia asks. "How does that make sense? I don't understand-"

"I killed six," TJ says, a grin spreading from cheek to cheek. I notice a graze on one of his cheeks.

Was he loitering, waiting to pounce at the optimum moment? I recall Rebecca said that one of the guards possessed the credentials to make a first-class stalker. Maybe TJ does, too.

"You only needed to shoot one," Sofia says. Her voice is deadpan. She isn't asking a question.

TJ holds his hands up. "I get that. But I took a life early and-"

"Wasn't it needless?" Sofia asks. "You may as well have killed innocent citizens?"

Sofia has popped TJ's bubble. Colour rises to his cheeks. "The guards didn't pull me out of the game. I was a sitting target. I was there to be shot. I had to shoot or-"

"Be shot," I say.

I turn to Sofia. "He had no choice."

Her eyes widen. She looks to TJ. "It's good to have you alive," she says.

I crack a smile. "So you shot six people, TJ. You didn't waste a single bullet."

"What can I say? I'm like Dirty Harry."

A door flings open at the back of the hall. Open-mouthed, I take a second look. It isn't the middle door, or the right door. It is the left door; it is the door that has previously been unopened.

"Right," Rebecca says. "Can you please make your way to the back of the hall? Our medical team await you."

******

The guards usher us through the third door. They've transformed the room, which is maybe fifteen feet or so squared, into a first aid room. The room reminds me of a budget hotel chain room; it is clean and clinical and devoid of any personality.

Three women in medical gowns guide each of us to a bed. With impeccable manners, they ask us to please undress to our waists. Displaying white smiles, they pull across plastic curtains, dividing us into our own cubicles.

My nurse, or doctor, or whatever she is, massages my burning thigh with long, nimble fingers. With a deep, soothing voice, she tells me that I've been such a brave boy. She warns me that this might hurt just a little.

Someone screams loudly. It takes me a moment to realise that I am that somebody.

It is the last thing I remember before drifting off into a deep, deep sleep.

******

Evening

"Ooh, so the sleeping beauty has awoken."

The words sound muffled, like I have earphones on. The words sound affectionate, though, like they emit from a friend and not a foe. I try to pull my chin from my chest. What the hell is going on? It feels like a weighted fishing line is hooked to my lip.

"Where am I? What have you done with me?"

The high-pitched female laughter is friendly. "What have we done with you? Oh you are funny, sweetheart. We haven't done *anything* with you. You are still in the game show. You haven't gone anywhere. We're just here to do your hair and makeup. And I do hope you'll agree that we have done an absolutely *marvellous* job?"

The thirty-something woman's straight, peroxide blonde hair contrasts delightfully with her flawless caramel skin. Beaming an electric smile, she uses a tissue to wipe dribble from the side of my mouth; I'm a toddler eating his first solid meal. The Indian woman to my right is younger, probably in her early to mid-twenties. Silky black hair falls just above her plump, upturned bottom. They tell me that everything is fine, but something *must* be wrong because - as far as I can tell - I don't have an uncontrollable erection.

"Am I in heaven?" I ask.

Despite the clouds in my mind, I *am* joking. Luckily, they pick up on my hilarity, for they throw back their heads, displaying their molars. My body is numb, like you could stab a needle in my thigh and I wouldn't flinch. Hold on. That is probably what happened to me.

"Where is the doctor? The nurse?"

The two women continue laughing. The Indian woman brushes her fingertips down my cheek. "She fixed your leg," she says.

I shake my head to try and wake up. My half-open eyes move away from the two beautiful women, to my own reflection. Where has my drab, dire black top gone? Hopefully it has been thrown in a fire. The top button of the sky-blue shirt is unbuttoned. I'm sporting a charcoal pair of slacks. I *feel* like I've woken from a coke-fuelled weekend of debauchery in Budapest, but I *look* fresher than I have all week.

"Why are you doing my hair and makeup?"

The older woman laughs. "Got to make you handsome for the audience, don't we, Andrew?"

I glance around. They've transformed the first aid room into some sort of dressing room. We are in tiny cubicles, with lopsided, wooden dividers. It's how I imagine a dingy changing room in a rundown theatre. I blink. TJ shot six contestants, didn't he? Was that today? There are three of us left. TJ and Sofia are probably here in the same room somewhere, hidden away in their own makeshift private cubicle. Rebecca said she needed two of us for the final day. One of us needs to die today.

"Audience?"

Muffled clapping drowns out my words. The

clapping intensifies, like somebody has removed the headphones. What is going on? One of the women has opened my door; the other wheels me out into the hall.

I glance at the man sat to my left. He's vaguely familiar, the type of guy I'd pass in the street and then, moments later, glance back over my shoulder. It takes me a moment to recognise him. The expensive, tailored navy suit extenuates TJ's broad, bullish shoulders. His moisturised skin glows healthily. He looks ready to take on the directors in the boardroom.

Leaning forward, I gaze further down the aisle. I gulp. If I were a romantic then I'd say butterflies flutter in my heart. As I'm not a romantic, I'll say that Sofia looks *hot.* Painted toes tease out of red heels. She crosses an impossibly long, bare leg over her smooth thigh. The black evening dress clings to the contours of her divine body; narrows at the waist and then plumps unexpectedly at the chest.

If this is indeed my time, then I'll die a happy, perverted man.

Neither Sofia nor TJ turn to me. Their eyes are fixed straight ahead, almost like they're in a trance. I follow their gaze. My eyes widen, too. The guards – or whoever else – have been busy whilst we slept. We *did* sleep, didn't we? They must have knocked us out. I recall my anguished shriek. The nurse must have plunged a needle filled with drugs into my body. They've constructed a wooden stand in the hall, converting the room into an auditorium.

Fifteen or so smiling, energetic faces perch on each row. Through the fog I estimate that there are maybe ten rows. I spot the occasional brown and black face, but predominately they are white. Squinting, I push my neck forward. The men outnumber the women maybe five to one. This is the place to be if you're a single lady on the prowl. Not that you'll find a high calibre of male. Most of the men are clad in tatty tee-shirts with messages or logos printed on the front.

"Ladies and gentlemen, my name is Jason and I'm your host for this evening's entertainment. Wow, do we have a sensational show for you tonight. We are here to interview the best of the best, the three surviving contestants..."

The audience claps and cheers. I turn to our host for this evening's entertainment. Light, blonde hair is parted floppily to one side. Faded, blue jeans fall just short of his suede shoes. His sky-blue shirt hangs loose. Turquoise eyes casually flicker.

"You – the audience – will decide which two contestants will make it through to the final day. I'm going to kick off proceedings by welcoming one of our favourites. Audience, can you please give a warm round of applause for...TJ."

******

Jason waits a few moments for the clapping to subside, before rising from his chair to shake TJ's hand. "A big well done from all of us, TJ. You are in the final three. That is truly an amazing feat."

A heavy-jawed TJ struggles to pull his eyes away from the audience. "Thank you, I guess."

"Are you surprised to get this far?"

TJ thumbs his tree-trunk thighs. When his hands reach his knees, he tangles and untangles his fingers. "Don't think so," he says. "No."

Jason's smile flickers from the side of his angled mouth. "Well, we certainly know what you're made of. It's not surprising that you're feeling confident." Jason refers to some scribbled notes. His eyes widen. "Remind me not to mess with you, TJ. It says here that you're a trained martial artist, and you have an amateur boxing record of seven wins and no defeats. I must say, you are quite the big, tough man, aren't you? You must be incredibly disciplined..."

"I am."

"Did you use any of the focus needed for the boxing ring to knock out any of your opponents in this contest?"

TJ stares absent-mindedly at the audience. A fly could disappear within his open mouth. "I guess so. I guess I did."

"Tell me. What was your proudest moment in the show?"

TJ glances to the ceiling. "It was when I stuck up for Kim." He gesticulates with his open hands, searching for the appropriate words. "You know, when we had that...that bedroom incident."

Jason lowers his hand to quieten the muffled giggles from the audience. "Between you and me, TJ, I found that scene very awkward. It was all *very* unfortunate. In all honesty though, the audience quite enjoyed the bedroom incident, as you called it..."

The giggles turn to laughter.

TJ turns away from the audience. His steely eyes fix on Jason. A film of sweat coats TJ's forehead. "Who *is* the audience? Who *are* these people?"

A gasp emits from the back of the hall. Much to their surprise, it seems TJ has asked the right questions.

Jason doesn't maintain eye contact. "We'll come to that at the right time. Don't worry about that. So why were you proud of that moment with Kim?"

"I stood up for her. The whole thing was out of order. I cracked some heads together. It had to be done."

Jason cups his chin in an upturned hand. "You really hate bullies, don't you, TJ?"

TJ doesn't miss a beat. "Yes. I do. They are the scum of the earth."

"So tell us about this mask you wear at all times, TJ?"

TJ looks at him nonplussed.

Jason leans forward in his seat. His tone is conspiring. "Let me put it more bluntly. You are a fraud, aren't you, TJ?"

TJ glances to Sofia, and then to me. His eyelids flicker. For the first time in six days on the show, he appears nervous. "What are you talking about? No offence, mate, but I have no idea what you're going on about."

Jason holds up defensive hands. "I apologise. That was quite a statement for me to make, wasn't it? I misjudged my approach. Clearly, I need to give some explanation first, to put things into context."

TJ stares at him blankly.

"What is your job, TJ?"

"My job?"

"Yes. You know, that thing you do for money. To pay the bills. To put a roof over your head."

There are a few stifled laughs from the audience. Jason glances at the culprits with a subtle warning.

TJ lowers his head. His muffled voice says that

he works in IT.

The host turns to the audience. "I'm sure you agree, that is a fine job, and something to be proud of?"

The audience shouts their approval.

"There is no reason to be bashful, TJ. That really isn't your personality. You don't just work in IT, do you? You run the IT department in a very prestigious company. In fact, the clothes you are wearing now are the clothes you wear every day when you enter the office. We've taken them straight from your wardrobe at home. You're an educated young man. Which leads me to ask a fundamental question. Why do you pretend to be such a dumbass?"

TJ shakes his head; the audience erupts with laughter. Our host pauses for a moment, deep in thought. "Sorry for my rudeness. I got carried away. But some of the contestants asked what you did for a living, and you told them you were a builder. Why have you pretended to be someone you are not?"

TJ lifts his head. He looks straight ahead. "Admittedly, I may have deliberately given a false perception at times..."

Jason turns to both of us. "How do you feel about TJ lying to you? After all, you placed your trust in him. You allowed him into your circle of trust."

Sofia's lips flutter, but no words escape.

I decide to fill the gap. "I'm sure we've all extended the truth at times. And there are worse things to lie about."

I may as well dig a hole for him to throw me in.

"There really are, aren't there, Andrew? I am glad that you've said that. We will come on to that later."

The promise – or maybe it is a threat - lingers in

the air for a few seconds.

Jason turns back to TJ. "Forgive me for pushing this, but I'm just trying to get to the bottom of why you'd lie about that, TJ. Tell me, what was your childhood like?"

TJ shoots him a look. "You think you're Freud or something? What does that have to do with anything?"

"I'm just curious. Nothing personal. Were your family poor?"

TJ wipes his brow. "I wouldn't exactly say we were poor."

"I wouldn't exactly say you were poor at all. You were far from poor, weren't you? Your dad worked hard to provide a good upbringing for you and your sisters, didn't he? And all of his children have done well. You come from a good family. So why do you pretend to be a thug, TJ?"

"I have no idea what-"

Jason interrupts him. "Were you popular in school?"

TJ shuffles in his seat. "Some kids liked me. Some kids didn't."

"I don't want to embarrass you, TJ, but I must say, you're an impressive height. I don't have a tape measure with me, but I'd say you are over six feet. Were you always tall?"

TJ shakes his head. "I had a late growth spurt, didn't I? I came back to school after the summer holidays when I was seventeen over a foot taller than when I left."

Jason eyes TJ's muscles. "You have such an impressive physique, too. I'm sure a few of the ladies here haven't failed to notice..."

A wolf whistle confirms that at least one has.

"When did you start working out?"

"When I was about eighteen."

Jason thumbs his chin. "So you were quite short until you were seventeen, and you didn't start working out until you were eighteen. And so you weren't exactly a physical specimen in school, were you? And my research team reliably inform me that you didn't develop your interest in boxing and martial arts until you were in your early twenties."

Saying nothing, TJ rubs the underside of his eyes.

We wait while Jason reads the card in his hand. He opens up his body to TJ. "Tell us about the incident in the changing rooms at school when you were twelve."

TJ straightens his back. "No."

"No?"

"No. Go fuck yourself. You'll have to shoot me before I tell you about that."

"I'm sure that can be arranged."

Jason gives TJ an apologetic look. "I think we are looking at this from the wrong angle-"

"There is only one angle to look at it."

"You look back at it with shame. I view it as a triumph. The counsellors believe this is the underlying reason you do so much to stand up to those awful bullies-"

"The counsellors talk shit..."

"They're trained professionals in their field of expertise. I appreciate that you are scared to tell the viewers here, and at home, about the incident-"

"I'm not scared of shit-"

"But they need to know, and if you don't tell them

then I will. A group of boys pulled you into the showers and they beat you up, didn't they TJ? And then, when you were lying naked and bruised on the wet, tiled floor, they proceeded to urinate all over you, and then some of them..."

TJ stands up. He casts a shadow over Jason. I suspect he could snap his body in half. "Nobody did a fucking thing to help me!" TJ shouts. "All the other boys sat on the changing room benches and didn't move a muscle. They were too scared to do anything. You know why I stick up for the victims? I'd like to think if I was one of those boys I'd have done something. I don't want to be like one of them..."

TJ's scowl vanishes when the audience applauds.

Jason edges out of his chair. Leaning forward, he massages TJ's arm. "See, I told you it wasn't such a bad thing." He turns to the audience. "We love TJ, don't we?"

A flicker of a smile crosses TJ's face; the audience shout their approval.

"You chose Fame as your reward. And you openly told the other contestants this, didn't you?"

"I did."

"You didn't tell the other contestants the real reason you chose Fame though, did you? You didn't tell the other contestants that you want your own show so you can raise awareness of the destructive impact childhood bullying can have on adults, did you?"

TJ shakes his head.

"This bad boy thing you have going on in here is all a bit of an act though, isn't it? Will you admit that for us?"

TJ stays silent.

Jason smiles warmly. "I suspect that your biggest secret, TJ, is that you are not actually such a bad guy after all. And that really isn't such an awful thing now, is it?"

TJ shrugs his wide shoulders.

Jason swivels to face the audience. "I think that wraps this interview up. One final round of applause for TJ, please."

He waits for the noise to die down. "I think we are ready to move to our second special guest. It is with great pleasure that I welcome Sofia..."

******

Jason follows the same routine with Sofia. He congratulates her on doing so well in the contest, flatters her until her cheeks burn red and then, with sharpened teeth, he leans forward for the kill.

"You really are as a mad as a bag of spanners, aren't you, Sofia?"

Jason opens his body to the audience. "*Naughty?* Who? Me? Never!"

Sofia's painted smile doesn't vanish. If anything, it widens. "I never pretended to be anything other than mad, Jason. At the earliest opportunity I literally told other contestants that I was insane. Andrew will confirm that for you."

I nod until I fret my head might fly off.

Exaggerated lines appear on Jason's forehead. "Credit where credit is due. You really did, didn't you? You were incredibly brave. I think you scared them with your brashness. They thought you might be dangerous, didn't they?"

"That wasn't my intention. But I still don't really

know whether I am dangerous. Maybe I am."

Jason rocks back and forth in his swivel chair. "You never told them that you were committed to an asylum though, did you? You kept that one quiet didn't you?"

Sofia uncrosses her legs. "That wasn't deliberate, either. It just never came up. Do you care to tell the audience when I was committed, Jason?"

Does Jason consider telling Sofia that he is the one asking the questions? He fails to maintain eye contact. "We don't seem to have that information to hand..."

"That's convenient. It was when my mother passed away. I appreciate your sympathy. Listen, I wouldn't have denied it if somebody had asked. On the one hand you are criticising me for being too open, on the other hand you are criticising me for being too discreet. I'm not sure what your game plan is here, Jason..."

"There's no game plan."

"And – just for the record - I think you will find that it is called a mental institution, and not an asylum. This isn't fucking Batman, Jason."

Jason's pearly whites disappear behind his plump lips. "Don't you just love her, ladies and gentlemen?"

The audience guffaws.

Clearly, Jason likes to be the one getting the laughs. He pretends to be absorbed by the facts on the card. He shakes his head, as if to indicate that the words are beyond belief.

"You believe that the world's leaders are reptiles..."

"I don't. I *did*, at one point. I was influenced by views on social media. I was an easy target. That was just a stage I went through when-"

"You recorded your boyfriend because you were paranoid he was having an affair..."

"He *was* having an affair, with my best friend."

"Was that before or after he realised you were completely mad?"

"It was when he realised my best friend had bigger tits than I did."

The audience breaks into laughter. Jason waves his cards in front of him.

Sofia purses her lips and emits a long sigh. "I do find your line of enquiry rather flawed, Jason."

Jason turns to the audience. "Line of enquiry? I am not a detective, Sofia."

"Just as well."

Jason fixes his eyes on Sofia. He holds the cards at chest level. He tears them in two. The pieces of card flutter to the floor. Jason thumps his fist against his heart. "This is much more like it, isn't it? Enough of these phony questions. My research team really need to do better. This is much more natural, isn't it?"

Sofia brushes a hand through her hair.

"I must say, I am much more drawn to you, Sofia, than I ever thought I would be. Looking in from the outside, I always found you somewhat aloof. You haven't really opened up with anyone apart from Andrew, have you? But you are actually kind of alluring. So tell me, why did you tell Andrew – your best friend in this show - that the pandemic killed your mum?"

A crimson flush appears on Sofia's sculpted cheeks. "The pandemic *did* kill my mum. It was on the death certificate."

Jason scrunches up his face. "That part is true.

But you didn't tell Andrew that your mother was already terminally ill with cancer, did you? And you didn't tell him that you paid for the trip around the world because you wanted to give your mother some final, wonderful memories before she departed this world."

The audience coos. Sofia shuffles in her seat. "I didn't want to go into detail. It was personal."

Jason beams. "Just like TJ, you really aren't this awful person you make out to be, are you, Sofia? Going back to a previous comment, I'm interested to know why you think our line of enquiry is flawed, though."

Sofia gives me a fleeting glance. What was that look etched across her face? Guilt? "You are suggesting that I'm mad. Guilty as charged. I have never pretended to be anything else. More to the point, though, isn't the fact that we are all slightly mad the reason we were chosen to be in this game?"

I plant my hands on my thighs. Sofia is right. We are all vulnerable. It wasn't chance that we were chosen.

Jason raises his eyebrows. He puts his hand to his ear. What are they saying to him? "Very good, Sofia. Very good. You may be onto something here. I think Andrew over there worked it out. It has something to do with the salvation line you all called?"

Of course. Kim called a salvation line, didn't she? We *all* did.

"What salvation line?" Sofia asks.

Jason smiles. "Exactly, Sofia. You didn't call a salvation line, did you?"

Reluctantly, she shakes her head. "Plenty of people called lines for me, but I've never, ever called one myself."

"You were too brave. No. We brought you on the show for a different reason, Sofia."

Sofia stands up. "What reason?"

Jason dismisses her question with a wave of the hand. "Ladies and gentlemen, a big round of applause for Sofia..."

He turns to me with a wolfish grin. "Last but definitely not least, let's move on to our final guest. Ladies and gentlemen, please welcome Andrew..."

******

Jason gets the niceties out of the way. This time he leans back in his chair before posing his first hard-hitting question.

"Andrew, is it out of line to say that you've thrived because the contestants are like the family you never had?"

"Yes, that's proper out of line. Maybe you should sack that research team? That's nonsensical. I had a wonderful family growing up-"

"Up to a certain age. Did you love your dad?"

I recall the man who took me to football on Saturday afternoons, who spent hours building a doll's house for my little sister. "When I was young, I loved him."

Jason's eyes narrow. "When you were young? So, what about when you were a little older?"

"He was not a good man when he was drinking."

"And was he often drinking?"

"He became an alcoholic. So, yes."

"Is that why you don't drink?"

"Yes."

Jason opens up his body to the audience. "That's

very commendable, don't you think?"

They clap their hands.

"I must say, Andrew, we were very impressed by your fighting skills. Did your dad have anything to do with that? Did he teach you some funky moves?"

I maintain eye contact. "In a roundabout way, my dad can take some credit for that. I learnt to fight to stop him kicking the shit out of my mum."

Jason nods. "Where is your dad now?"

I raise one eyebrow. "You don't know?"

"Humour us."

"He's dead."

"I'm very sorry to hear of your loss."

"No you're not."

Jason puts his hand to his heart. He gasps with shock offence. "Who is the first person you phone when you are down, when you are struggling?"

I don't flinch. Not for one moment. "I phone my sister. I phone Frances."

Jason elaborately takes a second look at the card. "I'm sorry, I'm confused. Please forgive me. This is most unprofessional of me. You phone your sister?"

I nod.

"That can't be right."

I shrug my shrunken shoulders.

"Why do you phone your sister when she died from anorexia three years ago, Andrew?"

The audience gasps. I sense Sofia's eyes burning into my cheeks. Does she do so out of anger? Or worse: does she do so out of pity?

Jason tells the audience to please quieten. "Answer the question, Andrew."

I clear my throat. "I like to hear the sound of her

voice. She has a voicemail."

Jason coughs. "But she is dead?"

I clasp my hands together. "I know she is dead. I paid for her phone bill when she was alive. I never cancelled the phone. I like to hear her voice. It makes me feel stronger."

"Do you miss her?"

I wipe my eyes. "I miss her every day. And I haven't heard her voice for six days. It breaks my heart."

Jason pulls his chair closer. He'd better not get too close, or I'll knock him out. "You tried to help her, didn't you?"

I look away.

"Tell us how you tried to help her."

I raise my head. "I got her sectioned. It was for her own good."

"And how long after she went into the hospital did she die, Andrew?"

I take a deep breath. "Three weeks."

"So you tried to help Frances, and she died. You tried to help Kim, and she's dead now, too. You don't have a great track record for helping people, do you, Andrew?"

I bury my head in my hands. In the background, Jason wraps up the interview. The audience cheers and claps.

"This is where the fun really begins, ladies and gentlemen. I'm going to call out each of the contestants' names. Please hold up the sponge thumbs if you want them to stay."

I lift my hand. Rising to my feet, I shake TJ's hand. He slaps my back. I lean over and kiss Sofia's cheek. She whispers that I did so well, that she is so proud.

Jason stands up. "Put your thumb in the air if you want TJ to stay..."

A handful of thumbs go up.

Turning to TJ with a pained face, Jason says that he may just be too much of a nice guy.

Twenty or so of the audience raise their thumbs when Jason asks if they want Sofia to stay.

"Congratulations, Sofia. You are through to the final round."

He asks the audience to put their thumbs up if they want Andrew to stay. I already know the outcome. The majority of the audience haven't raised the prop yet.

They want me to stay.

I close my eyes. I dig my fingers into my trousers.

A gun fires.

TJ drops from his chair, dead.

******

Now there are only two of us.

The audience dispersed hours ago. I sit with Sofia on the top tier of the wooden stand, looking down at the hall.

"You and TJ had something significant in common," I say. "You were both much better people than you pretended to be in this show."

Sofia's beautiful eyes scan my face. She raises her eyebrows, a sign of acceptance. "I guess so," she says. "For TJ, at least. I think it is wonderful that TJ died knowing that at least you and me knew that he was a good person."

I straighten my back, try to loosen my shoulders. "A wise man once said something to me. Admittedly, it turns out that this wise man existed only in my head."

Sofia laughs. "Jake the Snake? Well, he did seem like a wise man indeed. And you said that he helped you, and so I like him. Even if (strictly speaking), he was your invisible friend, wasn't he?"

I bring my hand to my mouth, stifling a cough. "Well, I wouldn't say he was my invisible friend as such, more of a mentor who helped me through some difficult times."

"I agree," Sofia says. "A mentor who helped you through some difficult times, who just happened to be your friend. And invisible."

"Right. Well, Jake said that it is better to pretend not to care, than to pretend to care. I think that applied to both you and TJ in this show. Don't you? Can I ask why you took that approach?"

A cluster of horizontal lines appear on Sofia's forehead. She is silent for a few moments. "I don't think I did pretend. I have done some bad things in my life. I could be a better person in so many ways. I just don't pretend to be any better than I am. Okay, I hide some of the good things I've done, but that is just so I don't deceive people into thinking I'm any better than I really am."

I arch an eyebrow, prompting to her tell me more.

"You know when a person in the media appears to have a halo over their head? And they are always quick to share their self-righteous views when somebody else doesn't live up to their mighty moral expectations? And then – low and behold - it turns out that these angelic people aren't actually perfect, after all. They hide a dark secret. I feel sorry for them."

I pull a face. "You feel sorry for them?"

Sofia nods. "Don't you think it must be fucking exhausting to keep up that pretence? Don't you think it must be exhausting to pretend to be perfect, when really you are just as flawed as every other person on this planet?"

"I get what you're saying, Sofia."

"And not only that. Don't you think it would be terrifying? They must live in fear that their dark secret will finally be exposed, that their whole world will come crushing down. I choose not to live like that. I'd prefer people to hate me for who I actually am, than love me for something I'm not. And, just maybe, I go over the top with this. Sometimes they'll be pleasantly surprised that I'm not quite the horrible little bitch that they think I am."

I squeeze Sofia's hand. God, this woman is amazing. "And what was your motivation for being here? Was it really just Fortune?"

Sofia turns to me with red-rimmed eyes. "Nah. I had to choose one reward, didn't I? I didn't fancy going to another country. And sometimes I think I'm super human. Imagine if I suddenly had a following of millions? I'd turn into Donald Trump."

I chuckle.

Sofia sniffs. "Like I said when we first met; I was lonely. I desperately wanted some people to talk to."

The words float peacefully in the air.

I longed for people to talk to in the middle of the pandemic. I walked the aisles of the local supermarket one Saturday night, trying to catch the eye of another masked shopper. Their glazed eyes looked through me. I felt invisible. I felt pointless. Absentmindedly, I browsed the bookshelves. I thumbed a few covers. My eyes rotated. I focused on the bestsellers. I fixed on a cover. Picking up a paperback, I leafed through the pages. I turned to the acknowledgments.

"I would like to thank my first mentor, Andrew

Macintosh. Without his incredible support and belief I would never have been able to write this book."

John had published a book. It was a bestseller. I knew – deep from my core – that his words were authentic, that he really couldn't have achieved something so monumental without my guidance. I realised that I wasn't pointless after all.

I'd been thinking about this over the last torrid, exceptional six days. After all, I've had plenty of time to reflect on the past, to ponder the future. And I've decided that – if I get the chance – I'd like a future. Not only that, but I long to grasp it with both hands, to make up for all the wasted, futile time, the endless missed opportunities. I'm going to quit my job and become a lecturer again. I helped John to make something of his life, didn't I? I will make it my mission to help others just like him.

"Could you share the bed with me tonight, Andrew? We can just hold each other."

I gulp. I try to flatten my smile. "If you insist; I'll do that for you."

Sofia playfully slaps my arm. She guides me down the wooden benches, all the way to her warm, waiting bed.

DAY SEVEN

Contestants eliminated: 48
Contestants remaining: 2

Morning

After six days creating the world, God rested on the seventh day. On the seventh day He reflected on what He had completed.

This is our seventh day in this world they created. The creators of this travesty (whoever they are) have been playing god with human lives for six days. They haven't been creating life; they have been destroying life. They are not going to rest today. They are not going to reflect on the harm they've caused.

On the seventh day, they are going to remove one final life. Only one of us will survive. Only one of us will leave this world they created alive. The one who survives will likely spend the rest of their life mourning the life they took away.

Fuck you, The F-Word Reality Show.

******

I daren't open my eyes.

I know that it is morning, and I know it has been morning for quite some time. I recall waking on a sofa in a shared household one Monday morning. I was aware of the frantic activity all around me – the opening and closing of cupboards, toast popping from the toaster, the front door slamming – and all the time I pretended it wasn't happening, I pretended they couldn't see me when – of course – I stood out like a sixth toe.

I don't know how many of them occupy the hall but, from the clattering feet, the whispers and the conspiring laughter, it's definitely a crowd. There's never really been a hiding place in this game, has there? Sure, there are no cameras in the showers, but you still have other contestants peeking at your naked, glistening body. And they continued to close the bedroom shutters twice a day: but how could we trust that after Kim's humiliation? And even though – clearly – the show isn't televised to the general public at home, TJ was right; the cameras have a purpose. Surely we have been watched by someone, somewhere?

And of course, whoever is out there now can see inside my bedroom. They are watching me. They are watching *us.* My naked back presses against the window. Sofia's angled body nestles against mine. My hot breath tingles the delicate hairs on the back of her neck.

I daren't open my eyes, not just because I don't want to face whatever awaits me out there, but because I don't want this moment to end.

At first, the clapping is muted; it is barely audible. Over time it swells and grows until rapturous applause vibrates around the hall.

This is our signal.

Untangling our bodies, we silently dress. Planting

a kiss on Sofia's lips, I run my thumb down her moist cheek. And then, raising our heads for the first time, we step out of the bedroom, ready to take on anything and everything that awaits us.

******

Every inch of the makeshift wooden stand is occupied. They've rolled out two reclining leather chairs, the swanky type you'd likely find in a CEO's office at a large investment bank. Just like yesterday, they are the audience, and we are the entertainment.

We saunter out of the bedroom; the clapping turns to boisterous cheers. Rebecca greets us with a warm, painted smile. She is dressed for business today; a navy, lapel collar blazer hangs over tailored slacks. "Look at you two love birds." She turns to the audience. "Isn't it sweet?"

The audience coo.

Rebecca gives me a wink, the type you'd expect from your mates down the pub. "Did you give Sofia a good time last night, Andrew?"

I look away.

"Right, welcome to the final day of the show. You've both done fantastically well to get this far. Why don't we give them both a warm round of applause?"

Clapping spreads across the hall.

"I could patronise you and say that there are no winners and losers in this show, but I respect both of you too much to do that. After all, if you don't win today, then you'll be dead tomorrow."

Isolated sections of the crowd laugh at this.

Rebecca turns to me. "Andrew. Please can you

do me the honour of choosing the third and final Truth Card?"

A guard appears with the box. My hand disappears within, pulling out the card. I read the words. I'm sure my forehead furrows.

"Don't leave us in suspense, Andrew. You may or may not have noticed, but we have quite a few guests with us today. Tell us what the card says..."

I read the words that are written on the card. "Rebecca is a fictional character in this reality show."

Gripping Sofia's hand, we both take a seat on the reclining leather chairs. Sofia crosses one leg over the other. We turn to Rebecca with open faces. "Well?" Sofia says. "What exactly does *that* mean, Rebecca?"

Rebecca's jaw drops. If she had a cigarette in her mouth it would have dropped to the floor. She flaps her hands around madly. "Oh darlings, that's news to me. Honestly, I have no idea what that means at all."

Somebody steps out from the crowd. Standing over six feet tall, his beefy shoulders stretch his tee-shirt. He moves to within touching distance. His heartfelt smile signals familiarity. Momentarily, I'm wrong-footed by the casual denim jeans that hang from his hips. It is like bumping into the postman down the pub. He dressed differently last time. The bombshell drops. I know who it is. The last time I met him was the *only* time I've met him.

It is the man from the canal. It is the man who started this horrific journey. Involuntarily – like a spasm I just can't control – I return his smile.

"Andrew," he says, flicking his attention between me and the crowd. "The last time we met you asked for my name and I was – to put it bluntly – a bit dismissive. And so it's time to properly introduce myself. I'm Keith, and I'm one of the organisers of this extravaganza."

Any initial artificial warmness I felt towards this guy instantly evaporates.

Holding out upturned hands, Keith turns to Rebecca. "Both Andrew and Sofia deserve an explanation. We've given you the opportunity to do the honourable thing here. Are you going to tell them?"

Rebecca clenches her jaw. "That wasn't part of the deal. You never mentioned any of this to me. Why are you doing this to me?"

Keith looms over her; he must be a foot taller than her. "I'll give you one last chance. Are you going to tell them? If not, then I will."

Rebecca shrugs her shoulders. I notice that she moves a few steps further away from us.

Keith turns to the audience with a subtle smile creasing his lips. "I am sure you will agree that there is good news and bad news about Rebecca."

There are a few bemused shakes of the head amongst the nods and guffaws. On cue, one of the audience shouts that it is *all* bad news; this prompts hearty laughter.

"Don't be so harsh," Keith says, displaying his molars. "This show has repeatedly shown us that every cloud has a silver lining. The good news is that the Truth Card does as it says on the tin: it tells the truth. Rebecca is just a character. The bad news is that the actress depicting Rebecca is a fucking monster."

He turns to us expecting questions. I imagine that our glares speak louder than words.

"It's been fascinating listening to you trying to work out Rebecca's role. Is she a puppet? Is she a puppeteer? No offence, but this isn't a Punch and Judy show..."

Keith waves away the laughter.

"With all due respect, it was as dull as dishwater sympathetically listening to your whines of self-pity on the salvation line. We let most of you poor sods jump in front of the train. We noted the telephone details of those showing promise, and probed you for more and more information. Good Samaritans? Don't offend me. We only wanted the details so we could use it against you on the show. We were merely cunning. But then a few weeks into the process, Rebecca called the line. We knew straight away that she was the jewel in the crown, that she was special."

I turn to Rebecca. She stands with one leg slightly forward, her eyes glued to Keith. I search for a flicker of emotion, some sort of involuntary spasm. I cannot find one.

"Who *are* you?" I ask.

Rebecca jerks her head flamboyantly to the side, like she is a catwalk model. Her subtle smile makes me flinch. "I'm your worst nightmare, Andrew."

Keith takes a few long strides towards me. "She becomes whatever you want her to become, Andrew. Just like you did that day on the railway platform, Rebecca shared with us all her problems. And just like you did, Rebecca told us about all the harm and misery she'd inflicted on those closest and dearest to her. However, credit where credit is due, you showed remorse for practically killing your poor little sister. And your dear, deceased friend Dylan; well, he blubbered about betraying his wife, didn't he? Rebecca did none of this. She didn't call us seeking help. Rebecca merely sought an audience to gloat to. She longed to repulse and appall us. She craved reassurance, but not the usual type. Rebecca wanted us to reassure her that she was the most despicable, cruel person we'd had the misfortune of speaking to. And she didn't need to try very hard to convince us."

Sofia leans forward with clenched, whitened knuckles. "What did that bitch tell you?"

Keith glances at Sofia and then turns to the audience. "In retrospect, she barely told us anything. It was the way she told it. You may have figured, but we aren't-"

"We?" Sofia says.

Keith holds his hand up. "We're not resistant to causing a certain degree of pain ourselves, and we recognised that Rebecca barely scratched the surface with what she told us. She is calculated. She's conniving. She knew she'd get into serious trouble if she told us too much. She merely planted a seed. Of course, she had no idea who we were. After that initial call, it was *us* who contacted Rebecca. It was *us* who propositioned her."

"Stop talking in riddles," Sofia says.

Keith smiles. "We met with Rebecca and Duncan - the only other hired help – at a disused scout hall. The flimsy, brown carpets stunk of damp and the paper-thin windows rattled from the wind. We'd researched both of them. We made it clear that, as a last resort, we were prepared to expose the blood they had on their hands. We didn't want it to come to that. We wanted it to be amenable. We told them we wanted them to play a role in the show and we'd pay them handsomely if they did."

"And that's exactly what I did," Rebecca says, turning to us and waving her hands. "I played the villain. Believe me; it broke my heart to do those things. But it wasn't me. You have every right to despise Rebecca – trust me, I did too – but hate *her*, not me."

Sofia's eyes flicker. Her mind is in conflict with her heart.

We glance up. Keith slow claps. "She is good, isn't she? Every word she utters is diced with logic. Only, here's the thing. The character we created wasn't anywhere near as horrendous as the one she played. This sadistic woman thrived in the role because she was able to kill with no consequences..."

"Who *is* she?" I ask.

Keith walks up and down the imaginary stage. He takes a deep breath. "We have reason to believe that this person you know as Rebecca has taken at least five innocent lives, even before she entered this arena."

We gasp.

Keith strides past me. Releasing a deep breath, he tries to take Sofia's hand. She brushes it away. His face remains placid. "Sofia, have you wondered how come the other contestants called our salvation line and you didn't?"

She opens her mouth, ready to utter that of course she has; she merely nods.

"We brought you in as a link to Rebecca."

Sofia shakes her head. "I've never met her before. You've got it wrong. You've dragged me into your sick show by mistake."

"Rebecca's real name is Denise Edwards. We can't be definite about four of her killings, but we are certain that Denise took her first victim, David Shanklin, when she was only fourteen..."

The words linger in the air. Silence fills the hall. My eyes fix on Sofia. She appears numb. Colour drains from her face. She glances at Keith. Solemnly, he nods.

"She killed my dad?"

******

Sofia springs from the chair and lunges at Rebecca, who swipes out with flailing legs. Sofia grabs Rebecca by the throat before Keith, and three guards, tear the two women apart.

"You dirty, murdering little bitch!"

Keith tells her that she'll have her chance, warns her that she needs to calm down, just for now.

"I don't want to wait! I want her dead!"

The guards escort Rebecca to the far side of the hall. Reluctantly, Sofia returns to her chair. I take the opportunity to embrace her. She sobs in my ear. "She killed my dad," she says. "I never even met him. I was still in my mummy's belly."

I jerk my head to the side. I want to divert attention away from Rebecca. I fix on Keith. "Tell us who you are," I say.

Keith nods. "The time has come. I'll pass you over to my good friend Simone, who I believe you've already met."

Keith returns to the stand. The woman who interviewed me when we landed at the venue bounces towards the stage. She leans forward to give me a kiss on the cheek but – not surprisingly – I flinch. The crowd laughs and cajoles.

"Fair enough, handsome. So you want to know who we are? Well, we are nobody and everybody all at the same time," Simone says. Her eyes scan the room. The audience greet her words with approving murmurs and claps. "On our own we are nobody. Frankly, we are the type of people who struggle to get served in a busy bar. And yet together we could buy the bar and serve whoever we want."

I glance at Sofia. Her body shakes. I don't even know if she is taking in anything this woman says.

"We're just everyday people, the type you'd pass on the street without giving a second glance. I work in a factory. Dennis over there stacks shelves in a supermarket. And Janet – she is hidden away in the audience somewhere, bless her - Janet provides exemplary customer service in a call centre. Let's just say that Janet made a fantastic contribution to our salvation helpline, which each and every one of you, with the exception of Sophia, called when you were feeling a little down in the dumps. We are all in this together. The guards. The croupier. Jason, who interviewed you yesterday. Everyone."

Sweeping a handful of stray hair from her flushed face, Sofia lifts her backside from her chair just a few inches. "The contestants weren't part of your scheme though, were they? They called you at their lowest point. They needed your help to keep the razor from their veins and the rope from their neck. And this is how you repay them?"

Simone pouts sympathetic lips. "I'm not sure you're the voice of reason on this subject, darling. You never actually utilised our services, did you?

Anyway, we kept our callers alive, or at least the ones we chose for the show. We offered them hope."

Smirking, Simone turns to me. Her hazel eyes, flecked with green, fixate on mine. "I said that you were one of my favourites, Andrew, when I interviewed you, and I meant it. Strip away the layers and we have similar beliefs. We represent the little man and woman on the street. And we deliberately go unnoticed, Andrew. That is why we are so successful, and that is why we are so deadly. We don't broadcast what we do, and we definitely don't brag or gloat. We don't care if people approve or disapprove of us. And we remain a secret to everybody but those who seek us out. We only appeal to a select audience, and to those people we are blood to a vampire."

I hold my hands up, exasperated. "Why all of this? Why do you need to resort to murder?"

Simone arches her eyebrow. "I think it is merely a matter of supply and demand. I assure you that it is nothing personal. You and I know that the real world isn't interesting enough for most people. Most of these people get their thrills from a fake world. They watch films and play video games and read books to get their fix of murder and violence and-"

"Nobody dies from those things!" Sofia stabs an accusing middle finger at Simone.

Simone flattens her hands. "The games, films and books satisfy the cravings of most of these people. And if their cravings aren't met, then most of them don't have the funds, the courage or the inclination to seek anything else." Simone takes a moment. She lowers her microphone to her side. "But then there is a select group of people who do have the funds, the courage and the inclination. And that is where we come into the fray. We offer the services they desire. We offer the services they crave."

I shake my head. "This isn't real."

Simone's heels click on the polished floor and stops close enough for her shadow to eclipse me. "For now, this game is as close to reality as you are going to get. Your best friends really *did* die in here, Andrew."

My knuckles whiten as I grip the sides of my chair. My whole body shakes. I look up. "What exactly is it that you're running here?" I ask.

"We operate on the dark web. I'm sure you've both guessed that part."

We nod our dazed heads.

"Our tagline was – how shall I put this without causing any undue offence – highly enticing to our target audience. We said that viewers could pay to watch fifty suicidal contestants fight to stay alive for seven days. The irony of it all never fails to make me chuckle."

Guffaws emit from the audience.

Sofia spits out her words. "That's sick."

Simone turns her smile upside down. "I think that is the point, darling. We appealed to a sick sort of person. It was an excellent business plan. We charged £10,000 just to subscribe to watch."

I glance at the cameras. "So how many sick people actually watched us?"

"Tens of thousands, dear. But they were merely the equivalent of ticket sales. We were taking a big risk; the stakes were high. We had to think outside the box to make big money." Simone peers into the audience. "I think you came up with the idea, didn't you, Janice? What was your idea, darling?"

A middle-aged woman straightens her back and pumps out her (not insignificant) chest. "Bidding."

Simone turns back to us with a self-satisfied smile, like she had just told a fantastic joke that had the audience in stitches. "The simplest ideas are always the best, aren't they? Bidding gave our viewers the opportunity to be part of the show. They bid on everything and anything. What you ate for breakfast. The shocking clothes Rebecca wore. The Truth Cards. The games you played. I could go on and on. Oh, and don't go thinking your misery wasn't for a good cause. Someone bid £100,000 for the shutters to go back up when Kim lured that boy to her bedroom. And we made £50,000 when Duncan tried to slice that man's head off. That was a real crowd-pleaser."

"How much did somebody bid for Duncan to kill me?"

How much value was my life?

Taking a few steps towards me, Simone's hand smooths my thigh. "You didn't come cheap, darling. A viewer bid £125,000 for that. We didn't refund the money, either. Duncan *did* try his best, bless him."

Sofia sighs. "So it was all about the money?"

Simone turns to the audience. "*Was* it all about the money?"

It takes a few moments for anybody to respond, and then the responses come from all directions. Some say that – yes – it was all about the money. Others say that the money was a means to an end. Some say it was the excitement. Others say that it was about the power, about playing god.

Simone turns to us with pouted lips. "Does that

help?"

I turn away from her. I face the audience. I have a better question to ask. "Do you have any regrets?"

This time there is no inconsistency. The answer is clear, bold and loud.

"No."

******

Blowing air from her cheeks, Simone rubs her hands together. "It's time for the final game. It's time to find out which one of you two darlings wins your reward..."

She turns to the giant screen on the wall. "Our loyal subscribers have been bidding all morning. They've been bidding to decide what happens to you two."

Every member of the audience stands. They start clapping.

"We are going to count down from ten," Simone says. "You guessed it. When we reach zero, the highest bidder wins."

The audience chant the numbers. Ever-increasing numbers flash on the screen. The top bid keeps changing. The numbers rebound in my head. I can't keep up. I close my eyes.

Sofia turns to me. "I'm going to kill Rebecca. I don't care what this game is, or what happens to me. But I'm going to kill her." Her whitened fingers tug at my sleeve.

Gasps emit around the hall as the timer reduces to zero.

"We have a nice round five hundred grand for the highest bid," a beaming Simone says.

Rebecca has snaked even further away. She presses her flat hands against the exit door. When she removes her hands, there is a smudged imprint on the glass.

Sofia rises to her feet. Instinctively, I pull at her arm. The guards stand in line with raised guns, blocking her path.

A grinning Simone glances in the direction of Rebecca's turned back. "Look at her go. Run rabbit, run rabbit, run, run, run..." The audience breaks into hysterics.

Simone narrows her eyes to absorb the details of the highest bid. "How exciting!" she says, opening her arms to us. "We are all going to be allowed to run wild. You won't have any weapons. We won't have any weapons. The only cameras will be those on our helmets, so the loyal viewers at home can view the action as it unfolds."

She turns to the crowd. "I'll keep calling her Rebecca, if you'll forgive me? Things could get awfully confusing if we don't." Her words are met by approving guffaws. "Rebecca, bless her; she will leave first. Rebecca has a sixty second head start before the contestants are allowed to leave. *We* aren't interested in Rebecca. *We* won't hunt her down. But – and this is entirely optional – our two remaining contestants can. And I get the distinct impression one of the two contestants might decide that is a good option."

The white smiles widen. Next to me, Sofia snarls like a dog ready to be left off her leash.

"Personally, we are going to give the contestants three minutes before we hunt them down. Remember, there are hundreds of us and only two of them." She turns to both of us. "I'm only saying this in your best interest, darlings, but you might decide to split. The last one standing is the winner. But if we catch both of you together – and we will catch you – then we'll attack both of you. We'll only stop when we beat one of you to death."

I glance at Sofia. Her eyes remain fixed on Rebecca. She bangs the back of her fist against the glass. I imagine drool trickling down her chin.

Leaning forward, Simone holds out a manicured hand. "On your feet please, my darlings. Let's get this show on the road."

The audience counts down from ten. The doors flick open, and Rebecca disappears outside.

Absentmindedly, I stare at the numbers on the digital clock. My body is numb. My mind is blank. I don't know what I am going to do when I get out there. I blink. Focus. The numbers stop moving. We reach number ten. With jelly legs, I move to the door, not letting go of Sofia's hand.

The buzzer sounds. The doors flick open.

And we disappear outside. For one of us this will be the last time we see the outside world.

******

Our heads rested against the dry, faded grass. Occasionally I sheltered my eyes from the sun that seeped through the cracks in the trees. Absentmindedly, I rolled balls of hardened mud between my thumb and forefinger before flicking it through the air. From the corner of my eye, I glimpsed the tips of my sister's raised knees, pressed together. At the time, her sun-kissed legs were coated with a healthy layer of fat.

"I don't want to go home."

I angled my head to the side. "Is it school? You don't want to go back to school?"

Frances shook her head. "It's not that. Things are different here. I don't want this to end."

I squinted. The sun stung the side of my face. "I get that. We've had a good time."

She angled her body so that she faced me. "It's more than that. Mum and Dad don't argue here, Andrew."

I nodded. I'd thought the same. It was almost like different rules applied because we were in a different location. "How do you know they will start arguing when we get home?"

She stared over my shoulder, probably because she didn't want to look at me when she uttered the cold, hard truth that neither of us really wanted to hear. "Because they always do."

I wasn't going to try and argue against that.

I sensed my sister's eyes rise as I got to my feet. "Where are you going?"

I dug deep inside the pocket of my jean shorts. Frances pushed herself up from the floor. I flicked my wrist. Her eyes widened. "What are you doing, Andrew?"

I turned my back. With the knife held delicately between my fingertips, I carved my initials into the tree with the widest trunk. "Your turn," I said.

Frances snatched the blade. She took longer than me. Biding her time, she made sure the lines were straight and consistent. Smiling, she took a step back and admired her handiwork.

"You've added the year," I said.

The sparkle in her eyes had returned. She nodded. "We can add the year every time we return. It will help when we are back home, knowing that we are a day closer to coming back."

I shook her hand. "Deal."

It wasn't that we intended to break the deal. We just had no choice.

Mum and Dad *did* argue when we returned home, only it became more and more toxic. Dad's drinking worsened. Mum's health deteriorated. We never returned to the holiday camp.

******

As soon as the crisp air hits my cheeks, Sofia lets go of my hand. With her hair swinging from side to side, her retreating back gets smaller and smaller. For a second or two, I just watch her. Have I swallowed my tongue? Am I physically unable to speak?

"Sofia! Come back!" I shout.

Turning, she heads towards me with raised hands. "I'm sorry, Andrew, but I need you to leave me alone..."

I take a step forward. She slaps her flat hands against my chest. "Go away! I'm going to hunt her down, and I'm going to kill her!"

"What good will *that* do?"

Sofia's eyes widen. She looks at me like she wants to claw her fingernails down the side of my face. "Don't you understand, Andrew? That woman killed my dad! I was still in my mum's belly. Can you even imagine that? I never even met him. My mum lived the rest of her life not knowing what happened to her. She loved him. What good do you *think* it will do?"

I nod. "And then what?"

Sofia slants her face to one side.

"They'll kill you if you stay on your own," I say.

Sofia nods. "Yes. They will. One of us has to die. That is why you need to leave. I don't want you to die, too."

"I'm not going to leave you, Sofia."

"I'm warning you!"

I grab hold of her wrists. I sense her strength – and her anger - dissolve. Seconds pass; I release my grip. Sofia's shoulders slump. She parts the hair at the sides and then plants a kiss on my forehead. Her lips brush against my right lobe. She whispers in my ear, "I love you, Andrew, but I don't want you to come with me. I am going to kill that bitch. It is going to be the last thing I do. They'll catch me. I'm prepared for that. There is no reason for you to die, too. You deserve to live."

I pull away. Gently, I press the tip of my nose against hers. "I've been here before."

She arches an eyebrow. "What do you mean? *Here*?"

I take a deep breath. I've been longing to say these words for days – compelled to utter them, to shut them from the rooftops – but I resisted the temptation. I imagine Dylan looking down - for if there is a Heaven and Hell then he'll definitely be looking down – and nodding his approval. "This camp. I have been to this camp before. As a kid. I was here with Frances and my mum and my dad."

Her jaw drops. "Why haven't you told me before? Why have you kept this from me?"

I grip her arms. "I couldn't tell you in there, and God knows I wanted to. I couldn't tell you, because of the cameras. They would have shot us. They would never have let us out."

Sofia sighs. She looks around, looking for Rebecca. "What difference does it make if you've been here before? They're coming to find us. They're going to kill one of us. We're running out of time. Please. Let me find the bitch and let me kill her."

My grip on her arms tightens. "Trust me. I don't think we should try and hide."

Sofia angles her face. "What should we do then? Fight? There are too many of them. We'll both end up dead."

Shaking my head, I release my grip on her arms. "We should try and escape. Come with me."

Sofia pushes at my chest. "And if we can't escape? What happens then?"

I gulp. "Then we die together."

Sofia narrows her eyes. It feels like too many seconds pass. Cupping the underside of my chin, she kisses my lips. "I'll die with you, Andy," she says. She takes hold of my hand.

"Let that madness seeping inside you be your friend," I say.

She allows herself a smile. "What are you talking about?"

"Become that superhero," I say. "Become whatever superhero you want to be. And let's make it out of here."

My childhood memories are vague. They are blurred. Running through the overgrown grass, we pass the tree with our initials engraved in the trunk. Rain spits against my cheeks. My heart sinks as we manoeuvre around the crumbling block of flats where Dylan died. With the car park to my right, I fleetingly recall the excitement of arriving at the park that Friday afternoon, thirty years or so ago. "This way." I tug Sofia's hand. We head towards the brick wall with metal spikes on top. The sound of the horn emitting from the hall is like a dagger to the heart.

They are coming to get us.

"We can't get over that wall," Sofia breathlessly says. "Why have you taken me here?"

"We aren't going over," I say. "We are going under."

Only, I don't know where the tunnel is, do I? My scrambled brain can't find it; there are phantoms in my crumbling mind. Never before have I so wanted to stay alive. I want to stay alive with this woman. I pull at the grass. I kick at the ground. Glancing at Sofia, I shrug my shoulders. She merely gives me a sympathetic look. The look tells me that it isn't my fault, that I tried my best. In a daze, I pull at a tree branch.

"Here," I say. "Look behind here."

I turn to Sofia, but my gaze is disorientated. Sofia scurries towards me. I glance over her shoulder. My mouth drops.

Not now. We don't have time for this now. They are coming for us. I can sense their footsteps. They can already smell the blood.

"Stay away," I say.

Turning, Sofia stops dead in her tracks. Rebecca creeps closer to us, like a dog checking to see if she has been forgiven for jumping on the sofa. She appears more diminutive and fragile than ever, like a bird with a broken wing. Only, she isn't fragile. She isn't the bullied; she is the bully. She is a killer. She killed Sofia's dad.

Rebecca plants her hands together in a praying gesture. "I'm so sorry. It wasn't me in there," she says. "I was just playing a role. I was an actress. I had no choice. "

I stab my finger at Rebecca. "Turn around and run, before this girl tears you apart."

Sofia brushes my arm. "She might as well come," she says.

I gaze at her like I'm the mad one. "She killed your dad."

She blows air from her lips. "We don't have time, Andy. I'm done caring with her. She can't hold us back. If she doesn't come then she'll tell them where we are. I just want to escape. I want to stay alive."

"Sure?"

"Sure."

Soundlessly, we let Rebecca wait in line, like a good little girl waiting for her bottle of milk in the classroom.

I lower my hands to the ground. They stick to the mud, to the damp soil. I take a deep breath. The tunnel is dark. There is no end in sight. I start crawling. Glancing over my shoulders, Sofia already has her hands flat to the ground, ready to follow me.

I imagine the tunnel shrinking around me, just like in my nightmares. I imagine losing my breath. I imagine gasping for breath. It is all in my head. I keep moving forward. My hands slip against the rising, dirty water. I stare ahead, desperate for light. There *is* no light. I'm surrounded by darkness, everywhere I look, and in every direction.

I shudder. What was that?

Screams echo around the tunnel.

"No! No!"

Should I turn around? There isn't room. I can't.
She might be dead. Rebecca might be dead. Sofia
might be dead.

They *both* might be dead.

I have to keep going forward. I blank it out. I keep
moving forward. There is a sliver of light. It is no
longer total darkness. My arms are heavier, and yet
they move faster. My breathing quickens. I imagine
Frances telling me that I can do this. She did it, and *I*
can do it. I imagine Mum calling my name from the
other side.

Andy.

I'm going to make it. I'm going to do it. For me.
For Frances. For Mum. For Sofia.

Sofia.

I pull myself out at the other side of the tunnel.

With my hand pressed against the brick wall, I
straighten my back. I splutter out a mouthful of dirty,
contaminated water. I peer back inside the tunnel. I
can see nothing. I can hear nothing.

Hold on. I *can* hear something. Only, it isn't
coming from inside the tunnel. It is coming from the
other side of the wall.

"Where *are* they?"

"There are hundreds of us. There are only so
many hiding places. Keep looking."

"Maybe they aren't hiding?"

"What are you talking about?"

"Maybe they escaped?"

"*Can* they escape?"

"Maybe they can. Maybe they found a way out.
Look on the ground. Look for a hole, a tunnel. Look
for *something*."

I stare down the dark tunnel. They are going to

find us. Come on. Hurry up. There are only so many seconds we can hold off. I can't go back inside the tunnel, because I won't be able to turn around to come back. I may need to go without her.

Do I *want* to live without her?

The spluttering alerts me. I pull on both damp, sodden hands. She looks up at me with loving eyes.

"Sofia!"

Our embrace is quick. It is fleeting. I glance back in the tunnel.

"Rebecca won't be joining us," Sofia says.

******

I remember the town. There was *definitely* a town.

We strolled to the town in the evenings, just as the blistering sun began to fade. For once, we were just like any other family, giddy from too much sun and ice cream. The shops appeared identical, all selling buckets and spades and water guns and fridge magnets. My legs were shorter and the world felt bigger, but we *definitely* walked there. It was one long, straight road.

How far was it?

I don't know. I don't think I knew then, and I absolutely do not know now. I can only estimate. I need to be realistic, but I need to give Sofia a glimmer of hope.

"The town is three miles away," I say.

Sofia looks at me with a pinched forehead. She wipes her forearm across her brow. She already appears exhausted.

The voices from the other side of the wall seem louder. They seem closer. I squeeze Sofia's shoulders. "We can do it. We just need to keep running. It is three miles between us living and us dying. I haven't come this far to die, Sofia."

"What difference will it make? What will we do when we get there?"

I take a deep breath. I remember the stretch of shops. I don't remember much else. Would the shops still be there? What time is it? Would the shops be open? There would be houses. There *would* be houses, surely?

"There will be people around. We will shout from the rooftops that we were captured, that we were prisoners in a sick reality show. We will tell them that all the other contestants are now just dead bodies lying in the gutter."

Sofia stares at me with vacant eyes. She looks like she has nothing left to give. I shake her shoulders. "We have no choice! We are fighting against the clock, Sofia! They will realise that we have escaped and then they will hunt us down!"

I begin running. Overwhelming relief seeps through my body when I glimpse Sofia's shadow on the floor in front of me. We pick up the pace. My lungs feel like they are on fire. I glance over my shoulder. They are not following us. Something resembling hope overcomes me. We can do this. We can make it. We can live.

And then, Sofia begins to slow. She begins dragging her left shoe against the tarmac. Within a few hundred feet, she stops. Resting her hands on her slender hips, she raises her head to the heavens.

"What is it?"

"I didn't want to say anything. I was hoping I could overcome it. But I injured my foot in the tunnel. I can't run any further. I can't even walk."

Narrowing my eyes, I gaze over her shoulder. They have realised that we have escaped. They have found the tunnel. They are coming for us. "What shall we do?"

"You need to go on without me. You need to leave me here."

I laugh at her suggestion. I take hold of her from her waist. Swivelling my body, I place her in a fireman's lift.

I keep glancing over my shoulder. They grow larger. There are hundreds of them.

I feel like I have inherited Sofia's mythical superpowers. I could pull a truck with a rope tied around my waist. I could climb the highest mountain.

Only, I can't, and I don't. We move forward, but my heavy legs begin to weaken. Spluttering, I gasp for air. I gaze forward, searching for the town. I still can't see it. We have run maybe two miles, but there is still a mile or so to go. And that is if it even *is* three miles from the camp. Reluctantly, I look over my shoulder. The hunters – the predators – are no longer insignificant ants. They are now more like tigers, claws ready to savage their prey.

We aren't going to make it. They are going to catch us. They are going to beat us both to death.

I collapse on the floor.

"We tried," I say. "We gave it everything."

Sofia smiles. "Goddamn, we sure did try."

Maybe I lose consciousness for a few minutes, or maybe I just lose my mind.

My eyes blink into consciousness. They are gaining ground, getting closer and closer. They have blurred into a single entity, like a flock of birds or a swarm of wasps. Their anger is intense, roaring like an engine. They are almost within touching distance. I brace my body for the attack.

"Why are you lying in the middle of the road? What the hell is going on?"

I dare to open my eyes wider. A bulky man stands over me with his feet parted wide. His straw hair is rumpled like he has just got out of bed. Fleshy lips twist with concern.

"They are after us," I say, thumbing behind us.

The man pulls me to my feet. I stagger forwards on unsteady legs. He helps me into the back of his car. My heart flutters when I see Sofia sat next to me, her face drawn and pale and yet...and yet, still alive. I embrace her, and her breath is hot against my cheek. From the front, the stranger glances over his shoulder. "Where do you need to go?"

"At least a hundred miles from nowhere," I say.

The man smirks. "That's just where I was heading. Buckle up."

Sofia speaks to the man from the back of the car. "We don't have masks. Do you have spare masks?"

The man gives a dismissive wave of the hand. "I'll take my chances, now that they've found the vaccine..."

I turn to Sofia. She gives me a look which says that she told me so.

Over my shoulder, I stare through the window, flecked with bird shit. I wave at the figures, as they grow smaller and smaller.

I can't ever hold's Kim's hand, or Dylan's, or Frances's, or Dad's. I can hold Mum's, though. And I can hold Sofia's. I reach over and take hold of her hand. I don't ever want to let it go.

I have no idea where we're heading. I don't care. All I know is that we'll be heading there together, and we'll finally be free.

******

If you enjoyed THE F-WORD REALITY SHOW, make sure you read I AM HERE TO KILL YOU, a compelling psychological thriller with a stunning twist.

The members of a local support group in a sleepy welsh town are captivated by the new arrival, Sheena Strachan. Each member of the group has a reason for attending. Some hide dark, sinister secrets, and for others it is the highlight of their week.

But what are Sheena's motives for attending?

The group's leader, Rose, unexpectedly stops attending meetings. She goes into hiding, and quickly becomes an outcast. And then she is arrested for her estranged husband's murder.

Did Sheena really have no involvement in his killing?

With Sheena at the helm, the group goes from strength to strength, both in numbers and commitment. But their behaviour is changing. No story is to leave the room. They trust nobody. Men are the enemy. The residents of the previously peaceful town start turning against each other.

Was this Sheena's plan all along?

One mystery, however, stands out more than all the others.

Who is here to kill who…?

Acknowledgments

As always, I'd like to thank my wife, Elizabeth, for her wonderful ongoing support and belief.

Thank you to Jeff Jones, who provided expert proofreading services, and to Elizabeth Ponting of LP Designs & Art, for designing the perfect book cover.

Christine Hodgson and Claire Hall deserve a special mention, as they have provided invaluable feedback on my last four novels. And thank you to Noel Powell and Simon Prior, who provided some fantastic early insight.

Finally, thank you to my friend Ron Cox, who came up with some incredible ideas after work at the café across the road.

About the Author

Chris Westlake was born in Cardiff and brought up in Wick, a coastal village seven miles from Bridgend. He now resides in Birmingham with his wife, Elizabeth, and two young children, AJ and Chloe.

After completing a creative writing course, Chris's short story, *Welsh Lessons,* was awarded 1st place in the Global Short Story Award. He followed this up with 1st place in the Stringybark Erotic Fiction Award and 2nd place in the HASSRA Literary Award.

He has written four previous novels, *Just a Bit of Banter, Like, At Least the Pink Elephants are Laughing at Us, 30 Days in June, and I AM HERE TO KILL YOU.*

Chris is on schedule to publish his next novel in 2024.

You can find out more about Chris, and his novels, at his website, chriswestlakewriter.com.

CHRIS WESTLAKE

Printed in Great Britain
by Amazon

25939648R00192